SURGICAL HEIGHTS

By Paul E. Hardy, MD

Paul Hardy

Library and Archives Canada Cataloguing in Publication
Paul E. Hardy

ISBN 978-1-926747-63-7

To Contact Paul E. Hardy Write to him at:
Paul E. Hardy
#400 3939 – 50A Ave.
Red Deer, AB T4N 4E6
403-304-9290
Or email him at:
info@surgicalheights.com

Printed in Canada
www.firstchoicebooks.ca

For Janet

"If you do not tell the truth about yourself you cannot tell it about other people."

—Virginia Woolf, 1882-1941

Table of Contents

Preface

Transforming thoughts to paper has been a pleasurable experience. Improving the project has required help and support of friends, relatives and colleagues. I would especially like to thank those who reviewed my manuscript and gave valuable feedback including Janet Hardy, Trevor Theman, Fred Hansen, Barbara Hardy, Sylvia Gillespie, Rob Harrop, Jim Czegledi, Brian Keen, Joanne Glen, Dennis Jirsch and Bryan Caddy.

I would like to give special thanks to Dania Sheldon for her excellent editorial work and invaluable suggestions, which improved the novel significantly.

Teachers, health care colleagues, students and patients have all provided me with an enjoyable line of work. Such satisfaction has provided me the stimulus to write this book.

Thank you for the excellent work by Shy Riysat, Kyla Ferns and others at First Choice Books.

The following novel is based on real surgical cases. Names have been changed and details have been altered to protect confidentiality. I have done consulting work and worked for a medical licensing body. No cases or characters were derived from these lines of work.

Major characters in this novel are a product of my imagination and any resemblance to any individuals, living or dead, is purely coincidental. Some minor characters have been inspired by real people: highly respected colleagues or teachers.

Prologue: December 1979

The second he released the heavy front door from his gloved fingers, thirteen-year-old Jamie Smythe worried that he'd gone too far. Fortunately, fresh snow lined the doorway, so the expected crash was muted to a dull thud. Inside the house, he stomped his feet, both to shake the snow off his boots and to let his parents know that he was none too pleased about having to shovel the entire driveway and sidewalk. The last time he'd slammed a door that hard, he'd received a first-rate dressing down from his father.

"Jamie, I don't know how many times I've told you not to come crashing in here like that. Show some respect for me and your mother."

Jamie had been the target of more than a few of his father's lectures about temper recently. Apparently, Andrew Smythe was only willing to cut him a minimal amount of slack.

Andrew approached from the front hall as Jamie took off his hat and gloves. Jamie's straight blond hair had a sprinkle of snow around the edges. The flakes on his face were melting, leaving behind tiny water droplets on his red nose and cheeks. He slid his coat off, revealing his wiry frame, a stark contrast to his father's solid 230 pounds. At just under six feet tall, Jamie had nearly caught up to his father in height. He tucked his hat and gloves in one of his coat sleeves, and was just about to throw his coat into the corner of the front hall, but thought better of it and hung it on the hook just inside the door.

"Did you finish shovelling the driveway?"

"Sort of," Jamie mumbled, heading towards the family room.

"What do you mean, 'sort of'? Did you or didn't you?" His father followed him. "No idiot box until the driveway's finished!" The television had been a source of recent disputes. Andrew had made it quite clear he couldn't stand it when his son spent hours mindlessly watching TV. It didn't matter if it was Happy Days, The Rockford Files or Charlie's Angels—it was all a waste of time.

Jamie couldn't understand why his parents were so uptight about everything. His father was the worst; he suspected his mother only went along with it to keep the peace. The previous three months had been hell. His dad was going on about something all the time. When Jamie opposed his father's attempts to "whip him into shape", things only got worse. But he wasn't just going to take his father's dictatorial behaviour indefinitely. His father was never physically violent, but sometimes Jamie wondered how much longer he could stand the verbal attacks. Every few months, Dad would back off for a week or two, apparently sulking while Jamie's mother took over the role of family cop. Jamie was hoping for one of those breaks. It was easier to put up with his mother.

"I did the front walk, the steps, the sidewalk and three-quarters of the driveway. I need a break."

"Never mind. I'll finish it myself." Andrew put on his heavy coat, calling to Jamie, "Someday you'll understand. And no TV until after supper!"

Jamie felt a mixture of relief and guilt, knowing that his father was going out into the cold winter air to finish shovelling the driveway. When he heard the front door close, he relaxed. He'd finally have a few minutes of peace and quiet, even if he wasn't allowed to turn on the TV.

As an only child, Jamie wanted to be closer to his father, but the ongoing turmoil in his home troubled him. Andrew claimed it was always Jamie's fault. Sometimes Jamie wanted to ask his dad questions about life, to bond with his father as his friends did with theirs. But he always hesitated; he didn't want to risk his role as the rebellious teenager, a label he'd been given on his thirteenth birthday. No particular incident had earned Jamie the title; his father had implied that it was simply a culmination of several noteworthy events.

Jamie sat silently on the family room couch. It was best not to upset the balance. If he wanted to ask questions, there was always tomorrow.

But by the next day, his father was dead.

Chapter 1 ~ Bleeding

Present Day—September 16, 2010—8:00 p.m.

"I would say he has definitely lost his marbles." Dr. Katrina Jaworsky's thick Eastern-European accent, her formal attire and her serious demeanour did not foreshadow such a simplistic conclusion. She was a new staff psychiatrist, and although Jim Smythe had never met her before, he'd heard good things about her.

"Of course he has; otherwise, I wouldn't have asked you to see him," retorted Dr. Smythe. Regretting his sharpness, he added, "I'm interested in your opinion about whether we can compel him to have surgery despite the fact that he has withdrawn consent."

"Under normal circumstances, a person can be certified if they are suffering from a mental illness and are at risk of harming themselves or others. But these aren't exactly normal circumstances."

The patient, Rory Harbin, was a man in his twenties with no relatives in the area. He had refused to give his family members' phone numbers. Currently, he was lying in his intensive care unit bed, connected to monitors and tubes. He was breathing on his own—he had not yet been intubated—but each breath was painful and shallow. Smythe was not keen to wait to see what would happen next. Harbin's pulse rate was rapid at 110 beats per minute; his oxygen mask partially covered the pained expression on his face.

Smythe was not sure whether the expression was from Harbin's shoulder pain or from his paranoia. Harbin had appeared convinced the hospital staff did not have his best interest in mind. But that didn't matter to Smythe—such subtleties were for Jaworsky to figure out. Surgeons fixed things. If Smythe were paid to think, he would be a psychiatrist or an internal medicine specialist. Smythe *wanted* to fix Harbin, and he knew he *could* fix Harbin, but he didn't have permission. Soon, it could be too late.

Jaworsky clarified her previous statement: "You see, most often harm comes from an act of violence, such as attempted suicide. It's very unusual for me to be here in the intensive care unit in the first place. Psychiatrists usually consult after a patient has been stabilized medically and is out of danger—"

"But we can't wait for him to be stabilized; we need an answer in case his bleeding doesn't stop." Dr. Smythe always found it interesting to chat with an attractive co-worker such as Dr. Jaworsky. If he weren't married, he might even be interested in her. She was slender and brunette. Her hair was pulled back, her lips were full, and she wore just a touch of make-up—something he thought she really didn't need. He judged her to be in her late thirties.

Dr. Jaworsky said, "Your patient has internal bleeding. You are not absolutely certain, but you think it is from his spleen. There has been no history of trauma, which in itself is puzzling. From a psychiatric point of view, he could be declared mentally incompetent. So, it looks pretty straightforward—no?"

"Let's get on with the surgery."

"Although his life appeared to be in danger when he arrived a few hours ago, it's not quite so clear at the moment. His blood pressure was low and his pulse was more rapid, but he has responded to non-surgical treatment in the form of intravenous fluids. His vital signs have improved. He has not yet received blood but his hemoglobin remains only slightly below normal. You don't have a definite diagnosis and you can't be certain that he is going to continue to bleed. And, he has consented to blood transfusions, an option that has not yet been utilized."

"Too bad he's not a Jehovah's Witness," Smythe sighed. "At least they know the value of early surgical intervention." Jehovah's Witnesses' refusal to accept blood transfusions on religious grounds was often a source of irritation to surgeons like Smythe, but those patients were less likely to hesitate if an operation to stop bleeding was recommended.

It annoyed Smythe to hear non-surgeons expound logically on surgical topics. It was all very well for Jaworsky to have her opinions about surgical treatment, but *she* wouldn't have to take the heat for a bad surgical outcome. Smythe was still keen to perform surgery on Harbin. After all, it was much easier to sleep at night when one's patient had an incision on his belly than to wonder at three in the morning if an urgent phone call about a crashing patient was just around the corner. Surgeons rarely got in trouble for operating too early, especially for bleeding. But operating too late could be a disaster. Still, he'd learned long ago to pick his battles, and this was not one he was willing to fight—yet.

"It's only 8:00 p.m. right now. Your patient is reasonably stable at the moment. I would be willing to certify him—which would be the first step in permitting surgery—if he destabilizes. After he has had a couple of units of blood, if he still refuses surgery and his vitals indicate ongoing bleeding, call me. I can be back here in ten minutes."

Smythe wondered where she lived if she could be there in ten minutes. He thought Jaworsky was single, but he wasn't certain. The absence of a ring was not always an indicator of marital status in the hospital environment. He wondered, just for a second, what she'd look like less formally dressed. Or undressed. He shook himself out of his trance and said tersely, "Right then. Expect to hear from me. And thanks for seeing him."

Jim Smythe was forty-four years old, over six feet tall and of muscular build. Greying was only slightly visible amongst his predominantly blond hair, but it gave him the appearance of experience. His youthful features complemented his approachable personality. He'd heard that female staff found him attractive, especially since he'd gotten laser eye surgery and no longer wore glasses. As a general surgeon, he spent close to half his time doing operations and other medical procedures. Most of his surgery was in the abdomen, often on cancers or other serious conditions such as peritonitis or trauma. Even taking out an inflamed appendix gave Smythe a thrill; he'd rather be doing that any day than listening to tales of woe about a marital breakup, a skill he'd only half-learned many years ago as an intern.

* * *

September 16 had started out like any other day while Smythe was on call for the surgery service at the 360-bed Lakefield Regional Hospital. He had a few surgical follow-ups booked in the morning but was essentially free the rest of the day to deal with incoming emergencies. His on-call shift lasted until seven o'clock the next morning, after which he'd have to check on his new admissions and tend to more booked patients. Being on call for general surgery could be quiet or it could be hectic all day and night. Although it was not a common occurrence, in theory he could work thirty hours straight, between his twenty-four hours of on-call time and his regular work the next day.

At approximately 11:00 a.m. that day, he'd received a call from the emergency department about Mr. Harbin.

"Jim, I've got someone I'd like you to see regarding a possible intra-abdominal problem." Rick Abbott, a highly respected emergency physician, was currently starting his third and final year as Chief of Medical Staff at Lakefield Regional Hospital. In his administrative position, he often drew on his objective, calm approach when dealing with other doctors. He was also composed when it came to handling sick patients in the emergency department.

Abbott continued, "I have a twenty-eight-year-old male who came in with left shoulder pain, shortness of breath, tachycardia and hypotension." Tachycardia and hypotension—rapid heart rate and low blood pressure—were telltale signs of shock, which sometimes meant bleeding. *Now, this is getting interesting*, thought Smythe.

"He's just passing through town—been driving for sixteen hours straight, so with all that immobility, we originally thought he might have a pulmonary embolism. But his blood gases are normal. He was seen by internal medicine, and they don't think it's a PE. They say a blood clot of significant magnitude to the lungs would likely be incompatible with normal blood gases. So, we've just sent him to the CAT scanner for a pulmonary angio and an abdominal scan. That should sort it out, but I think it's his belly, so we'll be needing your services."

"What's his hemoglobin?" asked Smythe.

"Not back yet."

It drove Smythe crazy to be called to the emergency department before a patient's diagnostic work-up was complete. Why couldn't Abbott just call him after the CAT scan and the hemoglobin were done? Half the time, the tests came back normal, the doctors were back to square one and Smythe would be responsible for a patient who had a non-surgical problem. Last time he checked, a general surgeon wasn't the guy to treat heart attacks or blood clots. But Abbott had informed Smythe of this patient, and it was difficult to wiggle out of it now. Smythe knew better than to try to talk Abbott out of the referral; he'd done that a few too many times before. Worse than Abbott's premature emergency referral was the fact that he was often correct, and Smythe couldn't stand being wrong. Better to keep his mouth shut and see the patient.

"Have them call me when he's back from his CAT scan. I'm just around the corner in the clinic and will come see him right away." Smythe hung up the phone and got back to his surgical follow-ups.

About half an hour later, the phone call came. This time it was Jen

Boyer, a young emergency nurse. Smythe guessed she was about twenty-two. She had shoulder-length brown hair that was parted in the middle. Her dark, rectangular-framed glasses couldn't hide the beauty of her deep brown eyes. And her smile—men half his age must have been rendered defenseless on a regular basis.

"Dr. Smythe, it's Jen. Your patient is back from CAT scan." *Your patient*, thought Smythe. *Why is he "my patient" when I haven't yet seen him?*

"Do you know what the scan showed?" asked Smythe.

"No. Dr. Abbott just asked me to call you."

"I'll be right there."

Smythe hung up the phone and leaned against the wall. With his eyes closed, he grimaced. Opening his eyes to make sure no one was looking, he took some Maalox from his white coat pocket. Without spilling, he carefully filled the bottle cap with it. As he downed the antacid, he thought he really should do something about his heartburn. But not now; he had work to do.

When he arrived at the emergency department, Smythe found several people crowded around the X-ray display unit. Now that images were digital, X-rays were no longer on film and could be viewed just about anywhere in the hospital. Rick Abbott was scrolling through the abdominal CAT scan images, demonstrating the findings to his audience. His portly frame rested squarely in front of the X-ray monitor. Jen was peeking around his right shoulder to catch a glimpse. Several others—students, nurses and paramedics—were vying for position to scrutinize the pictures.

A couple of people parted and stepped back so Dr. Smythe could see the CAT scan. He slid up to the front beside Abbott, brushing Jen's arm in the process.

Abbott continued, "I spoke to the radiologist, Jim. It's not a pulmonary embolism. It looks like blood in his belly. Can't be certain, of course, but there's some kind of fluid that shouldn't be there. Radiology estimated about 750–1000 cc. It's around the spleen, under the left diaphragm, under the liver, and down in the pelvis. There's no obvious source of bleeding, but the spleen does look a bit enlarged and abnormal in texture."

"Any history of trauma? Is his belly tender?"

"No and no," replied Abbott. "I thought he'd have at least some abdominal tenderness with this amount of free fluid in his abdomen. But he does have left shoulder pain."

Smythe picked up on Dr. Abbott's courteous pause. This was Smythe's cue to impress the students in the crowd. It wasn't often a surgeon got to display his intellectual prowess to the team: a surgeon's hands constituted his most impressive assets, yet they were primarily used in the sanctuary of the operating room, far from the eyes of most hospital personnel.

"Sometimes the only symptom of blood accumulating in the abdomen is pain in one shoulder. It comes from irritation to the undersurface of the diaphragm. Some of the nerves that supply the shoulder join nerves from the diaphragm. The patient feels the pain coming from the shoulder, even though it's originating from elsewhere. It's called referred pain. It's similar to the shoulder pain after a laparoscopic gallbladder operation—irritation under the diaphragm from carbon dioxide gas and small amounts of blood." Aside from Smythe enjoying his own theatrics in front of the younger members of the team, the human body's quirks fascinated him. Others, like Abbott, seemed willing to allow Smythe his few minutes of fame; stroking a surgeon's ego now and then was a small price to pay for his service on a day-to-day basis.

"Well, when in doubt, look at the patient," said Smythe, starting towards the patient's cubicle. Jen snickered, revealing her awareness of Dr. Smythe's attempt to be humorous. The others didn't let on if they had any idea.

Dr. Smythe entered the cubicle with Jen at his heels. He introduced himself to Rory Harbin, who was lying on the stretcher, his heart rate and other vitals being continually monitored. When the patient didn't immediately take Smythe's outstretched hand, Smythe continued a large arc to ceremoniously scratch his forehead, as if he'd never intended a handshake.

Harbin had sandy brown hair around the edges of his central bald spot, and he wore circular, silver wire-rimmed glasses that reminded Smythe of John Lennon's. But Harbin's face looked nothing like Lennon's. Small, shifty dark eyes rested above puffy cheeks in a round face. Smythe judged him to be below average height and of slight build. At least he was thin. Smythe didn't relish the idea of being up to his elbows in a 300-pound patient's abdomen, trying to stop bleeding. Mr. Harbin's 145 pounds or so would help him avoid a significant pitfall of surgery on a larger man—poor exposure of the operative field. Smythe studied Harbin's physique, and thought about a gratifying operation for this man, who probably had internal bleeding.

"Mr. Harbin, I'm Dr. Smythe. I'm a surgeon, and Dr. Abbott has asked me to see you about possible internal bleeding. How long have you been feeling unwell?"

No answer.

"Is your shoulder painful? Do you have pain in your stomach?" Smythe looked at Harbin's vitals. His heart rate was down from 135 to 105, and his blood pressure had come up from 80 over 60 to 110 over 70. Obviously, the intravenous fluids were helping. "If you want me to help, you will need to answer my questions. Are you having pain?"

"Dr. Smythe is the surgeon we told you about, Rory. He's here to help you," Jen piped in.

"Yes." Rory's tense expression relaxed, his forehead wrinkles disappearing.

"Can you tell us about it?" Jen added.

Perhaps it was Jen's comparable age or her warm expression that helped Rory begin to open up. "I have pain in my left shoulder. It started at about 6:00 this morning while I was driving. It hasn't let up, and I started feeling dizzy, so I pulled into the hospital. I'm on my way to a convention, and I really need to get going."

"What convention?" Smythe found that showing interest in his patients' lives occasionally helped draw out more detail.

"It's personal."

So much for the "appear interested" approach. Jim Smythe continued with the interview and the examination, just as he'd done hundreds of times previously. In this case, his mind was already made up. Harbin needed surgery for suspected intra-abdominal bleeding. The interview and the exam henceforth were merely formalities to convince the patient that Smythe was not a knife-happy surgeon, but that he actually had a very good reason to operate, and operate soon. But when it came to examining Mr. Harbin's abdomen, Smythe didn't find much. It was flat and soft, and it wasn't tender—all findings one would not normally associate with an acute surgical abdomen. But Smythe knew bleeding into the abdominal cavity was different. He'd been amazed in the past by how much blood could hide between loops of intestine and under the diaphragm, without any overt signs on clinical examination.

"What about an MRI?" asked Harbin.

While refraining from rolling his eyes, Dr. Smythe calmly launched into his usual monologue about how MRIs—magnetic resonance imaging—were no more informative for this type of problem than a CAT scan. Smythe knew that an MRI would waste valuable time; how could any test make him more than 100 percent sure of his plan? But he also knew better than to share this degree of certainty with his patient. Although he should be perceived as confident, too quick a diagnosis could make a patient hesitate. Smythe continued, explaining that this could be a life-threatening situation due to internal bleeding, and that in this case, it was better to look and see, rather than wait and see. As Mr. Harbin's expression softened further, Dr. Smythe excused himself to check on operating room availability.

Jen, following close behind, asked, "Where could he be bleeding from?"

"His spleen," replied Smythe.

"But there's no history of trauma," countered Jen.

"Probably spontaneous splenic rupture. If the spleen is pathological it can rupture without any known history of trauma. A tumour in the spleen, or mononucleosis, can make it fragile enough to rupture in rare circumstances. And in such a situation, surgery is the best option."

Smythe enjoyed talking to anyone who would listen; he especially liked talking to Jen because she reminded him of his eldest daughter, Emily, who was now thirteen. Dr. Smythe would be delighted if Emily took a path like Jen's and went into nursing or even medical school, although he wasn't too keen on surgery for a young woman in his family. And, he wouldn't blame Emily or her younger sister Sara if they ran in the opposite direction of a career in surgery after seeing how often he was absent from his family due to work commitments. Although women were prominently represented in surgery these days, there was always a risk of conflict between work and family life, a clash he'd particularly observed with his female colleagues.

Smythe himself often felt conflicted, tugged between the desire to spend time with his family and his need to immerse himself in his surgical activities. At least he had Amanda to pick up the slack at home from time to time when life at the hospital got busy.

After phoning the operating room and putting Rory Harbin on the list for surgery, Dr. Smythe went back to see him and fill in the details of the interview. Further questioning didn't reveal any obvious reason for Harbin to be bleeding internally. Although he did not appear enthusiastic about surgery, he seemed resigned to it and signed the consent form Smythe presented to him.

* * *

At five o'clock in the afternoon, staff in the operating room were preparing for Mr. Harbin's upcoming operation. Everyone in the room wore a mask except Harbin, who lay on a narrow operating table at the room's centre. He was strapped on to the table so he wouldn't fall off either before or after induction of anesthetic. At the back table, two nurses counted instruments and sponges, ensuring the same number of items would come out of Harbin as went into him. Harbin's head was next to anesthesiologist Dr. Sandi Tremaine's elaborate array of monitoring equipment. She prepared medications and equipment to protect Harbin's airway and support parameters such as blood pressure and breathing while he was under anesthetic.

Sandi Tremaine, a divorced mother of two teenage boys, was one of twelve anesthesiologists at Lakefield Hospital. In addition to having in-depth knowledge and experience, she was self-assured. No one actually knew if it had been due to Sandi's strong personality or the fortitude of her lawyer, but it was clear she'd come out on top in the divorce proceedings. Not only had she secured custody of her boys, but she'd also extracted considerable child support payments from her ex-husband—even though he made half the money that she did. No one dared confront her on medical issues, fearing being rendered a travesty in front of their colleagues like her poor ex-husband had been in front of the courts. There were a few exceptions, of course—including Jim Smythe. Dr. Tremaine tightened her operating gown around her lean waistline, then checked to ensure her thick, light-brown hair was completely covered by her surgical cap before she drew up the next syringe full of medication for her patient.

Harbin stared up at the ceiling. The room was silent except for the nurses' monotonous counting at the back table. Many of the items in the operating room were wrapped or covered in green to signify sterility. The green sterile drapes were yet to be placed over Harbin's body after his abdomen was cleansed with disinfectant. After induction of anesthesia, the drapes would cover all but a window on the abdomen, through which Smythe would make his incision.

Sandi Tremaine connected cardiac monitoring electrodes to Harbin's chest, which added the rhythmic beeping of his heart to the background noise. His heart rate was 120 beats per minute—the rapidity probably a combination of his previous blood loss and his current nervousness. He now stared forty-five degrees to his left at a clear bag of saline dripping fluid one drop at a time, heading for a vein in his left arm. The cadence of the drips increased as Dr. Tremaine adjusted the intravenous infusion rate to prepare for induction of anesthesia. She then gently placed a mask over Harbin's face to maximize the oxygen in his bloodstream prior to putting him to sleep.

The nurses finished counting. Dr. Smythe began to tap his right foot as one of the nurses methodically tied his gown at the back. Even though

Harbin was not yet asleep, Smythe was demonstrating to the team it was time to get moving; he intended to start, whether they were ready for him or not. At that moment, Harbin grabbed at the oxygen mask in Dr. Tremaine's hand, trying to push it away from his face. Before Tremaine could give the usual assurance that it was just oxygen, Harbin said, "I've got to get up—just for a minute."

Dr. Tremaine slid the oxygen mask away from his face.

"You what?" she asked evenly.

"I have to get up, just for a minute," he repeated.

"That's what I thought you said," replied Dr. Tremaine. She turned to Smythe, "Jim?"

Smythe shrugged.

One of the nurses looked inquisitively above her surgical mask at Dr. Tremaine, who nodded and gave a wave of her hand, indicating that they should follow Harbin's wishes. To argue with Harbin or initiate a drug-induced sleep before he could repeat himself wouldn't be wise. He would surely remember his request after the surgery, and if Sandi Tremaine ignored it, there could be some potential for trouble. It was always easier to avoid a patient complaint than to have to respond to administration about it after the fact.

The nurse unstrapped Rory Harbin from the operating table. Without assistance, he swung his legs to the right and sat up. He paused for a few seconds with his legs over the side of the table. Then, he carefully stepped off the table onto the cold tile floor and stood up straight. All he wore was a baby-blue hospital gown that tied up the back and only covered his body to his mid-thighs. There were now six puzzled onlookers in the room—Drs. Smythe and Tremaine and surgical assistant Dr. Jared Chong, along with three nurses—all waiting to see what Harbin was going to do next.

He bent forward as if he were an Olympic sprinter before the biggest event of his lifetime. As his hands touched the floor, his hospital gown parted, displaying his buttocks to the operating team. Harbin pursed his lips, then expelled three staccato puffs of air, as if waiting for someone to announce, "On your mark . . ." Then, as if a false start had been called, he got up and paced three very tight circles.

Harbin looked Smythe squarely in the eyes and proclaimed, "No, I don't think I'll go through with this."

Smythe had seen a lot over the years, but he'd never seen a patient get up off the operating table and declare the operation cancelled. If Mr. Harbin had been actively bleeding or showing signs of instability, Smythe would have pushed the issue. Instead, he simply asked, "Are you sure?"

"Yes, I'm certain. I know I'll be fine without the surgery. I'll be fine."

"But you've been bleeding internally," Smythe reminded him.

"No, I'll be fine. No surgery."

The staff all stared in silence toward the centre of the room at Rory Harbin. The three nurses glanced amongst themselves, and then simultaneously looked wide-eyed at Smythe. It was now 5:15 in the afternoon. Several surgical emergencies were waiting in line for the operating room, although no operation was as urgent as Harbin's.

"All right, send Mr. Harbin back to the ward." Tremaine's tone declared that there would be no further discussion. She'd often said that she had not gone to medical school to coddle patients. Anxiety about a surgical decision was something Tremaine expected to be addressed *before* a patient came to the operating room.

Tremaine leaned towards Smythe, coldly staring at him. "And he's not coming back for a second chance in the middle of the night. He's had his opportunity for an operation today."

We'll see about that, thought Smythe. Then, he announced, "Without surgery, we need to admit him to the intensive care unit for close observation and a second opinion." Occasionally, in uncertain circumstances, Smythe consulted with a general surgery colleague, but he had no doubts about this case. He wanted a consultation about Harbin's mental ability to make a decision about his health. Smythe wanted input from a psychiatrist for a change.

In the locker room a few minutes later, Jared asked why Smythe had given in so easily.

"We can't force him to have surgery. Not yet, anyway. He's very stable at the moment. But believe me, Jared, I'll be in there in no time if necessary."

Jared buttoned his dress shirt after tossing his greens in the laundry bin. Jared Chong was twenty-five years old, medium height and slim. His black hair was long enough at the front that he often had to sweep it across with his hand to keep it out of his eyes. He had the face of a sixteen-year-old with barely any dark stubble, and would likely hear the exclamation, "But you're too young to be a doctor!" for many years yet. He had graduated from medical school as the youngest in his class four years ago. After a residency in family medicine, he'd settled into Lakefield, doing occasional walk-in clinics and emergency room shifts when he could pick them up.

Over the last year, however, he'd told Smythe he wanted to help more often in the operating room. Although Smythe sometimes thought Jared was a little *too* eager to please—in contrast to many of the young doctors graduating these days—he liked Jared's enthusiasm. When he heard that Jared was thinking of going back into residency to become a surgeon, Smythe's interest in teaching was re-ignited. This intensified their relationship in the operating room, as Smythe viewed Jared's interest in a surgical career as an inclination worth fostering. Jared was married, with a three-year-old daughter and another child due in February. In five months, he'd be a father of two—not an ideal situation in which to start a surgery residency. But his wife, Hilary, was supportive.

Both fully dressed, Jared and Smythe left the O.R. locker room in opposite directions, likely to cross paths later that evening.

*　*　*

Smythe was not a big fan of bureaucracy. In fact, he was suspicious of anything put forward by administration—except for the annual Western Canada Medical Awards dinner. Held in late January each year, it was seen by most doctors as a pleasant social event to lift them out of the winter blues, while at the same time recognizing the achievements of a select few. For those like Smythe who were in the top percentile for ability and commitment to their job, it stood for more. Five years ago, he had won the Clinician of the Year Award. Since medical colleagues, not bureaucrats, were the voters, the choice took on an importance for Smythe above what administration could ever acknowledge.

Although the awards were supported by administration, he viewed being selected by one's professional cohort as validation of the process. If the unfortunate rule that one could never win the Clinician of the Year Award more than once were not in place, Smythe might have won it repeatedly. Instead, he had been shut out of the awards for the last four years and would likely continue in this trend—unless a rumour that he was up for this year's Lifetime Achievement Award turned out to be true. Normally presented to physicians nearing retirement or death, it had never been awarded to a doctor under fifty. For administration to recognize him in such a way, Smythe was willing to make an exception in his general opinion about all things administrative.

With a few spare minutes, Smythe took the short walk across the street to his office. While on call, he enjoyed the opportunity to get away from the hospital environment. With a small kitchen, including a microwave, he could heat up a quick meal—but only if he remembered to stock the cupboard. Today, he found only some noodle soup—not much to call a meal. He really should have his secretary top up the supply for him from time to time. He'd talk to her about that.

Smythe was startled to hear Moira's voice behind him. Still in the office at 6:30 . . . he should give her a raise.

"Jim, did you really mean to call the Hudspeth family 'these bastards'?" Moira asked in her usual high-pitched tone. Unmarried and in her late forties, Moira was staunchly loyal to Smythe in her position as his sole office employee.

"What do you mean?" Smythe asked. Before she had a chance to reply, he added, "Of course not!"

"It's just that in your letter to the referring doc, you're saying 'Mrs. Hudspeth and her family needs to think it over, and these bastards will get back to me when they've decided if they want to go ahead with surgery.' I think your voice recognition software is going a little wonky these days. You know, I don't mind typing your letters if this kind of thing is the alternative."

Smythe ran a hand through his hair. "We've got to do something, that's for sure. When my letter went out referring to a 'Luke ileostomy' instead of a 'loop ileostomy', it's likely no one noticed. Even when I referred to heart 'murmurs' as 'moaners', probably most people missed it and a few had a chuckle. But *'these bastards'*—and in perfect context!" He shook his head. "It's not good."

"What did you actually say, Jim?"

"I have no idea." His eyes brightening, he added, "We have to add a disclaimer after my signature, indicating any errors could be due to voice recognition software."

"I can add that," Moira said reassuringly.

"If that letter slipped through and someone who doesn't know me read it, they could think I'm a lunatic. They might even complain to the Medical Licensing Authority!"

"I'll fix it first thing tomorrow." Slipping on her jacket and looking at the floor, she added, "Oh, this arrived late today." She thrust a letter abruptly into Smythe's hands and turned toward the doorway.

Without looking at the letter, Smythe wished Moira a good evening and walked down the hall, glancing into the empty room next to his consulting office. Such a waste of space. He thought he should get some exercise equipment. A small gym would be good for burning off excess energy while waiting for an operation. Smythe was convinced there was more than one type of energy, and that no matter how hard one worked, there was always some pent-up vitality waiting to be released. He'd order a rowing machine next week.

His office was neat and sparsely furnished. Surgical textbooks were displayed behind his large, mahogany desk, which had a big, comfortable swivel chair. Two chairs were across the desk, for a patient and a patient's family member. There were a couple of smaller stools to pull up to the desk if more family members were present. A few anatomical posters decorated the wall. A door to Smythe's left led to a small examining room.

As he sat down at his desk to do some quick paperwork, he looked at the plain white envelope Moira had handed him before she left: PRIVATE AND CONFIDENTIAL. His heart rate increased. The return address—Medical Licensing Authority—could cause any doctor's pulse rate and blood pressure to rise, no matter how confident he was. Smythe speculated that some sadistic employee at the Licensing Authority took great pleasure sending all its mail—even Christmas cards—stamped PRIVATE AND CONFIDENTIAL.

As he slit open the letter, his eyes widened. This was the real thing. His attention jumped to words and phrases across the page, without taking in the whole picture: COMPLAINT—Mrs. Hazel Kowalchuk—ALLEGATIONS—MISSED DIAGNOSIS—DAMAGES—RESPONSE WITHIN THIRTY DAYS—LEGAL COUNSEL—POWER TO REVOKE MEDICAL LICENSE.

His mind raced. If there was anything good in the letter, Smythe had missed it. Whatever happened to "innocent until proven guilty"? Who *was* Hazel Kowalchuk? He looked her up on his office computer. She wasn't there; he must have seen her over ten months ago, which was when he'd transitioned his office to a paperless system. Suddenly, the security of his role as a surgeon was shaken. One serious complaint, if justified, could result in the loss of his medical license. And his license was what defined him. A threat to his ability to do surgery was an attack on his entire self.

Hazel Kowalchuk's name had the ring of familiarity, but he couldn't remember who she was. Smythe wasn't so good at remembering to bring home milk or bread, but given a surgical case, his powers of recollection were phenomenal. He could be wakened at 2:00 in the morning, remembering everything about a patient he hadn't seen for five years—as long as he was given enough to start the process. Now, he just needed a clue to trigger everything he knew about Hazel Kowalchuk. He'd ask Moira to pull the paper chart. Smythe put the letter back in the envelope and thrust it into his desk drawer, which he locked.

Then he reached for a bottle of Maalox as his mind turned back to Rory Harbin and the anticipated psychiatric opinion from Dr. Jaworsky.

Chapter 2 ~ All Bleeding Eventually Stops

September 16 – 8:15 p.m.

Smythe reflected on Dr. Katrina Jaworsky's recent words in the intensive care unit. What was it she'd said—"lost his marbles"? Smythe mulled it over. Rory Harbin had told Dr. Jaworsky that he'd refused surgery because God would protect him from death due to internal bleeding. Although a strong belief in God was not in itself delusional, Dr. Jaworsky extracted a few other bits of information that confirmed Mr. Harbin was out of touch with reality. He had been hearing voices for the last three weeks. He'd hear people *speak to him directly* over his car radio. Soon after Harbin's pain had started this morning, God told him on the radio that He was going to protect Harbin from whatever was ailing him. This was a key feature of psychosis: the presence of delusions or unequivocally false beliefs.

Jim Smythe watched Dr. Jaworsky walk down the long corridor to the exit of the intensive care unit. It was only 8:15 p.m. but he was already tired. He had spent most of the day running from one cubicle to another in the emergency department, assessing several new referrals with abdominal pain. He had taken out one appendix and admitted three other patients for observation, but Harbin was his most interesting case of the day.

Smythe watched Harbin from across the intensive care unit, wondering why this patient was so out of touch that he would decline a life-saving operation. Smythe contemplated the medical history: a twenty-eight-year-old male, presenting with signs of shock, and showing fluid in his belly on a CAT scan. It had to be blood—what else could it be? Pus would look different, accompanied by inflammatory "stranding" on the images. Bowel content from a perforation would have contained air. But in Harbin's case, it looked like blood. Apart from a previous episode of pancreatitis, he'd been healthy. The pancreas could become inflamed due to gallstones, heavy alcohol consumption or other causes. Harbin hadn't admitted to drinking alcohol, but he wasn't giving away a whole lot about his medical history. He didn't admit to a personal or family history of mental illness, either.

Yet his paranoid attitude and his withdrawal of consent for surgery were obviously delusional. Harbin had even refused an angiogram, a less invasive procedure using X-rays to diagnose and possibly treat the bleeding site. Jaworsky's conclusion about Harbin's mental health was spot-on, as far as Smythe was concerned.

What troubled Smythe was not Harbin's current condition, but what might develop over the next few hours. Sometimes internal bleeding would start and stop. The body's natural defense against bleeding—low blood pressure—was the result of the bleeding itself. This allowed a clot to form at the hemorrhage site. In most circumstances, this defense was successful. But in other cases, it was only temporary. In those situations, the initial bleed was referred to as a "herald bleed"—heralding the torrential hemorrhage that was yet to come.

But for now, his patient was stable; he had probably stopped bleeding, and he had explicitly stated he did not want surgery. Despite the shaky grounds upon which Harbin was making this decision, Smythe would wait on this one for a while—reluctantly.

* * *

Having just drained an abscess in the emergency department, Smythe was finishing up paperwork fifteen minutes after midnight when his cell phone rang. The anxious voice on the other end belonged to Frieda, an experienced ICU nurse. Rory Harbin had destabilized.

Everything had been quite unremarkable until midnight, at which point Mr. Harbin's pulse rate began to climb, he became anxious and his blood pressure dropped to 90 systolic. At the same time, he decided to test his legs by walking around his small private area in the ICU. Fortunately, his "private" area included a clear view from the nursing station through glass walls, and continual monitoring of vital signs such as pulse rate, blood pressure and oxygen saturation. When Harbin's knees buckled and he crashed to the floor, Frieda was already running into the room before any alarm bells commenced.

Frieda and a couple of co-workers assisted Harbin back into bed. He appeared pale and his skin was clammy. Prior to phoning Smythe, Frieda had turned up the intravenous fluids. Despite this measure, when Smythe answered the phone, the patient's blood pressure was dropping rather than rising.

"We've just started a bolus of Ringer's lactate, wide open, yet his BP has now dropped to 70 systolic and he doesn't look good," Frieda reported.

"I'll be right there. Get him ready for surgery immediately. Transfuse two units of red blood cells as soon as possible." Jim Smythe was excited to finally get Harbin where he needed to be—in an operating room. "I'll call the O.R. and then come up to the ICU straight away."

"What about consent for surgery?"

Fuck the consent, thought Smythe. He thought of Katrina's blue-grey eyes, her soft facial features and the curves he imagined under her business suit and white lab coat. She'd said she could be there in ten minutes. "Call Dr. Jaworsky and let her know what's happening. If she can do her part for the consent by the time we're ready for the O.R., great. If not, we go anyway." Several nurses hastily organized Harbin a second time for an operation. Jaworsky arrived to find that Harbin had signed the consent at the last minute.

Twenty minutes later, the team was in the operating room. There was a fresh batch of nurses on the night shift, but the physicians were unchanged, all being on call for the twenty-four-hour period.

Dr. Sandi Tremaine refrained from further comments. Harbin was clearly ill—in fact, unstable. Her prior declaration that Harbin had missed his chance to get an operation while she was on call had clearly been a bluff. In a case like this, there was never a question.

Although Smythe and Dr. Jared Chong had a sense of déjà vu, the atmosphere was altogether different this time around. The nurses completed their counting ritual at twice the speed. Dr. Tremaine ran third and fourth units of blood though pressure bags into intravenous lines in each arm. Harbin lay in the centre of the room with both arms out at ninety degrees. His body took the shape of a crucifix, an ironic symbol that was not lost on Smythe. A respiratory technician quickly inserted an arterial line into Harbin's left radial artery for beat-to-beat blood pressure monitoring, while Sandi Tremaine prepared to insert a large-bore intravenous catheter into Harbin's right internal jugular vein.

Dr. Smythe, his arms dripping from his second scrub for Rory Harbin, wondered why all these lines hadn't been inserted in the ICU hours before. The ICU staff had said something about reluctance on the part of the patient. Patient-focused care had gone a little too far, thought Smythe, when patient "comfort" superseded patient safety. Jim's mind wandered as the team frantically prepared for the surgery. Smythe knew that as soon as the anesthetic was commenced and the abdomen opened, Harbin's blood pressure would drop again until the bleeding was controlled. It was therefore necessary to optimize all factors possible before surgery began.

The risks and the challenges excited Smythe, and he was becoming elated with anticipation. He considered himself anything but brilliant, but he knew he had common sense. Plus, he had experience and the guts to make a decision. He did not know what he was going to find, but he knew he had to be in there to find it and fix it. Emergency surgery was like one question on a true-false test: to operate or not to operate? But one rarely got it wrong by choosing to operate. Dithering or failing to act were far more serious transgressions.

As he had done thousands of times before, Smythe took a green towel from the scrub nurse and dried his hands, taking care not to touch them to anything unsterile, including himself. As the nurse dressed him in his sterile gown and gloves, he took a deep breath in and his surgical mask was drawn against his face. Now, he was not tired in the slightest. Despite being awake since six o'clock in the morning, Smythe was ready to go.

Rory Harbin was now under anesthetic. An endotracheal tube—a breathing tube in his windpipe—was the latest addition to his dependency on medical technology. He had survived the induction of anesthetic with minimal change in vital signs. Sandi Tremaine's administration of blood, fluid and blood-pressure-supporting medication prior to induction seemed to have quelled the expected precipitous drop in blood pressure that often accompanied the onset of anesthesia. The next insult to Mr. Harbin's physiology would be Smythe opening the abdomen, a compartment whose internal pressure had provided some measure of protection against rapid, ongoing bleeding.

Sterile green drapes covered Harbin, save for a rectangular window on his abdomen. His abdominal hair had been rapidly clipped and his skin painted brown with iodine disinfectant prior to draping. Now, his abdomen was visibly distended, no longer able to hide the volume of blood he had lost. His head was exposed for Dr. Tremaine to manage his airway and anesthetic.

Smythe glanced over at Dr. Tremaine and asked, "May we start?" Normally, the question was one of courtesy; this time, it was vitally important that Sandi Tremaine had all parameters optimized before Smythe started the operation. She simply nodded in his direction.

With one decisive stroke of his scalpel, Jim Smythe cut through the midline down to the final layer before entering the abdominal cavity. The incision went from just below the ribs to below Harbin's umbilicus. There was no place for laparoscopic or "keyhole" surgery in circumstances like these. Having parsed the midline perfectly, avoiding Mr. Harbin's rectus muscles on either side, Smythe now opened the tough midline layer, or linea alba, with electrocautery. With similar swiftness, he opened the final layer, entering a cavity brimming with dark, mostly unclotted blood. It had been a long time since Smythe had seen this much blood all at once.

He and Jared Chong worked quickly to pack all four quadrants of the abdomen with surgical sponges, while using two large suction devices to catch the overflow. Harbin's blood pressure dropped quite suddenly, and in response Sandi Tremaine pushed in more blood and medication to keep the pressure at an acceptable level. Once the abdomen was tightly packed with sponges, the bleeding appeared to be under control.

Smythe looked over at Tremaine's monitors. Blood pressure had dropped to 40 systolic for a brief period—a life-threatening situation—but now it was up to 85 systolic. Smythe gave Tremaine time to catch up.

"He's now had a total of twelve units of red blood cells, and we're starting plasma to improve his clotting." Sandi Tremaine's breathing was rapid and her voice was tense. "If you can leave those packs in for a few minutes, we might be better prepared for the next little challenge." Tremaine was obviously aware that when the surgeons did not know where the bleeding was coming from, their attempts to find out would likely result in more tumultuous drops in blood pressure.

Smythe contemplated his next move. The usual course of action would be to remove packs one quadrant at a time, starting where he suspected the bleeding was *not* occurring. If all went well, as each quadrant was freed of the pressure from the surgical sponges, the trouble quadrant would be identified. Smythe thought the bleeding source was in Rory Harbin's left upper quadrant. When swiftly and gently sliding sponges in every possible crevice at the beginning of surgery, he had been able to feel major organs and eliminate some possibilities fairly quickly. Smythe had *not* detected any cracks or tumours in the liver or spleen. A subtle, underlying pathology must be causing substantial bleeding.

Without further words, Smythe and Jared Chong began tentatively removing surgical sponges from the lower abdomen, one by one. Starting on the right side, they withdrew fourteen blood-soaked sponges with no adverse effect. The left lower quadrant was similarly unburdened, and no further blood loss occurred. By this time, Harbin's blood pressure had improved to 90 systolic, and his pulse rate had come down to 100. Just as

Smythe was contemplating Dr. Tremaine's relative success in improving Harbin's numbers, she spoke. "Jim, he's doing better, but I've now given him eighteen units of blood. If you get into any more periods of heavy blood loss, he's likely to get DIC pretty soon."

DIC—disseminated intravascular coagulation—would be a disaster. The culmination of massive hemorrhage and its treatment, DIC was the feared final pathway of most fatal bleeding. When ongoing bleeding occurred, ultimately clotting factors were entirely consumed, resulting in blood leaking from any and all surfaces. By that time, it was too late. Why did Tremaine have to bring that up now? "Perhaps we could visualize success rather than failure, Sandi," Smythe said tersely.

It was time to unpack the final quadrant. With bleeding temporarily under control, hopefully Smythe would see where any bright red, fresh blood was originating and control it. Rare causes of spontaneous hemorrhage ran through Smythe's mind as he started to remove sponges from in front of the spleen. No new bleeding. The patient's thinness allowed visualization of the spleen without much difficulty. Just medial to the spleen, the space behind the stomach called the lesser sac seemed to be filled with blood. This became more apparent as each sponge was removed, relieving the lesser sac of pressure from the front. Getting in the space behind the stomach was just a matter of separating one layer of tissue that loosely attached the stomach to the transverse colon. Smythe used cautery to open this thin layer, a maneuver he had done a hundred times before under less pressing circumstances. As the lesser sac was opened, clotted and liquid blood emanated, again dropping Harbin's blood pressure and raising Tremaine's. With manual pressure on sponges placed in the lesser sac, Smythe pressed firmly on the body of the pancreas, which seemed to be controlling the situation. He had found the source of Rory Harbin's trouble.

It was only afterward in the locker room that Smythe explained to Jared Chong the exact steps he had completed to stop Harbin's hemorrhage. Smythe had been standing on the patient's right side, opposite Chong. Reaching behind the spleen without visualization, he was able to feel attachments to the outside of the spleen through which no blood vessels traveled. With long scissors, Smythe had then cut these attachments without actually seeing them, pulling the spleen and the tail of the pancreas with it up into the front of the surgical field. The spleen's major blood supplier was the splenic artery, a robust vessel that ran along the back side of the upper border of the pancreas from the midline to the left. With his fingers tightly compressing the tail of the pancreas, Smythe had fired the surgical stapler, deploying four rows of staples across the pancreas and its neighbour, the splenic artery. At the same time, a blade within the stapler had cut between the middle two rows of staples. The pancreas and splenic artery were now completely divided and the ends stapled. It was only a matter of minutes before Smythe handed off the spleen and the tail of the pancreas to the scrub nurse. With only minor suturing, Rory Harbin's bleeding had been stopped.

In the locker room at three o'clock in the morning, Jared savoured a large bottle of Diet Coke. He could not contain his excitement about Smythe's performance. "How did you know that would work?"

Smythe was euphoric. "There aren't many causes of spontaneous hemorrhage in the abdomen, Jared. There really weren't many choices to make."

"But it happened so fast."

"Splenic artery aneurysm can be a rare source of bleeding with no obvious cause. Since pressure on the pancreas seemed to control the bleeding, and since the spleen was normal, an aneurysm of the splenic artery was the only thing left I could think of. Because the bleeding was controlled by firm pressure on the pancreas and splenic artery, I knew the problem—that is, the aneurysm—would be removed with the specimen."

"I thought it was great, especially after Tremaine was about ready to call the mortician. You showed her!"

"Yeah, Sandi can be opinionated and downright mean at times. In this case, she was okay, because we had to give this patient a chance whether he made it or not. But as a piece of advice, Jared, if you ever cross her, be certain you're right. When she wins a confrontation, she always makes sure the loser is roadkill. And it's usually not pretty."

"Good advice. I'll be careful around Sandi." Jared paused and took another drink. "So, why did a young guy like Harbin get it? Aren't aneurysms for old people?"

An aneurysm, or a ballooning of a section of a blood vessel, was possible almost anywhere in the body. Spontaneous rupture and bleeding could be fatal, and this time it had been close.

"Splenic artery aneurysms are exceedingly rare, and are more common in women than men. But I suspect his previous pancreatitis was an underlying cause. We'll see what the pathologist tells us."

Rory Harbin's pathology report came back a week later and confirmed Smythe's theory. But it really didn't matter, thought Smythe. The bleeding was stopped, so whatever the pathologist said was immaterial. The amount of pancreatic tissue removed would not be a problem, and he would not be diabetic as a result. Rory Harbin would now live life without his spleen, an innocent bystander organ that had to go during treatment of a major bleed. A couple of vaccines to replace the immunity benefits of the spleen, and Harbin would lead a normal life—as normal as he could, thought Smythe.

Harbin had been remarkably appreciative after the surgery. On daily ward rounds, Smythe was able to get an occasional smile out of him. It was like the major bleeding had jolted Harbin's mental health back to normal, as if by electroshock therapy. Dr. Jaworsky came back to see Harbin on one occasion, but his paranoid thoughts seemed to be well hidden and he didn't need her help.

On the eighth day after surgery, Harbin was ready to go home, wherever that was. Smythe was surprised to see the guarded expression back on Harbin's face. It seemed that any goodwill Harbin displayed the week after surgery had evaporated. Smythe gave his usual instructions about diet and activity, prior to writing the final discharge orders.

"God will judge you for what you have done," Harbin calmly stated.

Unfazed, Smythe shook Rory Harbin's hand and wished him well. Jim Smythe was at the top of his game these days, and it would take more than simple words to unsettle his good mood or his confidence.

But earlier in his training, Smythe had been as green and hesitant as any other medical student. It was only after many hours of study and years of experience that he had reached this level—a stage he considered the best of his career so far.

Chapter 3 ~ Greener Days

July 3, 1990

Never again, she thought. NEVER! Twenty-three year-old Amanda Berringer had just dumped her third boyfriend in ten months. Would she ever learn? That's the last guy I date for his needs, she thought. Next time it'll be me. My needs.

Standing in front of the large metallic sink, she slipped her surgical top into her green pants, accentuating her figure, then caught a reassuring glance in the mirror, her eyes beaming as she suppressed a smile behind her surgical mask. I can do better than Dwayne, she thought. She tucked her silky brown hair under her surgical cap before starting to scrub. From now on, she would avoid taking on guys who needed rescuing.

At the end of her scrub, Amanda sequentially ran each arm under the water for the final time, preparing herself for the upcoming surgery. As she held her hands as far away from her body as possible, water dripped down her vertically positioned forearms to her elbows and then into the sink. Observing the rules of sterility, she walked backwards, pushing open the swinging operating room doors with her gluteus maximi muscles, and entering the brightly lit operating theatre, all the while keeping her hands away from anything that might contaminate them.

Today she was with Dr. Steinberg, alternating between operations as scrub nurse and circulating nurse. Sakura, the circulating nurse, tied Amanda's gown from behind. As the scrub nurse, Amanda was responsible for passing the appropriate instruments to the surgeon. She put on her sterile gloves, the final barrier between her body and any instrument to be used in the operation.

Meticulously, she completed the ritual of counting instruments. Waiting for Sakura to paint the patient's abdomen with iodine solution, Amanda continued to punish herself over her latest romantic folly. Perhaps it was the nurse in her that made her feel she needed to help people. Dwayne, her most recent dud, was probably the biggest loser she'd hung out with in a long time. The young dentist was unfortunately in the habit of bringing home Valium from his office and self-medicating. Her willingness to stick around as Dwayne tried to sort out the "issues" that led to his drug use bothered her most. She should have dropped him right then and there two months ago. But no, Amanda accepted all the excuses about the family pressures that caused Dwayne's problems. She repeatedly chose her boyfriends by how appealing a rehabilitation project they seemed to be. This troubled Amanda.

Having received her R.N. diploma two years previously, Amanda was where she wanted to be—in the operating room where all the action was. If only she could get her personal life sorted out. She didn't have difficulty being asked out by guys. In fact, she was constantly turning down invitations for dates. Next time, she'd be careful not to turn away someone for being too "normal". So what if the guy wasn't needy? Based on her recent experiences, "normal" would be a much safer bet. Even though it made Amanda feel good to help people, she should leave that at work and be more selfish in her personal life.

Prior to this operation, Amanda had met the two latest med students who were being oriented in the O.R. administrative office. Both were blond, but she found the one with curly hair especially cute. The other one—Jim, was it?—was taller and gangly; he looked like a bit of a nerd. Better stay away from him. Or better yet, stay away from both for now. After Dwayne, the last thing Amanda needed was to get sucked into another relationship without having a clear head.

"What are we waiting for?" Dr. Steinberg's booming voice brought Amanda back to reality.

* * *

Jim Smythe and his clerkship partner, Steve Buchanan, put on their surgical greens with a mixture of anxiety and excitement at the beginning of their surgical rotation. Since Monday had been a holiday they met instead on July 3—Tuesday morning—in the operating room. The clerkship year marked the real transition towards becoming a medical doctor; this was the year the students would move through all the core hospital rotations, eternally grateful they would never have to sit through the unending days of lectures again. Although neither of them knew this, it would be another couple of years of medical school, followed by five years of surgical residency training before Smythe could call himself a surgeon. Steve Buchanan was fairly certain of his fate, heading for a career as a family doctor.

Steve was six feet tall and athletic. As if his superior intellect were not enough, his blond curly hair and warm smile both helped him perform well in the teaching hospital environment. Jim always found it a challenge to look good next to a guy like Steve.

Surgery had a reputation for being the toughest rotation for students and resident doctors, so Jim thought it wasn't a bad idea to get it over with at the beginning of the third year. A 6:00 a.m. start was not popular with most neophytes, especially since the average day often continued until after 6:00 p.m. With night and weekend on-call responsibilities in addition to twelve-hour days, medical students usually viewed the eight weeks of surgery with some degree of trepidation.

After carefully tying on his green surgical cap, Jim slid on his disposable paper booties. They didn't quite fit over his large shoes, but with a little tugging he managed to achieve good enough coverage to head into the operating room hallway, with Steve right behind him. Outside room number four, they tied on their surgical masks and tentatively slipped into the operating room, excited to find a real operation—a hernia repair—underway. They had just endured the one-hour orientation by the nurse administrator, a pleasant but elderly lady who went into great detail about too many rules that had to be remembered. Missing the first operation and being parachuted into Dr. Steinberg's second case of the day compounded the agony of the past hour.

Dr. Steinberg peered over his glasses across the room at the two new students. "Well, here's a couple of green ones, if I've ever seen green!"

Jim realized that "green" referred to his and Steve's inexperience, yet he had no idea what gave them away so promptly.

"Dr. Steinberg, we're starting surgery today. I'm with you and Steve is with Dr. O'Brien."

Dr. Steinberg leaned over to look more closely at Jim Smythe's nametag. "Okay, Jimmy-boy, what are you waiting for? Get scrubbed and join us! Amanda—get Jimmy-boy washed up and back in here before this patient's wound has healed!" He turned slightly and added, "Steve, you're with Dr. O'Brien? He's down the hall in Theatre Seven. And a piece of advice about Dr. O'Brien: don't ever be late, Steve."

Amanda escorted both Jim and Steve out of the room. She sent Steve off to find Dr. O'Brien, and then showed Jim how to scrub. But Amanda's first task was to have Jim remove his mask and put it on properly this time—not upside down.

The mask was the first of many missteps. When scrubbing before surgery, the trick was to carefully clean one's hands and then get into a sterile gown and gloves without touching something non-sterile. It was a rite of passage to learn this technique while being kept in check by the nursing staff. The longer the scrub, the more satisfying it was for a nurse to point out that the young medical student's left elbow had come in contact with something outside the sterile field. It was back to the scrub sink for another five minutes, before donning a fresh sterile gown. Amanda pointed out these lapses in sterility several times to Jim that day, telling him it was better to teach good habits early in his medical education. He was reminded of the chain of command several times.

Despite these obligatory rituals, Jim's first day in the operating room was the best day of medical school so far. He got to "assist" in six operations: two hernias, two gallbladders, a breast biopsy and a hemorrhoidectomy, enough to keep Jim excited all week. Assisting the first time as a medical student meant mostly watching, but occasionally Jim was called upon to cut sutures or hold a retractor to expose the relevant tissues to the attending surgeon. Jim was even allowed to stitch a drain to the skin at the end of one of the gallbladder operations. Such a task was enough to make him feel like an integral part of the team. At about four o'clock in the afternoon, with all the elective surgery for the day completed, the team went up to the wards to check on the inpatients. On Unit 5-West, the surgery ward, four resident doctors and two medical students congregated to do afternoon sign-out rounds. At the beginning of this session, the Chief Resident, Dr. Mary Halliday, introduced the rotation to Jim and Steve.

Dr. Halliday was just twelve months from the end-of-residency surgery exams that would qualify her to work as a full-fledged general surgeon. Five years of residency training at the end of medical school was arduous but worth it to those who completed it—or so they said. Mary had bags under her eyes—an obvious manifestation of overwork for anyone in her late twenties. Her brusque manner and lack of camaraderie with younger members of the team complemented her tired appearance. Had he known it would be another seven years before he would be ready for his yet-unchosen field, Jim might have quit right on the spot.

As it was, Mary's serious explanation to Jim and Steve about the next eight weeks stirred up Jim's enthusiasm for surgery. Each morning started at 6:00, with the team meeting on Unit 5-West. With Mary in the lead, the team would split into two groups of residents and students to personally visit and write orders for the fifty or so inpatients on the surgery service. The necessity of finishing morning rounds before the operating room started elective surgery at 8:00 justified the early start. But many residents and students alike discovered that 6:00 a.m. was also a time when patients were likely to be in bed, not ask too many questions and most importantly, not have family members present to ask even more questions. The team of residents and students—or house staff—covered the eight general surgeons' patients. The staff surgeons usually did ward rounds later and got stuck answering questions or waiting for patients to come out of the washroom.

Back in those days, general surgery was male-dominated: all eight general surgeons at the University Hospital were men. Surgical specialties such as plastics and gynecology had significantly more female representation. Mary Halliday was in the minority at the time: a female breaking into the masculine ranks.

During morning ward rounds, the team split into smaller groups, going from bed to bed and room to room as quickly as possible. Tests or treatments were ordered for each patient. Carts carried the patients' charts for orders to be written at the bedside. The medical student's job was to catch everything called out by the resident and write it down in the patient's chart swiftly enough to avoid confusion when orders were tossed out for the next patient.

At the end of the first week, Dr. Halliday paused at Luigi Lorenzo's bedside with another resident, a nurse and Jim in attendance. Mr. Lorenzo was nearly fully recovered from a long abdominal operation to remove a locally advanced colon cancer. He scratched his grey stubble, looking intently at Dr. Halliday, but probably not understanding a word she said.

Halliday turned to Jim. "We need Mr. Lorenzo's internal jugular line removed. Can you do that for us later today?"

Jim didn't understand much more than Mr. Lorenzo. "Sure, what do I do?" he asked.

"See that four-inch plastic catheter sticking out of his neck? That's going into his right internal jugular vein. You'll need to remove that."

"No problem," said Jim, still not knowing exactly what he had to do.

"Just clean it off at the skin, cut the stitch and pull out the line. Then put a pressure dressing on and keep him in bed for twenty minutes after you pull it out. The vein seals up fairly quickly. Come back with Steve after the O.R. and do it together."

Looking directly at Mr. Lorenzo and speaking at twice his normal volume, Jim exclaimed, "I – be – back." Mr. Lorenzo and Jim smiled at each other, nodding and saying, "Yes, yes," until Mary interrupted their conversation by dragging the team along to the next patient.

Later that day, Jim learned as much about central lines as he could. A large-bore intravenous catheter was used for monitoring purposes in the intensive care unit after surgery. It was also used for administration of drugs and nutritional elements into a larger vessel. High concentrations of fluids going into a big vein were much safer and better tolerated through a central line. Now that Mr. Lorenzo's big surgery was behind him, he no longer needed his line. It was a bit like an iceberg. Much more lay below the surface—the catheter was going via the internal jugular vein into Mr. Lorenzo's superior vena cava. The tip of the catheter was located in the cava, the largest vein draining blood from the top half of the body and returning it to the heart.

At four o'clock, Jim and Steve approached Mr. Lorenzo, who was smiling, nodding and saying, "Yes, yes," as he had earlier. Jim again explained how they were going to remove his catheter. Neither Jim nor Steve had even seen one of these catheters removed before. The procedure's complexity was considered minimal, and therefore no formal teaching was required. Strangely, nurses who had worked with these lines for years were not allowed to remove the catheters, so the task fell to medical students, who were always delighted to enhance their experiences by doing new procedures.

With the head of the bed elevated at forty-five degrees, Mr. Lorenzo was lying with his left side down, trying to cooperate as best he could. Mask now in place and dressed in his crisp surgical gown and sterile gloves, Jim carefully cleansed Mr. Lorenzo's neck with iodine solution. Then he covered the area around the catheter with sterile disposable paper drapes. Steve also wore a sterile gown and gloves as he hovered over Mr. Lorenzo's neck. Using sterile scissors, Jim decisively cut the stitch, the only obvious attachment between Mr. Lorenzo and his central line.

"Do you want to pull it out, or should I?" Jim politely asked.

"Hey, you're the one who has half a chance of going into surgery. Go for it."

Jim gently pulled the catheter towards the ceiling. Mr. Lorenzo's skin tented up with the catheter at the insertion site, on the right side of his neck. Jim hesitated. He then pulled a little more firmly; again the skin seemed adherent to the catheter. There was no reason why it simply shouldn't slide out, thought Jim. He looked over at Steve. Jim could tell that Steve was smiling confidently under his surgical mask.

"Go for it," Steve said again.

As Jim tugged harder, the catheter snapped just above the skin. For one helpless half-second, Jim and Steve watched as the remaining one-quarter inch of visible catheter disappeared under the skin of Mr. Lorenzo's neck. Jim quickly placed his hand on the skin where the catheter still made a visible impression, remaining evident from the entry point for about three or four inches down Mr. Lorenzo's neck. While still holding onto the catheter with his left hand, Jim stared in disbelief at the broken plastic end. Redirecting his attention to his patient, Jim was reassured that if he could at least feel the piece of the catheter under Mr. Lorenzo's skin, he would know it was not making its short journey into the right side of the patient's heart. But what if that happened? Jim feared that Mr. Lorenzo's life might be in danger. He looked across at Steve's serene eyes above his mask. Steve was probably feeling both lucky and happy that he wasn't the one who had just pulled on Mr. Lorenzo's central line.

Steve took a moment to reassure Mr. Lorenzo that this was all routine—all part of the plan—and that they would be done in a few minutes, after he made a quick phone call. With Jim's right hand still gently palpating Mr. Lorenzo's neck, Steve was off to call Dr. David Coulter, the junior resident.

"Dr. Coulter, it's Steve," he said sheepishly. "We have a bit of a problem up here on 5-West. That central line broke off and most of it is still inside Mr. Lorenzo. What? No, I'm not kidding."

Within minutes, Dr. Coulter was standing beside Steve, looking at Jim and Mr. Lorenzo. By now, a few nurses bustled around the room, mostly watching this interesting complication. One of the older nurses kept repeating, "I've never seen this before."

Dr. Coulter shrugged his shoulders and ran off muttering, "I'm going to phone Dr. Halliday."

Soon, Jim was still holding Mr. Lorenzo's neck as the bed was being wheeled down the corridor to the elevator. By now, Mr. Lorenzo's eyes were darting back and forth, suggesting he knew something was not quite right, despite Steve's confident reassurances to the contrary. Mr. Lorenzo shouted out questions in Italian while the team offered unrelated answers in English. There was no time to look for an interpreter. Mr. Lorenzo's son was on his way in, but he wouldn't be here for another half-hour.

As the elevator doors opened, the twelve nurses and doctors pushing Mr. Lorenzo's bed tried to squeeze in. Jim kept his hand firmly on the patient's neck to provide ongoing assurance that the catheter had not budged. With no room to stand in the elevator, Jim climbed onto Mr. Lorenzo's bed, all the while holding his neck. By this time, any pretense of normalcy that Steve had tried to convey was lost. With his hands tightly clasped, Mr. Lorenzo appeared to be praying to God in Italian as loudly and thoroughly as he knew how.

The elevator door opened just outside the operating room. It was not long before Dr. Steinberg and his team were surgically exploring Mr. Lorenzo's neck, retrieving the six inches of catheter that Jim had broken off twenty minutes earlier.

In the O.R. lounge, after the remaining piece of the catheter had been successfully retrieved, Dr. Steinberg reassured Jim that it was not his fault. "It must have been kinked, Jim. This type of thing just shouldn't happen. It wasn't anything you did. Don't worry about it."

Jim couldn't help but think what would have happened if the catheter had dislodged and moved into Mr. Lorenzo's heart. But the stress he'd experienced over this case diminished over the next few weeks, and Jim had all but forgotten about Mr. Lorenzo after a month. There was too much other excitement to keep him distracted. It wasn't long before Jim was seriously thinking about becoming a surgeon.

Despite his unexpected interest in surgery, Jim was determined not to get as wrapped up in the whole application process as he had back in his pre-med days. He couldn't remember much from the two years before he was accepted into medical school, other than it being a desperate time, when he and hundreds of others obsessed about their chances of "getting in".

The only serious trouble Jim had had in pre-med involved a brush with the law. Just before Christmas, he and some friends from his fraternity house were planning a big party. As part of the preparations, Jim and Mike Hawthorne were in charge of decorations. One night, the two quietly went out scavenging for items, and without much of a plan, stole a large flag from the front of the British Embassy. Having a few beers didn't help their escape. Getting caught by the police was not only an embarrassment—especially for Jim, who was using the flag to cover his naked body while he paraded down Main Street—it was also a substantial threat to the young students' futures. Fortunately for Jim, Mike was trying to get into law school, and a negative outcome from this incident could keep him out for life. A few quick phone calls from Mike's uncle to the right people, and the charges were dropped. Still, perhaps it was a good thing that Jim's memories of pre-med were a little fuzzy.

* * *

Jim's surgery rotation was over half-completed four-and-a-half weeks in. As he sat in the O.R. lounge with Dr. Dave Coulter, waiting to start an appendectomy, Jim mustered the courage to question Dave about surgery.

"Are you glad you're a surgery resident, Dave?"

"Very glad."

Jim said, "I'm kind of thinking of surgery myself. I know it's a bit early, but what do you think?" Jim was afraid Dave's response would crush his plans, but he felt a junior resident would be a better person to ask than someone higher up the totem pole.

"Surgery is great. You do things. Our patients generally get better. And there is nothing better than the operating room. It's pure, unadulterated fun."

"What about the lifestyle—isn't it a hard life?"

"Would you rather spend all your time doing something you like, or not? To me, the answer is obvious. Surgery is where it's at. Sure, surgeons aren't considered as intellectual as internal medicine or other specialists. But we know we've got common sense and practicality on our side."

"I like the way surgeons think, from what I've seen so far," mused Jim.

"No doubt about it, surgeons and internists are quite different. Some people say that surgery residency changes you. Others prefer to think that surgery selects out those medical students with a certain personality. But no matter what your interpretation, surgeons *are* different. We're more self-critical. We also expect as much from any team member as we do from ourselves. Sometimes we yell. And occasionally, God forbid, we throw instruments in the operating room. But it's usually not without good reason. All you have to do is picture *your mother* on the operating room table, and everything that can go wrong. We often start with relatively well patients, subject them to risk through surgery in the hopes of making them better—taking out a cancer, for example. But they don't always get better. Sometimes they die, having walked into the hospital in reasonably good shape. What's worse is that surgeons' patients can die from an operation for a benign disease—even taking out a gallbladder can result in death if things go bad.

"Internists, on the other hand, take sick people and try to make them better with medication. The only internists who come close to subjecting their patients to the same amount of risk that surgeons do are oncologists. They can kill their patients with one decision to give chemotherapy. But it's *always* for cancer and they often work in teams; the blame can be spread around. With surgeons, the buck stops here. That's why we are the way we are."

Jim was both excited and intimidated by Coulter's rant. He didn't know what to say.

Coulter changed the subject. "Do you golf?"

"No, why?"

"It doesn't hurt to get to know these guys if you want to get into a surgery residency. Golfing's a sure way to get to know them."

"Fulfilling my career choice depends on whether or not I golf?"

"Just a thought. Another strategy is to do a bang-up job on education rounds the last week of your rotation. You *are* presenting then, aren't you?"

"Yup. That's three weeks away. I haven't got a topic yet."

"Let me give you a piece of advice. Rehearse, rehearse, rehearse. These guys want you to know it cold. Know your patient, and know your topic—cold."

"What d'ya mean?"

"You must memorize everything—no notes. Know your patient's age, blood work, shoe size—everything—so when you present it, no one can ask you a question you can't answer."

"Seems a little silly to have to memorize all those facts and numbers. Are you sure, no notes?"

"One hundred percent sure. So you have to jump through a few hoops to impress the boys to get into a surgery residency. It's well worth it."

Jim would have to think of a topic soon. He was beginning to feel he wanted surgery more than anything.

* * *

Three weeks later, at 6:00 a.m., surgery education rounds were about to begin. There would be about twenty-five people present to hear the medical students and junior residents present interesting cases and topics. The senior residents and staff had an opportunity to display their own knowledge and have fun at the expense of the more junior team members. The questions could be fierce and the consequences harsh if correct answers weren't forthcoming.

The session started well, with Dr. Coulter and another junior resident giving slick presentations about unusual cases seen in early July. Steve got up and did a fairly good job talking about his patient who had cholecystitis—inflammation of the gallbladder—and giving a ten-minute exposition on treatment of bile duct stones.

As Steve walked quickly back to his seat, Jim made his way up the centre aisle, running his topic through his mind. His talk was about acid reflux and an operation to correct it called the Nissen fundoplication.

When acid from the stomach occasionally made its way back up the esophagus, it could cause heartburn. Medicine to reduce acid often controlled the symptoms. However, some individuals benefited from surgery to recreate a valve-like effect at the lower esophagus. The operation wrapped the stomach around the lower esophagus, eliminating acid reflux and regurgitation. It was quite a successful operation if done in the right patient and when accurate diagnostic information was confirmed before surgery.

Jim planned to describe a woman in her forties who'd had a Nissen fundoplication, with complications relating to the new "valve" being too tight. Although she was no longer suffering from backward flow of stomach acid, food didn't go down and was continually getting stuck.

As Jim turned to face his audience, he noticed all of the individuals focused directly on him. The room became very warm. Then a wave of nausea hit him and his knees buckled. As he was about to launch into his description of the patient, his mind went blank. He reached for the table beside him, steadied himself and decided to talk about the operation first. He could bring up the case report when it came to mind. Just as he was about to share his knowledge, he forgot the name of the operation.

Jim excused himself, ran down the aisle and started digging though his knapsack, looking for his notes. After pulling out a smelly pair of socks and gym shorts, he finally located his five pages of scrawled information that he had carefully rehearsed for days before. He returned to the front, and with help from his papers, went through the topic as planned.

His presentation didn't go badly, but Jim was devastated. It didn't help that all the prior speakers had done well. The surgeons, like vultures, had been circling for an opportunity, and Jim was it. Dr. O'Brien tore into him with question after question about what Jim "actually knew" about his topic. He informed Jim that book knowledge was not the same as experience, and perhaps he should have chosen a topic of which he had a little more first-hand information.

Jim was upset from then until his last day of surgery rotation. As he sat in the lounge, Dr. Coulter tried to console him.

"You've actually done pretty well this rotation. But your choice of topics last week was awful. How could you think a talk on Nissen fundoplication could be pulled off by a third-year medical student?"

"I thought that if I picked a difficult topic, and really nailed it, I'd be looking at a position in a surgery residency some day."

"It wasn't just the topic, Jim. The case report was a shitty choice. Here you're talking to a bunch of surgeons, and you bring up one of O'Brien's failed operations. How did you think he was going to respond?"

The point had never occurred to Jim. He felt even worse.

"You know, Dave, I've had my ups and downs these past eight weeks. When Lorenzo's central line broke off, I was not a happy camper. But we can laugh about that now. But this Nissen thing—this Nissen fiasco—I'm ashamed of that and will be for a long time."

"Get over it, Jim. It'll be okay."

The eight weeks of surgery seemed to have gone by quickly. His last afternoon, Jim was down in the emergency department assessing an eleven-year-old boy with possible appendicitis. After taking a careful history, doing a physical exam and reviewing the lab work, Jim was certain of his diagnosis. He relayed the information over the phone to Dr. Steinberg. Once Dr. Coulter had checked Jim's assessment, the child was booked for an appendectomy. It was now four o'clock and Jim was supposed to receive his surgery evaluation from Dr. Steinberg that day, but he was more concerned with whether or not this kid actually had appendicitis. He asked Dr. Steinberg if it was all right to stay late and assist on the operation. Dr. Steinberg agreed.

At seven o'clock, as Dave Coulter was putting in the final skin stitches, Dr. Steinberg took off his gown and gloves and exclaimed, "Well, you called this one right, Jimmy-boy. Another few hours and it would have ruptured." And then to Dr. Coulter, "You know, Dave, I think he's one of us. Yup, Jimmy just might be one of us."

Dave handed the needle driver over to Jim and said, "Here, why don't you put in the last couple of stitches." Jim Smythe's heart fluttered with excitement as he reached for the instrument that Dave had just offered.

That night at eight o'clock, Jim's surgery rotation evaluation with Dr. Steinberg went very well. "I don't think he dislikes you," Steinberg reassured Jim, speaking of Dr. O'Brien. "Don't repeat this, but Dr. O'Brien's a bit of a tight-ass. I think you didn't do yourself any favours by talking about his one bad outcome of the year with a Nissen. But *I'm the one* who does your evaluation. And as far as I'm concerned, 'you done good'." He reached and shook Jim's hand until it started to hurt.

Jim left the hospital on a high note. It felt like getting out of school for summer holidays. He knew he'd miss the team atmosphere of surgery, but was certain he'd be back.

Jim was also very happy these days for more personal reasons: he had just started dating that pretty O.R. nurse named Amanda.

Chapter 4 ~ Home Life

Present Day—October 2010

In her bathrobe, Amanda Smythe leaned slightly forward over the sink, staring into the bathroom mirror. Her tan and freckles had faded somewhat since the summer vacation. She could hear the electric garage door closing as Jim headed off to work. Carefully placing her toothbrush on the counter, she inspected her teeth and in the process couldn't help noticing the crinkles bracketing her eyes. When she closed her lips and pouted, her facial skin smoothed, the wrinkles disappearing. *As long as I don't smile*, she thought. Or perhaps a little Botox would do the trick. No, she would *never* resort to Botox.

She smoothed her straight brown hair with some water on the palm of her hand, attempting to restore the part in the middle. The shower would have to wait until after her workout. Besides, a shower six hours earlier ensured she was at least clean, although slightly dishevelled by morning when her husband woke, dressing in the darkened bedroom. Why Jim bothered to get dressed in a suit and tie before he hopped on his bike to work puzzled Amanda. He was only going to change into greens on arrival at the hospital, anyway. *But perhaps that's what makes him Jim*, she thought. He had to project an image of perfection—as if his surgical skills weren't enough to establish his position as the top general surgeon in Lakefield, if not the province.

Mixed feelings accompanied Amanda's pride in Jim. His surgical career was not without cost. Never mind that she had given up a busy life in nursing to raise their children; Amanda had done that without question.

It was the *in-between time*, as she liked to call it, that was often lacking.

When they were on holiday as a family, or playing touch football after a street barbeque, Jim was great. His enthusiasm was infectious. Parties with his co-workers and their families were always fun. Everyone loved Jim, and when Jim and Amanda were alone, he never failed to demonstrate his appreciation for her. When he'd woken her just before midnight the previous night for some intimate moments, it was satisfying as always—but it sometimes imposed a hollow feeling in her, leaving her to wonder when they would have time to simply relax together. She craved sitting down to chat over a cup of coffee or going for a walk in the ravine behind their house. It was this in-between time—not in a group and not alone in the bedroom—that Amanda desired.

* * *

Jim sniffed the cool autumn air as the leaves whizzed past his right shoulder. Despite the darkness, he could see they were yellow and starting to fall off the trees. He enjoyed riding his bike to work as long as the weather would permit. Last year he had pushed it into early December, trying hard to ignore the occasional snowfall, until he simply could no longer ride. He allowed himself to glide the last half block, having come down a substantial hill leading to the hospital's back entrance. He was cold but refreshed—a great way to get going before a full day of operating.

He would have to be better equipped this year so he could ride a little longer through the winter snow, even if it was only a few days a week. He couldn't ride when he was on call—it was too unpredictable whether he'd get home for supper, and it would not be good to be stuck at the hospital with only a bicycle to get up the big hill and back home at night. By car, it was a seven-minute drive from Lakefield Regional Hospital to his house. On his bike, it was about sixteen minutes, a little over half an hour on foot.

There was no way he could have had it this good if he'd stayed at the university after he'd finished residency. Jim had liked the idea of moving to a smaller city, and it suited Amanda as well. They had endured the five years of surgical residency, having been married in the four-week interval between medical school and surgical training. In his final year of residency, Emily was born. Two years later, Sara joined the family. Caring for an infant during surgical training could strain any marriage, but they survived.

The couple had talked about staying put after Jim's training, but Amanda's parents were still in Lakefield. Besides, "the big city" was only ninety minutes away if they wanted to go to a show or a football game.

Jim recalled sitting down with his long-time mentor, Dr. Steinberg, and breaking the news that he'd be going to Lakefield. Steinberg had repeatedly suggested that Jim go off and get a couple of extra years of training to bring a "special skill" back to the University Hospital. Despite feeling some obligation to Steinberg, Jim could not be tempted.

"I like general surgery too much. I'd miss out on the variety if I stayed at the U."

"Well, Jim, I know you'll do well wherever you go, and Lakefield will be lucky to have you. I'm sure you'll be busy. I bet that hospital draws from a population of 200,000 or so. How many will be in your group?"

"Six."

"Six general surgeons, that's a good size," Steinberg had said. "Just about the right amount of being on call, if you ask me."

"And if I can stand being *just a general surgeon,*" Jim had quipped, "I'll be fine." This was always a bit of a sore point for Jim. After completing five years of specialty residency training following four years of medical school, the name "general surgeon" implied not being a specialist. General surgery included most abdominal surgery, surgical treatment of breast cancer and some neck surgery, in addition to other bits here and there. Sure, thought Jim, he could do a couple of extra years to *sub*-specialize *within* general surgery—get a particular area of expertise—but that would also narrow his scope and deprive him of so many areas in which he loved to work.

There was another important factor in Jim's decision: the relative lack of residents doing surgical training. It wasn't that Jim didn't like teaching; he loved to teach. He just didn't like the loss of control, supervising a resident doing *his* operation on *his* patient. He was much happier with medical students, or family medicine residents, where he didn't have to give away his surgery. These students were much easier to please—delighted to put in a few stitches, just as Jim had been years before.

He occasionally wondered, however, if he might one day regret not striving for the uppermost echelons of surgical achievement: research, a professorship, transplant surgery . . .

His mind came back to the present as he locked his bike at the hospital rear entrance. It had been two weeks since Rory Harbin had left the hospital. Smythe expected he'd never see Harbin again, but he certainly thought about him and that "great case" of splenic artery aneurysm. He'd probably never have another one like it.

This was Smythe's favourite day of the week: Monday, his O.R. day. Although he did procedures at other times during the week, Monday was elective—non-emergency—surgery all day long. He loved the relative sanctuary of the operating room, where patients and other physicians couldn't easily get hold of him. Smythe enjoyed cranking up the music in his O.R. and doing five or six operations undisturbed. Today, he had a bowel resection for Crohn's disease, two laparoscopic gallbladder operations, a hernia repair and two breast biopsies.

Jared was assisting him for most of the day. Smythe enjoyed having him around, and he'd certainly miss his young assistant if Jared went back into surgical training. But Smythe was encouraging the idea. He'd love to see Jared come back in five years to join the group as a surgeon.

"Now's the time. It won't get any easier," Smythe said about once a week.

With a little girl at home and another one on the way, Jared had said he was a bit torn, but he had finally made up his mind. He was going to apply for a position in surgery residency for next July.

Smythe was delighted to quiz Jared at any opportunity. Even the nurses enjoyed listening as Jared was led through a multitude of scenarios that were relevant to the current operation.

"What's Crohn's disease?" Smythe posed the question just as he made an incision in the lower midline of the abdomen. This operation could have been done with the assistance of a laparoscope, except that this patient had scar tissue on his abdomen from several previous surgeries.

"It's an inflammation of the intestine, which occurs mostly in the small or large bowel," Jared replied.

"Where else can it occur?"

"They say it can show up anywhere from the mouth to the anus."

"Yes, but where does Crohn's disease *usually* occur?"

"Most often in the small intestine, sometimes in the colon or occasionally both."

"What causes it?"

"I'm not sure anybody really knows, but they think it might be related to a person's immune response to a particular bacterium—possibly one related to T.B."

"What does it look like? In the operating room."

"The small bowel is inflamed—red and thickened—and there is creeping fat. Mesenteric fat looks like it's growing over the small intestine."

"When is surgery required for Crohn's disease?"

"Same as for other gastrointestinal operations—complications of the disease such as bleeding, perforation or obstruction. Also, failure of medication and inability to exclude malignancy."

"Excellent. You'll make a great surgeon one day."

This particular patient's surgery was for incomplete bowel obstruction despite ongoing attempts to settle down inflammation with medication. Like all Smythe's operations—on that day at least—this one went well.

On his way home, Smythe suddenly remembered the envelope in his locked drawer, from the Medical Licensing Authority. He got off his bike, took out his cell phone and immediately called his office. How on earth could he have forgotten that letter? What had it said? RESPOND WITHIN THIRTY DAYS. It must have been fifteen already. When the familiar voice message ended, he spoke into his phone: "Moira, it's Jim. I'm leaving this message while I remember it. Can you pull Hazel Kowalchuk's paper chart for me and put it on my desk? I need to review her case and couldn't find her on the computer. And while I think of it, can you get the cupboard stocked with some food for when I'm on call? Oh, and can you remind me to order that rowing machine? Thanks." He climbed back on his bike and cycled up the hill, heading for home by six o'clock.

At home, Jim parked his bike in the garage and then unlocked the front door. As he smelled supper, his mouth watered. He noticed the house was immaculate as he walked in towards the kitchen.

"To what do I owe this pleasant surprise?" Amanda gave Jim a big hug and a kiss as he appeared in the doorway much earlier than usual.

"Just a little good luck," he said, prolonging the kiss.

"Gross! Leave each other alone!" Sara shrieked as she ran up and hugged her parents. Sara loved it when her dad came home for dinner, although it was not as frequently as she would have liked.

"Do you like my new outfit?" Sara pirouetted, showing off her bright yellow tracksuit, her short blond pigtails flying wildly behind her.

"It's wonderful, sweetie," Jim said, picking her up off the floor.

"Hi, Dad," Emily said in her usual matter-of-fact tone.

"Hi, Emily. Don't you look glad to see me!" He winked, but Emily was already walking in the opposite direction.

Jim and Amanda moved into the kitchen. Amanda was as athletic in her appearance as her husband, only she had a bit more time to get out and put her fitness to work. In addition to attending a gym regularly, she participated on several sports teams. She still worked part-time in nursing—although very seldom as of late. The last couple of years, Amanda had become increasingly occupied with volunteer work, her parents and her children's after-school activities. It seemed that whenever the hospital called for her to pick up a shift, a previous arrangement prevented it. As a result, requests to work at the hospital were less frequent. She reached her arms around her husband and gave him another hug. Her hair was tied in a ponytail, just the way Jim liked it. Jim stared into her green eyes and smiled. It felt good to be home.

They made the usual small talk about their days. More serious discussion was usually deferred until the children had gone to bed. Amanda told Jim about when someone had nearly crashed into her in traffic. She talked about the gym and her afternoon tennis game. Just as she ran out of things to tell him, Amanda added, "I'm sorry, how was *your* day?"

Jim told her about the operation on the man with Crohn's disease—how it went well and how they didn't need to bring the patient's bowel out to an ileostomy bag on the abdominal wall.

"I bet he'll be pleased about that," she said.

"For sure, but he knew it was a possibility. He would've accepted a temporary bag if he woke up with it. He'd have no choice. I just hope he doesn't leak—then he'd need a bag."

Jim went on to explain some of the other operations he'd done that day. When it came to the breast biopsies, he always added twenty-five years to the patients' ages. If Amanda knew Jim was doing a biopsy for a possible breast cancer on a thirty-year-old, Amanda would worry about herself and her two daughters for the next two months. A fifty-five-year-old sounded much less threatening. Her nursing background only exacerbated her understanding of all the terrible things Jim saw at work on a day-to-day basis.

Jim never gave away the identity of patients, even to Amanda, although acquaintances in the community assumed Jim shared all the details of his patients at home. Amanda became well versed in faking it when a familiar face would approach her in the grocery store, loudly exclaiming how Jim had fixed a bad hemorrhoid problem. Amanda maintained a fine balance between allowing people to feel important and known, without making them think their confidentiality had been breached. She crafted her responses on a case-by-case basis. Generally, the older people in town assumed Jim came home with vivid descriptions and photographs of their operations, names and phone numbers included.

The only time photographs had made it into Jim's home occurred when he borrowed a memory card belonging to one of his endoscopy colleagues. The card contained 1500 high-resolution photos of the insides of hundreds of patients' colons, rectums and stomachs, showing tumours, ulcers, blood, mucus and feces. Jim was interested in copying only one or two pictures for presentations he had to give. But when he inserted the memory card and gave the appropriate mouse clicks to permit saving it onto his computer, all 1500 photos were downloaded. To add insult to injury, they were now unintentionally part of the family's screen saver, brightly displaying a new picture every twenty seconds. At a three-to-two ratio, the Smythe screen saver randomly alternated family screen shots with nameless intestinal tracts of Lakefield's finest citizens. Jim knew he'd have to fix this; it was just a matter of finding the time to do so. Until then, the screen saver was a great source of both horror and amusement for the Smythe children and their close friends.

The family was still cheerful from their recent vacation to the Grand Canyon in August. Jim had seemed to make up for lost time, devoting his entire attention during vacation to "his three girls". He was always first up in the morning, preparing the day's activities. Now, they were home and back at school, not seeing their dad as often.

With Emily and Sara settled into bed, Amanda announced that she needed to talk with Jim. Her nervous appearance surprised him. They sat down touching each other on the family room couch. Just as Jim was settling in, Amanda clicked off the television.

"What's up, sunshine?" he said.

"Something is worrying me."

"So what else is new?" He managed to slide in a big grin before it was too late.

"No, I'm serious, Jim. I'm worried about you."

"Me? You're worried about *me*? What for?"

"Your health. I'm worried about your health."

"I'm fine! I've never felt better in my life." Jim stood up.

"No, seriously. You've lost weight. You must've lost fifteen or twenty pounds in the last six months. At first, I kind of liked that you lost that little extra roll you had. But this is getting to be a bit much."

"I'm fit. What's the matter with that?" he said, steadily turning 360 degrees with miniscule steps, his biceps flexed and stomach sucked in.

"You know what I mean, don't you, Jim?"

"No, what?" He sat back down again. "Why don't you just spell it out for me?"

"Cancer. Unexplained weight loss means cancer until proven otherwise. You should know that."

"Don't let your nursing background get the better of you. Sometimes a bit of knowledge can be a bad thing," he said, patting her on the knee.

"Don't patronize me, Jim. I've seen it too many times before—and so have you." She took his hand and asked, "When was the last time—or have you *ever*—had a full check-up?"

"When we moved here." He paused and then added, "I'm just working hard and not finding the time for proper food. I'd rather not eat than eat some junk out of a machine at 10:30 at night."

"But Jim—" Her lower lip started to quiver.

"Look, I don't smoke. I exercise when I can. I'm fine."

"Honey, if not for me, at least for the children." She was now sobbing quietly into a Kleenex. He knew this meant he had to do something. He put his arm around her.

"What do you want me to do?"

"Go to the doctor and get checked out. If everything's fine, I'll feel much better. If not, I'd rather know so I can prepare myself—" She burst into a full-out cry, gasping into Jim's chest.

"Okay, I'll go. I will."

"When?"

"Next week. I don't actually have a doctor, you know. I'll talk to one of the guys at work and arrange a check-up. If it makes you happy, I'm glad to do it. But I feel great, I really do."

* * *

One week later, Jim came home from the hospital with a bounce in his step. He had just been to see Barry Sanderson, one of the family doctors in town. Jim was happy, not because of what Barry had said, but because it had been another great Monday in the operating room. He had practically forgotten about his visit to Dr. Sanderson.

In the front hallway, Amanda greeted her husband with an expression of relief. "By the look on your face, it must be good news," she said.

"What?"

Amanda's face tightened. "The doctor. You did see Barry today, didn't you?"

"Oh, yeah, that. I saw him about an hour ago. I had the full check-up, and I mean *full*. He says he doesn't think there's anything seriously wrong. I got some blood drawn for testing—all routine, of course."

"What did he say?" she asked.

"I'm fine. He said I'm fine."

"That's all?" she pressed.

"That's all. What's for supper?"

* * *

The following morning, Amanda got up early to catch Jim before he headed off to work. She sipped from her coffee mug as they sat across from each other at the breakfast table. Out of the blue, she calmly stated, "Jim, I don't care if you're the best surgeon in Lakefield or the entire region."

"And neither do I," replied Jim. He took a final gulp from his coffee cup and plunked it on the table.

"Oh yeah, right!"

"You know I'm content when I'm working. And yes, I have been working hard lately. But is that not a good thing?"

"Jim, there's nothing I want more than for us to be happy. But I think your method of achieving happiness is different from most. You have to be the best—the alpha male at the hospital. I know that's your most important goal, and I'm proud of the stature you hold in the medical commun—"

"I don't have to be the best. But sometimes I wonder . . ." He was staring sightlessly in the direction of a cupboard to his right.

Amanda reached across the table and placed both hands on his cheeks, bringing his gaze in line with hers. "I don't mind that you work hard. But you have to learn to keep a lid on it. If your family is not happy, you won't be either. And believe me, sometimes when I think you are married to the hospital, I'm not so happy."

"Okay, I'll try to be around more. I'll see what I can do."

"And besides, you *are* the best in Lakefield, by a long-shot. I'd like you to be around for us. Please follow up on those blood tests with Barry." That was the last time she mentioned it.

* * *

Although Jim always strived for perfection, early in their travels to the Grand Canyon in August he'd been reminded of his limitations as a doctor.

Stopping in a small city for lunch, Amanda and the girls were waiting in a restaurant while Jim picked up some supplies and filled the vehicle with gas. After buying gas and parking the vehicle within sight of the restaurant, Jim saw a commotion around a woman who was lying on the sidewalk. Being a doctor, he approached to see if he could help. He initially thought she was a homeless person, possibly intoxicated. Probably in her late fifties, she was lying on her side and only occasionally gasped for air. Her lips were blue. A man who identified himself as her husband pleaded with his unresponsive wife, "Stay with me, honey. Stay with me!"

Jim grasped the lady's jaw, lifting it forward to improve her airway as he asked the usual questions about recent symptoms and medical history. He felt for a pulse on her neck but wasn't sure he could identify one. A by-stander was calling 911 on his cell phone when a young lady came along saying, "I'm an off-duty paramedic. Can I help?"

Jim was relieved to have some assistance and before he could answer, she was barking orders at several others to help position the lady on her back while she stabilized the neck. She then pulled a pair of latex gloves out of her purse, and shoved a wrapped plastic oral airway tube at Jim. As she was putting on her gloves she said to him, "Unwrap this," while to another, "Unbutton her shirt." Jim was glad he hadn't identified himself as a physician, since the paramedic was clearly taking charge. As a surgeon, Jim had dealt with his share of critically ill people, but in the field with no equipment, he felt helpless. Within a couple of minutes, a thirty-year-old lady who identified herself as a nurse was doing CPR, while the paramedic was bagging the lady through a small plastic mask. By now, there were at least fifteen people gathered around the unconscious woman, some helping while others simply observed. The husband was wringing his hands, standing in the second row of onlookers and helpers.

When the ambulance arrived, Jim felt relieved that this poor woman would be taken away where she'd likely get some help with real equipment at a hospital. But he realized it probably didn't matter, as she wasn't showing any signs of life despite their efforts over the last five minutes. Jim stepped back as one of the paramedics from the ambulance moved in. There was nothing Jim could do. Unnoticed, he calmly walked across the street to the restaurant where Amanda and the girls were sitting in a table by the front window.

"What was that all about?" Amanda asked. Jim explained in as little detail as possible, so as not to upset his daughters. Later, Amanda confided in Jim that for a few minutes, she had feared it was him lying on the sidewalk, as she could barely discern someone doing cardiac compressions amongst the crowd that had gathered.

Jim told her, "That's ridiculous, I'm fit and I'm forty-four." It bothered him only slightly that Amanda might have worried it was Jim lying there. What concerned him more was the fact that he'd felt powerless to help this woman. Outside of a hospital, Jim was unable to contribute anything; a paramedic clearly outperformed him. Troubled by the episode, he spent the next week trying not to think about it.

* * *

Smythe was walking down the long corridor towards the administrative wing to visit Rick Abbott. He had to bring up a few issues with Rick about efficiency in the emergency department. As the main physician hospital administrator, Abbott was often the lucky recipient of these concerns, things about which he could usually do nothing. But he was a good listener, and people often felt better when they left his office.

Down the hall, Smythe spotted Katrina Jaworsky approaching and could make out a big smile despite the fact that she was still very far away. When they met midway, they stopped to talk in the hallway. Jim glanced down at her left hand. To his slight disappointment, he noticed her wedding ring. *Oh well*, he thought. He didn't know why these things even popped into his mind. He *could not* and he *would not* ever act on any of this information.

"You know, Jim, you did a great job on Rory Harbin several weeks ago. Congratulations."

"Thank you."

"I didn't want you to think I wasn't supportive of you, but I really did think certification could wait until surgery became a more certain event."

"No problem, Katrina. I was glad to have your opinion and appreciate that you came to see him."

"You busy these days?"

"As always . . ." Before he could think of what to say next, Jim was jogging down the hall, hurrying to get on with his day.

Chapter 5 ~ Air

Smythe found himself on call yet another Friday night with a full moon. He knew people who would swear that the phase of the moon was a significant factor in determining what would transpire at work any given evening. He was undecided. What he found most interesting was the fact that this hypothesis transcended many disciplines, not only within medicine, but also across the community. Any experienced police officer or even a teacher would claim that a full moon was significant to their workload. Smythe, trying to be scientific about it, was always on the lookout for some statistical verification. He knew that if a bad case occurred and the moon was not full, human nature would encourage loss of the particular data point. Conversely, if a particularly notable stabbing or gunshot wound occurred and the moon happened to be full that night, the case would reverberate through the minds of all interested parties for weeks to come, only solidifying the theory that everyone knew, but could not prove, about phases of the moon.

*   *   *

Smythe reclined in his chair in the operating room lounge and reflected on his reasons for becoming a surgeon. Others had always considered him a high achiever—he knew he was meant to do something at least as demanding as surgery. Ever since he'd played hockey at a highly competitive level in his late teens, Smythe had needed to work hard. At age nineteen, when he abandoned his dream of professional sports and started to think about medicine as a career, he simply shifted his energy from athletics to academics. His friends envied him for his ability to master his goals, viewing him as determined and capable. For the most part, Smythe was satisfied with his abilities and considered himself lucky. But he was aware of a constant need to be striving for something. Occasionally, though, he interpreted this as an addiction to adrenaline and a curse. He was never satisfied unless he was busy, pushing the envelope. Now, he wondered if he'd ever be able to retire. He'd seen some of his surgical mentors have difficulty when the time came: a sixty-five-year-old who'd spent a lifetime in pursuit of the ultimate adrenaline rush did not always make a happy retiree. At least for Smythe that was a long way down the road. He had plenty of time to sort out his retirement strategy at some vague time in the future.

***

Dr. Jason Malcov studied the chest X-ray. Something wasn't right. Having just completed an extra emergency year in his family medicine residency, he was very keen but still somewhat hesitant. His boyish appearance matched his air of inexperience on the job but did not detract from his enthusiasm. He rubbed his double chin as he continued to gaze at the image of his young patient's chest, removed his thick glasses and squinted, then sighed as he put them back on.

Jen Boyer slid up behind Malcov. Looking at the images, she pointed to the left upper chest area and asked, "What's all that black stuff?"

Malcov's perplexed expression softened as he moved to his left, allowing Jen in beside him. His hand briefly touched her elbow as he maneuvered her into a more central position in front of the X-ray viewing monitor. Jen shuffled slightly to her right, increasing the distance between them to a few inches. "The heart and great vessels look fine to me." He then added, "See, this is the mediastinum—the midline structures—which all look fine. The left lung bothers me, though, especially here," he said, pointing to where Jen had questioned the "black stuff". "To me, that looks like air outside the lung. I think this man has a collapsed lung—a pneumothorax."

"Why's it all white at the bottom of the lung?" Jen asked, tilting her head to meet Malcov's eyes, just as he glanced down towards hers. She quickly looked back at the X-rays.

"I'm not sure. But this man needs a chest tube. I'm going to ask Dr. Smythe if he'll be on standby while I put it in."

***

Smythe was walking briskly down the long corridor when his phone rang.

"Smythe here."

"Jim, it's Jason." Malcov, one of the newest additions to the hospital staff, seemed unusually relaxed with Smythe and didn't attach his last name when identifying himself on the phone. Smythe was a little uncomfortable with the familiarity; some of these younger physicians might benefit from a little humility this early in their careers.

Smythe stopped walking and leaned against the wall. "What d'ya got?"

"I've got a guy down here who needs to have a chest tube. He has a big pneumothorax on the left side."

"Interesting."

"Yeah, spontaneous pneumothorax! This is the first one I've seen in practice."

A collapsed lung would require placement of a chest tube between the ribs to withdraw air from outside the lung, thus re-expanding it.

Malcov continued, "Would you mind consulting and being on standby for me while I'm putting in the tube? It's been a while since I did one in residency."

Smythe walked over to a nearby X-ray monitor. "What's the guy's name? I'll look at the images here." Smythe listened and then put his cell phone down on the counter briefly as he typed in the man's demographics. Picking up his phone, he added, "I've got his chest X-ray up now. That's a big pneumothorax." Smythe studied the image, noting a horizontal air-fluid level in the left chest that indicated more than a simple collapsed lung. "I think he might need more than just a chest tube, Jason. Why don't you get set up for the tube insertion and I'll be down there in a few minutes." Smythe slid his phone back into its holster and smiled.

***

Malcov rubbed his chin and turned to Jen. "Dr. Smythe said he'll be down here shortly. Can we get set up for a chest tube insertion?"

"I'll get everything ready. This is going to be fun!" Jen bent down, opening the lower drawer of the equipment cart. As the hem of her white top rose upward at the back, the T shape of a black thong riding above her nursing pants was clearly visible.

Malcov turned away as he attempted to stifle a broad grin.

A few minutes later, Smythe arrived in the department and sat down beside Malcov, who was completing paperwork at one of the emergency desks.

"So, what's the story?"

Malcov turned his chair sideways to face Smythe. "This is a twenty-year-old male who was out partying earlier tonight. He got sudden chest pain and his friends brought him in straight away."

"Any vomiting?"

"I think so."

"What do you mean, you think so? *Was he or wasn't he?*"

"Yes," Malcov responded tentatively.

"I bet he vomited quite a bit before his chest pain started," Smythe added.

"How do you know?"

"Let's put the chest tube in and we'll find out." Smythe leaped out of his chair and went over to the X-ray monitor, nodding as he reviewed the images.

Jen sauntered up beside Smythe and said to him, "We're ready for the chest tube in seven."

Upon opening the curtain of cubicle seven, Smythe had his suspicions confirmed. The patient, Vince, reeked of beer. He wasn't behaving as if he was intoxicated, but he did look unwell. Smythe introduced himself and asked a few questions about vomiting and what he'd had for supper, and whether he knew that Dr. Malcov was about to insert a tube the size of a garden hose between his ribs and into his left chest cavity.

Smythe listened to Vince's breathing. He felt the crunchy texture of the skin on Vince's upper chest, a telltale sign of air in the subcutaneous tissues. Smythe glared at Malcov. "You didn't tell me he had subcutaneous emphysema!"

"Oh yeah, I forgot to mention that."

"Will it hurt?" Vince asked.

"Not much. You'll get some sedation. I imagine things hurt quite a bit right now," Smythe added.

"You got that right," he gasped from behind his oxygen mask.

Malcov and Jen were on Vince's left side while Smythe watched the procedure from the right, giving sedation through the intravenous line and eyeing Vince's oxygen saturation monitor. Eighty-eight percent wasn't great for a young guy on oxygen, thought Smythe. He had other things to do throughout the hospital, but not for anything was he going to miss watching this chest tube experience.

Malcov cleansed Vince's left chest wall and draped it with sterile towels, intending to insert a tube between the fifth and sixth ribs at the level of the nipple, through the left side of the thoracic cage. He inserted a needle and froze the skin, muscle and surfaces of the two ribs he was going to penetrate between. He then looked across the patient at Smythe, who had just administered more sedation.

"Can I go ahead?"

"Anytime," Smythe said. Vince's snoring was interrupted by moaning as Malcov exerted considerable force with a Kelly clamp, trying to create a space between the two ribs.

"It's always tougher to get through than you'd expect," Smythe advised. Malcov continued on until Smythe added, "Remember, the left ventricle is not far away."

Malcov froze.

"Relax, Jason. Just be careful."

After a deep breath, Malcov proceeded. Vince was groaning through his sedation, and droplets of sweat formed on Malcov's forehead. Finally, his clamp popped between Vince's ribs. A small gush of dark fluid came around the instrument.

"Good, now follow that with your tube," Smythe directed.

The stench of beer was now unmistakable, as if Vince had a pint or two in his left thoracic cavity. Malcov drove the tube between the ribs to its destination in the pleural space. As Smythe had expected, dark fluid gushed from the chest cavity out the end of the tube, onto Malcov's shoes and pant legs. Smythe winced on Malcov's behalf. *Good thing he's wearing hospital greens*. Before any more fluid could gush out the end of the tube, Malcov clamped it and connected it to another tube, which drained into a plastic container. Jen placed the collection container on the floor at the bedside. When the tube was secured, Malcov released the clamp and more fluid flowed through the chest tube with each of Vince's exhaled breaths.

In addition to the smell and the dark fluid, a bit of solid material that drained out of Vince's chest and through the tube, like a helpless body hurtling down a set of rapids, clinched the diagnosis for Smythe. He had difficulty making a positive identification on the first solid object, which was nearly big enough to obstruct the end of the chest tube. As it made its way out of the tube and into the collection container, Smythe thought it was a mushroom. A black olive or an anchovy would be plausible alternatives.

"So, what's the diagnosis?" Smythe asked so loud that even Vince opened his eyes.

Malcov's expression was blank. He was clearly baffled by the solid material now flowing out, bit by bit, chunk by chunk, from Vince's chest tube. With a sudden flash of fear across his face, Malcov asked, "I couldn't have hit his stomach, could I?"

"Of course not. Haven't you heard of Boerhaave's syndrome?"

Malcov nearly smacked himself on the forehead with realization, but fortunately stopped short, as his previously sterile gloves were now covered in pizza-and-beer soup.

"He's ruptured his esophagus from vomiting so hard!" Malcov exclaimed.

"Of course he has. He's got a huge pneumothorax with a big air-fluid level on his chest X-ray after repeated vomiting. In this case, he's dumped his entire stomach-full through a rip in his esophagus into the left chest cavity."

Jen smiled from behind her mask.

"Next time, you won't need my help," Smythe added with a slight sneer in Malcov's direction.

Vince had begun breathing more comfortably, with oxygen saturations approaching 95 percent. And he was waking up. Startled, he gazed down at the collection container, which now had about two litres of stomach contents, including over one half of a large pizza in chunks, floating in beer. "No wonder I felt so bad," he said, closing his eyes and turning his head up to the ceiling.

"How much beer did you drink, anyway?" Malcov asked.

"About fifteen."

No one asked whether that was bottles, glasses or pints. Either way, it was obviously too much for Vince to safely consume.

After confirmatory imaging studies, Smythe and Malcov sent Vince out for definitive repair of his esophagus by a thoracic surgeon. A ruptured esophagus can lead to mediastinitis, or infection of the midline structures in the chest, which results in up to 50 percent mortality. Although diagnosed early, this was a case of "pizza and beer mediastinitis", and Smythe had no figures for survival of such an event. It would require judicious washout of Vince's chest cavity, esophageal repair, IV antibiotics and a healthy degree of paranoia about potential complications.

As it turned out, Vince did well, returning to Lakefield two weeks later with a lifelong vow to abstain from pizza and beer.

As the ambulance transported Vince an hour and a half up the road to the university, Smythe contemplated air. *It's interesting*, he thought. *Air can sustain life. In the wrong place it can be problematic. And it can even kill.*

*　　*　　*

Smythe used to think the tiniest of air bubbles in a vein would be instantly fatal. That was *before* he went to medical school. There, Smythe learned that small air bubbles accidentally introduced during medical procedures were usually reabsorbed into the bloodstream long before they could reach the right side of the heart, where they could cause damage by blocking circulation through the lungs.

When he had first started working in Lakefield about ten years ago, he'd had the chance to rethink intravenous air bubbles while inserting a pacemaker.

General surgeons, cardiac surgeons or cardiologists could all insert pacemakers. Shortly after Smythe finished his residency program, one of the internal medicine specialists in Lakefield asked him if he would train to insert pacemakers so the procedures could be done locally, rather than being sent to the university.

Insertion of a cardiac pacemaker was not all that complicated. The first step was to gain access to a large vein in the upper chest, usually the subclavian or the cephalic vein. Smythe was used to sticking a needle just under the collarbone, directly into the subclavian. Despite not being able to see the vein, it wasn't hard for him to find after some experience, and by the time Smythe started his practice, he had done over a hundred subclavian lines, so he didn't think safe access to the vein was really much of an issue. Sure, hitting the vein could be tricky, as could threading the guidewire down the vein towards the heart. But Smythe had encountered these little stumbling blocks many times; and with pacemaker insertions, he had the benefit of live X-ray imaging or fluoroscopy.

Smythe recalled the words of a cardiac surgeon from the university who was happy to mentor him for a day of observation in the operating room. "After you have access to the left subclavian vein under the left clavicle, you need to position the pacemaker lead." The surgeon demonstrated nine pacemaker procedures, making it a worthwhile experience for Smythe. Positioning the lead was a matter of watching the fluoroscopy monitor while fiddling with the lead just below the clavicle, where a small incision had been made under local anesthesia. "Once you get satisfactory measurements, your lead is in a good spot. You fixate it there and you're done!" Simple, thought Smythe, taking his newfound skills back to Lakefield Regional.

A couple of years after starting practice as a surgeon, Smythe added pacemakers to his list of surgical procedures. He started with single-chamber pacemakers and put in a series of seven with no problems whatsoever in the first two months after his educational field day. His eighth pacemaker patient was Mr. Bellini, a seventy-seven-year-old Italian man who spoke little English. He fleetingly reminded Smythe of Luigi Lorenzo, the man whose central line he'd broken off many years previously as a medical student.

"We need to put a pacemaker in to speed up your heart," Smythe told Mr. Bellini quite loudly.

"Yes, yes," Mr. Bellini responded.

Mr. Bellini's heart rate was 32 beats per minute from a third-degree heart block—a defect in the electrical conducting system within the heart. Such trouble could develop with age. Although Mr. Bellini maintained an adequate blood pressure, 32 beats per minute was certainly not enough, nor was it safe in the long term.

The operating room was quiet except for the slow, rhythmic beeping of Mr. Bellini's heart on the monitor. Smythe looked over at anesthesiologist Dr. Loh to see if it was okay to start. "Go ahead," she said quietly.

After injecting local anesthetic and making a two-inch incision just below the left clavicle, Smythe was ready to direct the needle into the left subclavian vein. In order to do this effectively, he had to put the patient in the Trendelenberg position by tipping the head of the operating room bed down ten to fifteen degrees. The reasons for Trendelenberg were twofold: if the vein was made bigger by distending it with the head-down position, it was an easier target to hit. Second, if the patient's head was down, then the increased venous pressure made it less likely that air would find its way into a vein and cause an air embolism.

Ever since first-year residency, Smythe had found Trendelenberg troubling. His residency colleague, Dr. Harley Blake, was inserting a central line one day in that first year, and put an elderly lady in Trendelenberg. With the head of her bed tipped down and her face mostly covered in sterile drapes, she turned blue, unbeknownst to Harley. She then had a cardiac arrest and was dead within two minutes, although the code team tried valiantly for half an hour to reverse that fact. Harley quit residency the next day and became a ship's doctor on a cruise line. He never put anyone in Trendelenberg again. In retrospect, anyone who died by having their head tilted down probably was going to die imminently anyway. But that fact didn't stop Harley Blake from a significant career change, nor did it prevent Smythe from having flashbacks of Harley each time he inserted a subclavian line. Smythe was always wary, erring on the side of caution by keeping Trendelenberg a mild tilt and doing it for the shortest time possible.

Mr. Bellini was fairly healthy, except that he had a degree of restrictive lung disease, which meant he required more effort to suck in air than the average person. He was breathing steadily as Smythe made his incision.

Pondering Harley, Smythe had Mr. Bellini in eight degrees of Trendelenberg. Despite the vein being distended, Smythe hit the subclavian artery twice. His needle identified bright red pulsatile blood, which signified blood moving under high pressure away from the heart, not draining passively towards it. He repositioned his needle, and with a third try, he hit the vein, sucking dark blood into his syringe. He passed a wire through the needle, preserving access to the vein. Over the wire, Smythe then inserted an introducer sheath, a small plastic catheter through which he was about to insert the pacemaker lead. That was when Mr. Bellini took a big breath in. The negative pressure in his thorax sucked air into the introducer sheath, now half in Mr. Bellini's left subclavian vein. Smythe thought nothing of this—it was such a small amount—and placed his finger over the sheath before he quickly inserted the pacemaker lead and directed it towards Mr. Bellini's right ventricle.

As the pitch of the beeping pulse oximeter sounded a continuous descent, Smythe knew something wasn't right. Within twenty seconds, Dr. Loh's nervous voice belted, "We have a problem here, Jim."

"What's going on?"

"His oxygen saturations have dropped. I can't measure them."

"Why's that?"

Without answering, Dr. Loh was chanting, "Mr. Bellini, Mr. Bellini, Mr. Bellini!" When someone had to say a patient's name three times in quick succession, it was always disconcerting to Smythe. He peered over the surgical drapes to see Mr. Bellini's unconscious, dusky face. He looked like he was dead.

"Jim, I'm going to have to intubate him."

"Go ahead." A tube in Mr. Bellini's airway couldn't hurt; *something* needed to be done. "I think a little air sucked down the catheter. I wonder if he's got an air embolism."

Dr. Loh shouted, "I have no blood pressure, Jim. You'd better start

CPR." As Smythe started cardiac compressions on Mr. Bellini's breastbone, the usual flurry of activity resulted, with nurses and technicians running in all directions, doing anything they could to help Smythe and poor Mr. Bellini. Each compression was accompanied by the sound and feel of Mr. Bellini's ribs cracking.

"I'm sure it's an air embolism. The end-tidal CO_2 monitor is reading zero. He's not perfusing his lungs." Measuring expired carbon dioxide confirmed the diagnosis. If any blood were going through his lungs, some carbon dioxide would be coming out. His entire blood flow through the lungs had been obstructed from what Smythe had thought was an inconsequential amount of air. What was he going to tell Mr. Bellini's family?

"Turn him left-side down!" Dr. Loh commanded. In theory, turning Mr. Bellini on his side would cause the air to rise within the heart, away from the entrance to the pulmonary system. Even more theoretical was the next step, in which an anesthesiologist could insert *another* central line—this time through the jugular vein—and try to suck air out of the heart. By this time, Smythe had just about lost all hope, but he was willing to go along with anything that might work.

While Smythe continued cardiac compressions, four nurses turned Mr. Bellini onto his left side. Doing CPR to somebody on his side was a bit like clapping with one hand, thought Smythe. Within seconds, however, the patient's colour improved from dusky blue to pink. It happened so quickly that Loh hadn't even gotten to the next step: sucking air out through the other central line.

"I can feel a pulse, not just from your compressions. You can stop CPR, Jim. The air bubbles must have risen away from the pulmonary artery and are dissolving as we speak."

The whole episode had lasted only a few minutes, but it seemed like longer to Smythe. He felt nauseated and flushed—not a feeling he'd had before in the O.R. It made him want to quit doing pacemakers, if not surgery altogether.

Within another two minutes, Mr. Bellini was on his back again, unconscious and intubated—but alive. His chest was cleansed and draped again. Smythe continued with the pacemaker procedure, his wave of nausea subsiding. After securing the lead, he buried the shiny new pacemaker under the skin, just below Mr. Bellini's clavicle. The bulge from the pacemaker resting on top of the pectoralis muscle was readily visible and would remain there as a palpable reminder of the commotion caused by an air embolism. Dr. Smythe only hoped Mr. Bellini would have the brain cells left to appreciate this new device.

"Do you think he'll be okay?"

"I think so, Jim." Dr. Loh tried to sound reassuring. "He was only down for a couple of minutes. I guess we'll find out tomorrow."

The patient left the operating room with a heart rate of 60, the pre-programmed rate of his new pacemaker. It would be hours before Mr. Bellini's medication wore off and anyone knew to what extent he'd wake up.

Smythe met with six of Mr. Bellini's family members. Crowded into the small conference room, he shook hands with Mrs. Bellini, her grown children and their spouses. Mrs. Bellini could not speak much more English than her husband, and one son, Giovanni, seemed to be the spokesperson for the family. He had just flown in, and the family had briefed him on how his father had felt faint and had been admitted with a low heart rate. His family also told him how Mr. Bellini had gone into the operating room talking, smiling and joking, but that there had been a problem.

Smythe opened the conversation, speaking tentatively. "The pacemaker went in smoothly. But there was a problem of air getting into a vein. He's unconscious and is going to the intensive care unit. We're not entirely certain of his overall prognosis."

"What do you mean, everything went well, but there was a problem?" Giovanni Bellini was at least as tall as Smythe and twice as wide. They sat almost knee-to-knee in their tiny conference area. Smythe didn't want to open the door because of privacy concerns, but the small room was getting warm and stuffy. All seven of them were seated on two small couches, with Smythe protected in a small armchair near the door. Giovanni wrung his hands and repeated the question: "What do you mean, *there was a problem*?"

It always fascinated Smythe that the most concerned family member was usually the one from farthest away. Perhaps the guilt of neglecting his parents over the last twenty years had finally caught up with Giovanni and he was going to make up for that in one fell swoop, whether his father was a medically-created brain-dead vegetable or not.

Smythe responded calmly, "Your father's heart rate was 30, which over the long term is not compatible with life. While we were inserting the pacemaker, he sucked in a small amount—"

"You mean *you* allowed him to suck in some air," Giovanni interrupted.

"A small amount of air got into a vein. His heart stopped pumping blood effectively, and he was in immediate danger. With the help of Dr. Loh and others, Mr. Bellini came around fairly quickly." Smythe always liked to mention the name of at least one other physician during these talks—not to spread blame, but to reassure family that he was not the only doctor involved.

"There could be some brain damage." Smythe swallowed hard. "But possibly he'll be fine."

By the end of the conversation, only Giovanni was still upset. Mrs. Bellini clutched Smythe's right hand in both of her own, uttering, "Thank you, thank you." Other family members filled a gradient of appreciation. Smythe left the room with nothing else to do but wait and see what happened to Mr. Bellini.

The next day, Smythe made his way up to the intensive care unit late in the morning, as he wanted to give the team a chance to extubate Mr. Bellini. With the breathing tube removed, he would be able to talk—if he hadn't sustained significant brain damage.

Before Smythe got to Mr. Bellini's room, Kent, the ICU nurse, came up to him beaming. "He wants to go home," he said.

"He what?" Smythe responded, dumbstruck.

"I'm telling you, he wants to go home," Kent repeated.

"How are his ribs? It can be painful after CPR when the ribs get cracked."

"He hasn't complained, and I haven't asked. He just wants to go home."

Smythe marched into the room with intense relief. Mr. Bellini's heart rate on the monitor was 60 beats per minute. Their eyes met. All they both could say was, "Yes, yes," with big smiles.

Smythe's fear of Trendelenberg was now a thing of the past; he'd accepted that Harley's experience was not typical. Although his own escapade was similarly unusual, Smythe had now seen an air embolism first-hand—one he had created. The experience humbled him. From then on, he never worried about a little bleeding while putting in a central line or a pacemaker. When nurses complained of the mess he made, he simply thought of Mr. Bellini. As long as blood was trickling out of the vein for that short part of the procedure, air was not getting in. Smythe still knew the tiniest of air bubbles wouldn't cause a problem, but how could you know what was tiny enough? Mr. Bellini had sucked in just the right amount of air that day, at just the right time: the combination had almost been fatal.

Chapter 6 ~ Urinary Flatulence

Jim Smythe had mixed feelings about seeing young people with bad diseases. They prompted thoughts about his mortality, or sometimes about delaying the inevitable. He had just operated for breast cancer on a thirty-six-year-old mother of four children. He'd tried not to think about Amanda and his own children when he delivered the bad news. When Smythe had started his surgical practice, he rarely ran into a patient with a life-threatening disease who was younger than he was. Now, at age forty-four, he seemed to encounter this scenario more frequently. Every time he treated a young person with cancer, Smythe felt as if he'd dodged a bullet himself, especially if the patient was a young man. It wasn't that Smythe was glad when a forty-year-old man developed colon cancer—but he knew how to treat it, enjoyed the challenge of doing the surgery and deep down felt a sense of relief that it was not *he* who had the disease. Occasionally, this sense of relief bordered on euphoria, which left Smythe feeling guilty.

One case was particularly troubling. A twenty-five-year-old had come into the emergency department after being smashed up in a car accident, and he went into cardiac arrest from internal bleeding. As a desperate maneuver, Smythe cut open his chest then and there in the emergency department and started open cardiac massage. The young fellow perked up, and they got him into the operating room. The team struggled for two hours, trying to stop the bleeding from behind his liver. Thirty-five units of blood later, the young man succumbed. As Smythe held the young man's dying heart in his hand, he experienced power and impotence simultaneously, and he felt guilt for prolonging this young man's life for two hours when death had been inevitable. But he kept these feelings to himself, thinking he was probably the only one in the medical profession who ever felt this way.

*   *   *

"Jim, you know that chart you wanted on Hazel Kowalchuk?" Moira startled Smythe as he was daydreaming, sitting at his office desk.

Smythe felt a fluttering in his chest as he recalled the Medical Licensing Authority: POWER TO REVOKE LICENSE—RESPOND WITHIN THIRTY DAYS. He drew in a deep breath and calmly said, "Oh, yes. I almost forgot about that."

"Well, it's over five years old, so it's in off-site storage. I can get it for you, but it may take a week or two."

Smythe looked at his calendar—it was already October 10. *I'd better see if I can get an extension,* he thought. "Let me know as soon as you have it." After Moira was down the hall, he closed his office door and unlocked the drawer. He located the letter under some scraps of paper and a bottle of pills, then picked up the telephone and tapped in the number for the Medical Licensing Authority. The grounds for more time were the remote date of the case and difficulty retrieving records. *Don't they have a statute of limitations on this type of thing?* he wondered. To his surprise, the extension was granted over the phone. His response was due December 15. That was much easier than he had anticipated.

*   *   *

"When you pee, have you ever passed air?" was one of the first questions Smythe had asked Cecil McNaughton. The day they'd met, close to three months ago, seemed like yesterday.

Most people would find the question unusual, but Cecil McNaughton didn't pause for a second. "Yes!" Cecil exclaimed. "It started like I was peeing soda water about two months ago. Now, it's sometimes like I'm farting out of my penis—big blasts of air. And the toilet water has brown bits of stringy tissue in it." He ran his fingers through his thick grey hair and gazed intently through the top half of his bifocals at Smythe, who was sitting on the other side of the large mahogany desk.

"How many times have you been treated for bladder infections in the past year?" Smythe inquired.

"I've had at least five prescriptions for antibiotics. At first, they said the infections were just from an enlarged prostate. When I first told my doctor I passed air out my penis, he told me that was unlikely. I'm glad *you're* asking. Finally, someone is taking this seriously."

To Smythe, this probably meant one diagnosis—a colovesical fistula.

When two surfaces abnormally connected or communicated, it was called a "fistula". "Colo-" was derived from the word "colon", the large intestine, and "vesical" indicated a vessel—or, in this case, the bladder. The term "pneumaturia" referred to passage of air in the urine, a phenomenon over 99.9 percent of the population would never experience. Smythe's mood brightened as he delved further into Cecil's symptoms and medical history. Another great surgical case was unfolding.

As Smythe collated the information, he realized Cecil was one of those people who looked better on the outside than he did on the inside. He'd had cardiac problems related to a congenital heart valve. At the tender age of twenty-five, Cecil had had an artificial heart valve implanted at the University Hospital to replace his own increasingly dysfunctional valve. He had been on blood thinning medication, warfarin, ever since, and he often bragged to his friends that he took "rat poison"—another common use of the drug.

The risk of an artificial heart valve was not insignificant, and being off warfarin even for a week could increase Cecil's risk of stroke. If a clot formed on the metallic inner surface of the artificial valve, then it was only a matter of time before a piece of clot would break off and take a left turn up to Cecil's brain. A blood clot there could be devastating, depending on the size of the clot and its location. So for Cecil, taking warfarin pills daily for life had been routine. *At least he doesn't smoke*, thought Smythe.

Cecil's heart wasn't great, but his colon was awful. Sixty-two years of a North American diet, combined with a little bad luck and sub-optimal genes, had left Cecil's colon riddled with diverticulosis. Over time, development of pockets or weak spots in the colon wall was not that serious. Until recently, Cecil had not experienced infection—or diverticulitis—in the pockets.

Antibiotics could usually successfully treat acute diverticulitis. Occasionally, surgery was required. In the case of a fistula to the bladder, the inflamed segment of colon ruptured and an abscess formed between the bladder and the colon. If the patient was unlucky, the perforation freely spread infection throughout the peritoneal cavity, resulting in peritonitis. If the person was less unlucky, then the infection was contained and one possible outcome was fistulization to the bladder. The person would have an ongoing connection less than one centimetre long between the colon and the bladder. The consequences ranged from frequent urinary tract infections to pneumaturia to more serious systemic infection. The last quarter of the colon, in the patient's abdominal left lower quadrant, was most commonly affected.

In Cecil McNaughton's case, the diagnosis was clear. Smythe completed a thorough history and physical examination in addition to ordering confirmatory tests. He also did a colonoscopy to make sure there were no polyps or tumours in the colon. Smythe was unable to get through the affected part of the colon with the colonoscope due to significant narrowing and inflammation, so he had to follow it up with a barium enema X-ray to check the upstream portion of the colon. A CAT scan of the abdomen showed an inflammatory mass in Cecil's left lower quadrant that was adherent to the bladder. Cystoscopy—or examination of the inside of the bladder with a scope—by one of Dr. Smythe's urological colleagues revealed a suspicious area, red from inflammation. Although cystoscopy did not demonstrate a definite connection between the bladder and the colon, a fistula was still considered highly likely.

It was not difficult for Cecil to decide to have the surgery, which took place in early August. The management of Mr. McNaughton's problem was not so easy for Smythe, however. Cecil's requirement to be on blood thinners increased the risk of bleeding during and after the surgery. Plus, his cardiac reserve would no doubt be somewhat diminished due to his age and his long-term artificial heart valve. Removing a segment of inflamed and infected colon after detaching it from the bladder was also not a simple undertaking.

Closing the hole in the bladder was less problematic. A single stitch would suffice, and as long as the bladder was drained with a catheter for ten days, the hole would heal. The potential difficulties lay more with the colon. After removing a one-foot section of Cecil's colon, Smythe could rejoin it with sutures or surgical staples. The more appropriate question was whether the colon *should* be reattached. If Smythe joined infected colon, the consequences could be disastrous. Should the bowel come apart at the join—an anastomotic leak—the condition would result in peritonitis and a life-threatening infection throughout Cecil's abdominal cavity. The only way of dealing with this was to go back, surgically clean up the mess and give him a colostomy.

Detaching the bladder from the colon, removing the infected segment of colon and bringing one end through the abdominal wall as a temporary colostomy was a safer approach. For Cecil to have bowel movements through a temporary colostomy into a bag, although not so pleasant for him, was preferable to an anastomotic leak. With all of these considerations in mind, Smythe prepared Cecil for his operation.

Cecil's lifelong need to be on blood thinners required a process called "bridging". He'd have to stop taking his longer half-life warfarin pills five days before surgery. From this time until the day before surgery, shorter acting, low molecular weight heparin injections would be given. From the surgery until Smythe deemed it safe to restart blood-thinning medication—usually two to four days after surgery—Cecil would be without anticoagulation. Throughout this time, his blood would be at normal thickness and he'd be at higher risk for blood clots and strokes, but he would not incur the higher chance of bleeding associated with warfarin. Bridging heparin injections would resume a few days after surgery, during the usual five days required for warfarin pills to reach maximal effectiveness.

It was a Monday morning in early August, the first operation for Smythe that day, and Jared Chong was assisting. Cecil was ready for his surgery. Getting out of bed six times a night to pass urine with air bubbles and fecal material was becoming intolerable. Just before he went under anesthetic, he looked in Smythe's direction and said, "I trust you."

With the patient asleep, fully prepared and draped, Smythe, at his right, made the vertical incision from the umbilicus to the pubis. Jared, on Cecil's left, provided exposure for Smythe's every move. In the abdominal cavity, they encountered a large, inflammatory mass that, as predicted, was the sigmoid colon. It was stuck to the bladder in the left lower quadrant of the abdomen.

"Tell me, Jared, who is more likely to get a colovesical fistula? A man or a woman?"

"I'm not sure."

"Men are more likely, although women who have had hysterectomies are also prone to them. You know why that is?" Before his assistant had a chance to answer, Smythe explained, "The uterus is a protection against colovesical fistula. By lying approximately between the bladder and the colon, it makes such fistulization less likely. It's a physical barrier."

"That's interesting."

"So, Jared, should we hook him back up or bring up a colostomy?" The segment of colon had been successfully removed, and a stitch had been placed in the tiny hole in the bladder. They were left with two ends of colon. They also had to decide whether or not to reattach the bowel today.

"I'm not sure. It would be nice for him if we could finish the job today. Then he wouldn't need a bag."

"It would also be nice for him if he doesn't leak five days from now."

"Yes, I suppose that's true."

"What would make him more likely to leak?"

"If the anastomosis is under tension, has a poor blood supply or is created in the presence of significant infection, the chance of a leak will increase."

"That's good, Jared. Well, what do you think?"

"I think we should give him a colostomy."

"Exactly what I was thinking."

Monday evening, Smythe went around to see his post-ops. The surgery day had gone well, and he was particularly pleased with Cecil McNaughton's operation.

"We had to give you a colostomy, Cecil. It was the safest thing to do."

"I trust you, Jim."

"We can reverse that in three months if that's what you want. At that time, conditions will be safer, when all the infection is long gone."

"What do you mean, if that's what I want?"

"Well it *is* another operation. You're not obliged to get rid of this colostomy. But we can talk about that another day."

Smythe visited most of his patients between 7:00 and 8:00 the morning following surgery. On Tuesday morning, Cecil McNaughton hardly looked like he'd had an operation. He was sitting up, reading the paper and asking when he could get his catheter out and start eating.

"Your catheter should stay in for seven to ten days, until the bladder has had a chance to heal. You can even go home with the catheter."

"When d'you think I can go home, doc?"

"Five days from the surgery, at the earliest. There's a good chance you'll be home by the weekend."

The next day, Mr. McNaughton looked similarly undisturbed by his recent surgery. He was already learning how to handle the colostomy bag, a task that many patients had to be prodded into tackling.

"You've been off blood thinners for a few days now," Smythe explained. "The surgery went well. We can start the heparin bridging injections today. The chance of bleeding at this stage is quite small."

On Wednesday Cecil's colostomy started to move gas, and not much later stool began to fill the bag. Smythe couldn't feed him fast enough. Everyone was pleased with Cecil's progress. He was discharged on Friday with his urinary catheter in place. Heparin injections would be administered at home until his warfarin tablets kicked in.

* * *

Smythe returned from vacation in late August, finding his office consultations a stark contrast to sixteen-hour days trekking with his girls in the Grand Canyon. His last appointment of the day was Cecil McNaughton. Smythe hadn't expected to see him for another month, but obviously Cecil was chomping at the bit to have his colostomy reversed. Mrs. McNaughton wasn't so sure. She shifted in her chair, rapidly alternating her gaze between Smythe and Cecil. She had grey hair, and a long pointy nose on which glasses were perched.

"I love my husband just the way he is," she said as she patted him on the tummy. "We call him Freddie," she said, pointing to his colostomy. Then, with a big smile, she looked Smythe in the eye and said, "What do *you* think, Jim?"

Smythe didn't mind being called by his first name by an occasional senior nurse or a long-time patient such as Cecil, but Mrs. McNaughton's familiarity didn't sit well with him.

"The decision is up to Cecil. As you know, there certainly are some risk factors. Although everything went extremely well when he was off the blood thinners, there's no guarantee that things will go as well when the colostomy is reversed. Having said that, he'd go into a colostomy reversal operation without infection and probably in better shape than last time, so I would expect a good outcome."

"Cecil is only one year from retirement. I'd like to keep him the way he is so we can enjoy many more years together."

"It's *my* colostomy."

"Yes, I know that, dear. It is ultimately your decision."

Cecil's surgery was scheduled for November, an interval Smythe insisted upon to allow proper healing before the next operation.

* * *

Present Day—October

The doctors' lounge was half full at eight-thirty in the morning. Some physicians had just finished ward rounds; others were about to start. A few were simply enjoying a cup of coffee or the newspaper before the workday started in earnest. Rick Abbott leaned back while redoing the lowest button on his white shirt, where his gut was trying to peek through the opening past his tie. Then he smoothed the thinning grey hair on top of his head and adjusted his glasses.

"All I'm saying, Jim, is that we need to formulate some guidelines on working hours. The back-to-back eighteen-hour days aren't going to last forever."

Smythe smiled slightly as he sat in a big armchair kitty-corner to Abbott. He secretly loved to banter with the Chief of Medical Staff. He'd deliberately bait Abbott, trying to draw him into an argument. It was fun to get under Abbott's skin, but it wasn't easy. They often faced off with familiar positions in their debates: Abbott represented administration and rules, whereas Smythe lamented the loss of doctors' autonomy and status. He'd speak fondly of the rigorous training that earned physicians respect in days gone by, while Abbott stressed promoting equality and teamwork amongst health care workers. Today, Abbott's cause was patient safety.

Various specialties had implemented a number of measures to improve conditions for their physicians and enhance patient safety. Surgery was working on a service model where surgeons did shifts rather than working a day and a night together. It had been years since anesthesiology started taking the day off after call. But even they had the potential to work twenty-four hours in a row in unusual circumstances. Abbott was trying to formalize the process and bring diverse groups together to effect these changes.

"Oh yeah, Rick. First guidelines, then rules."

"But—"

"Next thing you know, some kid will come in, smashed up on the highway, and there won't be a surgeon in the city to help because we've all had less than seven hours of sleep the night before."

"Take airline pilots—"

"I'm tired of this comparison," Jim interrupted again. "It's apples and oranges. Airline pilots simply have to avoid mistakes 99.9 percent of the time and they're okay."

"Jim, airline pilots have set schedules and limitations on the hours that they are allowed to work. To protect the public."

"Like I said, Rick, it's apples and oranges. We're not airline pilots."

"So, what's your point, Jim?" The other doctors in the room appeared to be taking notice, enjoying the entertainment.

"Airline pilots work in good conditions without bad things happening. That's the way it's supposed to be. We deal with crap every day. And we have no idea when the crap will descend upon us. It's not like we're paid to wait for crap to fall out of the sky. There wouldn't be enough of us around if we were all well rested, on standby, waiting for it to rain crap. And besides, avoiding mistakes simply isn't good enough for us."

"You've lost me, Jim."

"I could avoid mistakes and bad outcomes—no problem. Know how?"

"How?"

"Stop operating."

"I still don't get what you're trying to say. I'm talking about safe working hours."

"Let me put it another way, Rick. I did about 200 laparoscopic gallbladders in my last two years of residency. I could practically do them in my sleep. When I get a difficult gallbladder today, I rely on that experience."

"I'm talking about guidelines for working hours, Jim."

"Okay, Rick. Let's say ten years from now, you come in jaundiced with Mirizzi's syndrome. Do you want me to scrape a big mother of a gallstone off the front of your common bile duct? At least I've done a handful and seen a bunch of other weird stuff over the years. Or, do you want the young surgeon, who hasn't actually *seen* a case, but has eight hours of sleep each night and probably *read* about Mirizzi's syndrome? It just so happened that when the three cases came through the University Hospital during his five years of training, he was on enforced naptime. Do you want that Rick? *Do you?*"

"I was just asking about—"

"Never mind, I've gotta go."

Abbott scanned the physicians in the lounge, and then, looking directly at Smythe, pleaded, "What the hell is Mirizzi's syndrome, anyway?"

Smythe pretended to ignore Abbott's question and slammed the door. He chuckled as his long strides accelerated him down the corridor.

* * *

One of Smythe's least favourite places in the hospital was medical records. It wasn't the staff that bothered him: they were pleasant enough. The problem related to the work he had to tackle there about once or twice a month. He dutifully made a trek to the department in order to catch up on dictating and signing off charts, but usually only under a threat from administration. Every few weeks, Smythe would receive an intimidating letter indicating that if he didn't dictate thirty or forty charts, his hospital privileges would be temporarily suspended. For a surgeon, this meant no access to the operating room or other procedure rooms, and therefore the incentive to pay attention was significant. These required dictations were usually discharge summaries that entailed a narrative of a patient's recent hospitalization. After the physician spoke the information into a telephone, it would then be typed by a hospital transcriptionist and placed on the patient's file. Smythe and many of his colleagues viewed these summaries as irritants that were nonetheless necessary to maintain status as a member of the medical staff.

Enforcing the dictations many weeks after the patient had been discharged bothered Smythe. Compounding this delay, it often took six to eight weeks for a hospital typist to transcribe discharge summaries, as administration considered these documents to be low-priority. The purpose of the discharge summary, of course, was to document information for relevant caregivers, ultimately enhancing patient care. It was very beneficial for the family physician to know about events that transpired while a patient was in hospital.

In a perfect world, Smythe would dictate a discharge summary on the surgical unit immediately after releasing each patient, so details would be fresh. Completing a handful of summaries at a time would be manageable. But why bother if the hospital took eight weeks to type the documents? By that time, the patient could be dead! Smythe remembered a few instances when a discharge summary was distributed to interested parties long after its content had become irrelevant. So, Smythe waited for the threatening letter before making his way down to medical records, his own personal purgatory. He often wondered if hospital architects were secretly laughing at physicians when they designated these windowless, remote basement locations as the places doctors went to dictate charts to avoid losing hospital privileges.

There was another reason not to be too attentive to one's hospital charts. Smythe contemplated from time to time poor Dr. Lee as an example. A busy lung specialist at the Lakefield Hospital, Dr. Lee was notoriously bad at dictating charts. In his fifteen years on staff, he'd *never once* had his charts completely up to date. It became a joke amongst the medical staff. Lee cut it close all the time, and he was often within a day of being suspended. He'd usually manage to dictate the minimum required to keep his head just above water for another week.

Eight months ago, Dr. Lee had dropped dead of a heart attack at age fifty-two. It was a complete shock to his colleagues and family. There was considerable speculation over whether he knew about his heart condition or not. After the funeral, when the shock of the tragedy subsided, hospital staff became aware of Dr. Lee's final hours. He had spent four hours the night before his death completing all of his dictations, a feat he had *never* accomplished previously. Smythe wondered if Lee had known the end was imminent. Others hypothesized that the completion of his charts *caused* his demise. Smythe wasn't really sure, but he wasn't going to take any chances. He was at ease never being completely up to date, just in case.

This autumn, Smythe was far behind. Early Monday morning, he ventured down to the depths of the hospital to complete charts in response to the most recent threat. He settled into the uncomfortable chair in the small, dark room, estimating he must complete forty-five charts before starting surgery at 7:30 that morning. The stack was daunting. Smythe picked up the handset and typed the pertinent numbers into the telephone in preparation for summarizing his first patient.

It was a man who had been hospitalized for two weeks with a ruptured appendix. Smythe dictated as concisely as possible, then moved on to the second chart. As he typed the third patient's hospital number into the telephone at 7:15, he knew there was no way he'd finish on time. Yet if he didn't complete the required discharge summaries by 7:30, he'd risk being suspended within twenty-four hours. Why the hospital would jeopardize patient care over discharge summaries was beyond Smythe. Administration would say it was ultimately his responsibility, so the offending physician, not the hospital, was at fault.

Today, some faceless hospital staff member would check the computer dictation system and see how many charts Smythe had completed by the eight o'clock deadline. If he didn't hit the target, too bad—he'd have twenty-four hours' grace and then all non-emergency hospital activities for Smythe would cease.

He did some quick mental calculations. It took about fifteen seconds to type a patient's digits into the telephone. That was four per minute, or more than ten minutes *just to type in the numbers*. There was no way he'd finish on time! If each dictation took three minutes of speaking into the telephone, he'd take a couple of hours. That was more time than he could muster to complete dictations by the end of the grace period.

Smythe suddenly came up with a cunning idea. He rapidly typed the next patient's number. At the voice prompt to start dictating, he typed the code for the next patient. So what if the typist found his blank dictation eight weeks later? Smythe would simply claim some kind of technical problem and catch up when the threatening letter reached him later. In rapid succession, he typed the remaining forty-two patient numbers into the telephone, each time ignoring the voice prompt to start dictating. He finished them all in six minutes, with time to spare to get a cup of coffee on his way to the operating room.

As Smythe closed the door, exiting medical records for at least another two weeks, he smirked, picturing his name being removed from the black list by some unsuspecting staffer. But Smythe figured he'd better not try this trick too often. It was best reserved for dire circumstances.

Chapter 7 ~ Fortin

Smythe was on call the entire last weekend in October. This was all part of his effort to manage the ongoing conflict between work and family time. The surgeons normally split weekends, but he liked to have his work bunched up, allowing him more weekends off later on. So, he started his on-call shift Friday morning and continued right through until Monday morning.

At about 6:30 Friday evening, he took an outside call from a Dr. Karen Swain, an internal medicine specialist from out of town. "Dr. Smythe, this is Dr. Swain from Brandon. I know this is a bit of an unusual request, but a patient of mine needs some help. He's in your area, and from talking to your emergency physicians, I understand there has to be an admitting doctor if he needs hospitalization. His problem being closest to your area of expertise, they suggested I call you."

"Yes, how can I help?" So far, this was not promising to be interesting; Smythe hadn't heard anything so far to suggest a surgical problem.

"John Fortin is a thirty-two-year-old man who had surgery by Dr. Jefferies for rectal cancer—do you know Dr. Jefferies?"

"I've heard of him, but I've never met him," Smythe replied.

"John had a low anterior resection last year. Even though his pathology was reasonably good, since he was so young I referred him for post-operative radiation treatment. The problem now is that he's getting a lot of pelvic pain. We did a CAT scan three weeks ago, fully expecting to find a recurrence in the pelvis, but it was all clear. Yet he's having this terrible pain."

"What d'you think is going on?"

"I think it's either a recurrence of his cancer or that radiation has caused some delayed neuropathic pain. We'll likely get an MRI when he's back here."

"How can I help?" Smythe was becoming less interested by the moment.

"He's returning here early next week. We can run him through more tests if needed, but in the meantime he needs some pain control. He's in Lakefield visiting friends. I was wondering if you could admit him to your hospital and control his pain over the weekend. We'll take over when he's back here."

"Sure, I can have a look at him."

"He hasn't done well with morphine or Demerol. Probably the best would be to put him on intermittent IV hydromorphone. You can investigate if you want, but I don't think you'll find much."

"Just have him come to emergency and the nurses can page me. I'll see what I can do."

"Thanks very much, Dr. Smythe. I appreciate it."

"No problem," he lied. He wasn't too happy about babysitting someone with pelvic pain after another doctor's surgery.

Two hours later, Smythe's phone rang. The call came from just around the corner, at the emergency triage desk. As on most Friday nights on call, he was in the emergency department, sorting out a few people with belly pain. Nothing for the operating room yet, but he could hope.

"Dr. Smythe, there's a John Fortin here to see you, with lower abdominal pain. Can we put him in cubicle number three for you to assess?"

"Number three would be fine."

"Do you want any blood work?"

"No, I'll just pop over and see him."

Smythe introduced himself to John Fortin. John was a clean-cut, nice looking fellow who wore wire-frame glasses. His hair was thick and dark brown, and he appeared healthy. Smythe was looking for clues that he'd ever had cancer. He had a lower midline scar but no sign of a colostomy. The cancer must not have been too low to preclude reattachment of the bowel. Smythe was about to do a rectal exam to see if he could feel the stapled low anastomosis, but thought better of it. John probably wouldn't be keen on it, and what was Smythe going to do if he couldn't feel anything? That wouldn't enable any firm conclusions or change Smythe's management, anyway.

Smythe agreed to admit Fortin under his care over the weekend. He ordered some baseline blood work, along with IV hydromorphone every four hours, then promptly forgot about Fortin until the next morning.

On ward rounds Saturday morning, Smythe was to visit all the surgical patients under any of the surgeons who happened to be away. John was not in his room—probably in the washroom or the lounge, according to the nurse.

"How's his pain control?"

"Seems okay. He doesn't complain. He just takes his painkillers and keeps to himself."

"I'll catch him at the end of the morning."

Smythe was busy all morning and early afternoon in emergency. At two o'clock, he came up to Unit 23 to check on Fortin. The patient had been out of his room for a while. He'd last had hydromorphone at 1:30, so he might not be back in his room for a few hours if he was out visiting. Smythe returned to the emergency department; he'd see Fortin later.

The next morning, Smythe was in to do rounds again. He still hadn't seen Fortin since admitting him Friday night. This was a bit ridiculous. If he was going to be there getting hydromorphone, Smythe should have the opportunity to assess him periodically.

"Where is he now? Washroom again?" Smythe asked the nurse with a touch of sarcasm.

"He was here when you came on the unit, Dr. Smythe. I asked him to stay close by so that you could assess him," replied Lourdes.

"So, can you find him for me, or should we discharge him next time he comes looking for pain medication?"

"I'll call you as soon as I find him."

"I'll look forward to your call. Do we have any records from Brandon Hospital yet?"

"Nothing so far, Dr. Smythe. It is the weekend, you know."

"Yes, and it's also the twenty-first century. Don't they have fax machines in Brandon?"

Lourdes just shrugged. Smythe went downstairs to the doctors' lounge to make some phone calls.

"Yes, directory assistance for Brandon. I'd like the hospital. Connect me? That would be fine." *If you want something done around here, it's easier to do it yourself*, Smythe thought. "You're saying there's no record of a John Fortin at your hospital? He had surgery by Dr. Jefferies for rectal—" No, the details weren't really important, so Smythe added, "Do you have a Catholic hospital in your city? Perhaps there's another hospital I should be phoning." After hearing the negative response, he slammed down the phone.

It was all looking a little embarrassing at this point. Here was a guy in his hospital, posing as someone with pelvic pain, with no record to support it. The phone call from Dr. Swain had sounded so detailed and convincing. Smythe looked up Dr. Swain in the national physicians' registry. No Dr. Swain! This guy had completely duped Smythe with the help of an unknown accomplice over the phone. Smythe's first reaction was to simply discharge Fortin next time he showed up for pain medication. That would teach him. Or would it?

Smythe picked up the phone again and called the local police.

"What do you mean, you aren't interested? What the hell—what's that all about? This guy has broken several laws and you're not *interested?* I need to speak to someone who cares, please." The more Smythe was put off, the more he wanted to sink his teeth into this problem. So what if it wasn't actually a surgical problem? He was going to get to the bottom of it, no matter how long it took. He continued waiting on hold, formulating his strategy for the next person to take his call.

Eventually, two plain-clothes policemen showed up at Unit 23. They were taken to the conference room, where they were fed coffee and a potluck lunch, a tradition for Unit 23 on the last Sunday of each month. Lourdes told Fortin there was a slight delay getting his pain medication from the pharmacy, but if he'd wait in his room, they'd have it for him soon.

Fortin was then instructed to go to the conference room, where the two police officers closed the door behind him and started the interview. Smythe was still rounding on the unit, determined not to miss the outcome of this little encounter. The anticipation was almost too much for him. To Smythe, Fortin represented all the patients who had ever extracted narcotics from him under dubious circumstances. After about thirty minutes, the two police officers led Mr. Fortin out in handcuffs. Head down, Fortin refused to make eye contact with Smythe or any of the nurses.

Later, the cops gave Smythe more details. Fortin had been using fake ID and fake health care coverage. He was on parole, with explicit restrictions not to attend a hospital without notifying his parole officer first. Fortin wasn't from Brandon; apparently, he was from near Lakefield and had been seeking—and receiving—drugs for the last year in the vicinity. He'd visited a string of hospitals and physicians, giving a large repertoire of tales in exchange for narcotics. The use of an articulate accomplice on the phone had been particularly bold, but the final outcome was sufficient to make up for Smythe's foolishness in falling for Fortin's elaborate plan.

As Smythe was leaving the hospital, Lourdes beamed her congratulations. "Nice work, Dr. Häagen-Dazs! We'll have to think up a new nickname for you now, won't we? How about Dr. Dragnet or something?"

"You let me know. I'm holding my breath on this one."

Smythe knew Lourdes well, so he couldn't expect her to maintain formality all the time. As long as she didn't call him "Dr. Häagen-Dazs" in front of patients or younger staff, he was fine with a few jokes now and then.

About three years ago, Smythe had taken out the appendix of Samantha Howard, an attractive thirty-year-old woman. At the time, he thought she was either a little eccentric or mentally ill. His suspicions were confirmed the day she was discharged. Smythe was up on the unit doing paperwork, and Lourdes came up to him, grinning enthusiastically.

"I just came from Samantha's room, and you'll never guess what!"

"What?"

"She's lying on her bed naked, covered with chocolate ice cream!"

"I guess she's ready to go home, then."

"Wait, it gets better."

"Oh?"

"When I asked her how she got that way, she said it was your fault!"

"My fault?"

"Yes, she said, 'Dr. Smythe was examining me while eating an ice cream cone and it was dripping all over me.'" Lourdes was absolutely delighted.

Smythe simply smiled and muttered something about Häagen-Dazs ice cream. From then on, Lourdes and some of the other senior nurses affectionately and privately referred to him as Dr. Häagen-Dazs.

Smythe had a bit of a soft spot for the mentally ill, and the event seemed rather harmless. Of course, there was no truth to the story, but he was sufficiently concerned about the episode to put Ms. Howard on his DO NOT SEE list after he discharged her. This registry included those few patients Smythe would refuse to see if a consultation request arose in the future. Mr. John Fortin joined Ms. Howard on the list.

*   *   *

The following morning, Smythe jumped out of bed at 5:30. He was feeling rather smug—after all, he'd never been able to say he'd sent anyone off from the hospital in handcuffs before. The fact that Fortin had consumed hydromorphone by the wheelbarrow under Smythe's direction most of the weekend was a minor detail that wouldn't diminish Smythe's euphoric mood.

A few minutes before seven o'clock, Smythe's cell phone rang just as he was getting ready to hop on his bike for the short trip to work. It was Jason Malcov, finishing off the night shift in the emergency room. He wanted Smythe to see two people with probable appendicitis.

"They both probably have it. The first lady is a thirty-five-year-old—Gerri Kennedy. You may know her husband, a high-flying lawyer in town. The second one is a twenty-five-year-old mother of two—a bit disadvantaged financially, but a nice lady and healthy otherwise. They both started getting pain at lunchtime yesterday, both are tender in the right lower quadrant and they have the same white blood cell count: 16."

"No problem. I'll see them before the O.R. this morning."

Smythe did some quick calculations about how much time he had to assess these two women, and when he might fit each of them into the operating room. It was going to be tight. He'd have to do something about the way emergency doctors referred patients who came in through the night. It was a little haphazard, whether the patient was referred to the person finishing the twenty-four hour call or the surgeon starting on call at 7:00 a.m. Sometimes, he thought they bent the rules according to which surgeon was starting and which was finishing. In this case, it suited him fine—here were two bona fide surgical cases, patients Smythe could help with an operation. If Malcov had waited until after seven o'clock and referred the women to the doctor coming on call Monday, the two operations might have ended up bumping into Smythe's room and disrupting his day anyway. It was better if Smythe could put emergency operations into his own operating room from the outset. But if he wanted to get to his first operation on time, he'd have to hurry to the emergency department. Smythe started with the lawyer's wife, Gerri Kennedy. He had met her husband Frank once before, but it was a long time ago and Smythe couldn't recall where. He had a feeling Amanda wasn't keen on the couple. When he pulled the curtain and introduced himself to Gerri and Frank, he instantly remembered. He had met them at a community fundraiser for a new sports complex. He couldn't remember all the details, but it seemed to Smythe that Amanda and Gerri hadn't quite hit it off. Amanda later had said something about the Kennedys being uptight or stuck-up. Now he wished he knew the details, as both Gerri and Frank gave Smythe a cold stare as if to say, "Why the hell weren't you here at 4:00 a.m. when Dr. Malcov said he was going to ask a surgeon to consult on the case?" Smythe employed his usual strategy of ignoring the glares and being as polite and jovial as possible without being unprofessional.

"When did the pain start?"

"Like I told Dr. Malcov, it was at about noon yesterday—crampy pain all over my abdomen. At 10:30 last night, it shifted down to the right lower portion of my abdomen. I threw up once. It hurts to walk standing straight up. And the bumps in the car hurt like anything!"

Smythe wasn't sure whether Gerri had looked up appendicitis on the Internet before she came in, or whether her description of symptoms fit the textbook so closely because she had a classic case. When he examined her abdomen, he was even more convinced that she had a typical case, and that she should be having her appendix out that morning. She was tender in the right lower quadrant, and her muscles tensed involuntarily every time he tried to press down over the appendix. There was nothing else in the history or lab work to suggest an ovarian problem or tubal pregnancy. Smythe was as certain as he could be that this was appendicitis.

"You've got a classic case of appendicitis. I think we should book you into the operating room for sometime today. We could do it with a laparoscope and tiny incisions. If we leave it too long, it could rupture."

"What if it's not appendicitis? What then?" Gerri pressed, her husband nodding his approval.

"If it's not your appendix, we usually look for an alternate diagnosis, but we take the appendix out anyway if it's safe to do so. If the pain comes back or doesn't settle, then we know the appendix is out of the equation. If there is a different condition that requires treatment, then we go ahead and do it if it's reasonable. But I'm fairly certain it's your appendix."

"Do you know it's appendicitis?"

"No. One is never 100 percent certain in these situations."

"So, you're saying you are willing to do a potentially unnecessary operation on me without finding out ahead of time whether it's appendicitis? What about a CAT scan?"

Smythe covered his irritation by smiling at the couple and saying, "We can arrange a CAT scan. It will increase our certainty from 90 percent to about 98 percent."

"What do you think, hon?" Gerri looked at Frank, ignoring Smythe.

"I think we should get a CAT scan." He turned to Smythe. "Not that we don't trust you, Jim."

"No, of course not," added Gerri. "But I'd feel better if we knew what we were going in for."

"A CAT scan is very helpful, but it can be misleading in rare circumstances. Also, there's some radiation associated with it. If you're okay with that, we can arrange it."

"Sure, I'd feel better with a scan first."

Smythe knew there was no point trying to talk them into operating without a scan. After all, he could be wrong. Although it was unlikely, Gerri could have a problem that would get better without an operation, such as a viral infection or a subtle ovarian problem. He could just imagine the story Gerri would tell about her "unnecessary operation" if he took out her normal appendix. Word always travelled quickly, and there was never an opportunity for the health care provider to give the other side of the story; patient confidentiality precluded that.

"I'll put in the request. It'll be sometime this morning, I hope. If it shows appendicitis, we'll book surgery after that."

Smythe left the cubicle and looked at the clock. It was 7:30. If he was going to get the paperwork done and his second patient assessed before the operating room, he'd have to hurry. He peeked around the next curtain to find Tiffany Reynolds lying down, staring at the ceiling. Smythe thought he'd met her previously for another surgical problem; she reminded him that he'd taken care of one of her kids after a car accident. Smythe's assessment was a little quicker than with Gerri. It seemed as if Tiffany had read the textbook on appendicitis, too. The pain had started at noon yesterday and shifted to the right lower quadrant last evening. Her physical exam was also typical. In Smythe's opinion, she had appendicitis.

"You've likely got appendicitis. The only way to find out for sure is go to the operating room and have a look."

"Whatever you say. You're the doctor."

Smythe tossed around the idea of doing the surgery with a laparoscope, but the diagnosis was not likely wrong, so a traditional right lower quadrant open incision would do just fine. It was a little quicker than the laparoscopic approach, and this patient's thin abdominal wall would make it a small incision, not much bigger than the three cuts for the laparoscope. Smythe also couldn't imagine Tiffany getting hostile if he had the wrong diagnosis. He'd simply take out the normal appendix, look as best as he could through the small incision for an alternate cause of pain and after surgery inform the patient of what he'd found.

With the emergency consultations finished up, Smythe went to the operating room and put Tiffany on the list while Gerri Kennedy was waiting for her CAT scan.

At 10:30 in the morning, being a little ahead of schedule, Smythe slipped Tiffany's operation into his regular operating list and took out her inflamed appendix. Despite some incisional pain, by noon she was feeling better and enjoying a "wonderful" lunch of green Jell-O.

Gerri had her CAT scan at 11:30, and it showed another inflamed appendix. Smythe had a little more difficulty integrating her into his schedule. Due to increased anesthetic risk, the anesthesiologist was not keen on putting her to sleep only a couple of hours after she'd drunk the oral contrast fluids for her CAT scan. Plus, Smythe was starting a two-hour operation at 1:30. So, Gerri Kennedy waited impatiently for her laparoscopic appendectomy, having missed the opportunity to have it earlier. It looked like she'd have her operation at about 4:00 p.m., until a stat Caesarean section bumped into Smythe's room at the end of his list. With the day staff going home, Smythe started complaining that she must get her surgery. After all, it was now five o'clock and ten hours after Smythe had originally seen her.

Gerri's appendix was ruptured, but the operation went fine. Smythe couldn't say for sure whether it would have been that serious if she'd had her operation earlier. Leaning back in his recliner in the operating room lounge as he was writing her post-op orders, he paused and thought for a minute. Here he'd had two women with the same problem. The pushy one got high-tech investigation, while the meek one had a good old-fashioned operation based on clinical judgment alone. Although they'd both be fine, Gerri might end up staying a couple of extra days in the hospital. Smythe often wondered if technology was as useful as people thought. How many people had had a ruptured appendix because of the delay caused by a CAT scan? He moved over to a nearby computer terminal and did a quick search using the keywords CAT scan, appendicitis and delayed surgery. The top ten hits were not conclusive, but he was convinced the answer was not entirely straightforward. How many CAT scans would it take to cause one cancer from the radiation associated with the test? That was a more difficult question; certainly Smythe would have to leave that one up to the academics to answer. Another troubling thought came to mind: what would it be like a generation from now when the new surgeons were incapable of diagnosing appendicitis without a CAT scan because they grew up relying on technology? Smythe pondered these issues for the rest of the evening.

The following day, Smythe discharged Tiffany and anticipated another couple of days for Gerri to recover. Although he'd reflected on the overuse of technology the night before, today he recalled a time during his residency when a CAT scan would have been very useful, and only some persistent nurses had saved his butt.

As a second-year resident, Smythe had been called down to the emergency department to see a twenty-four-year-old woman who had accidentally sat on a stick a few hours earlier while out camping. It was a long time ago, so he couldn't remember her name, but he easily recalled the attractive redhead and the details of her case. It was a long, sharp stick, and it had penetrated her jeans, puncturing the skin about two inches from her anus, off to the left side. When he came down to see her, she looked fine and said she felt well—she had just come in for a tetanus shot. The emergency doctor had done an internal pelvic exam and hadn't seen any sign of injury inside the vagina, but he wanted an opinion from general surgery about possible injury to the rectum.

Smythe came down to the emergency department as quickly as he could—it was 6:00 p.m., and the lady with the puncture wound was his last task before going home.

"Do you have any pain?" he asked.

"Not really. I just came in to get the area checked and have a tetanus shot."

Smythe palpated her abdomen, which he found to be soft with no signs of trouble. He then had her turn on her side away from him as he looked at her buttocks and the small gash near her anal opening. It would be a freak occurrence to have a stick penetrate far enough up to injure something in the abdomen. An injury to the rectum was more likely.

"We should put a scope into your rectum, just to make sure you don't have any signs of damage there."

The woman, who was not much younger than Smythe at the time, was not convinced. "Do you have to?"

"I would recommend it. If everything's fine, you can go back to camping reassured that there's no internal damage." The words were so confidently stated that even Smythe was impressed with himself.

"I suppose. If you have to," she replied, blushing.

Within twenty minutes, Smythe had looked a couple feet up her rectum with a flexible sigmoidoscope and found nothing abnormal. He was on his way home, and she was on her way back to her campfire—or so he thought.

The next morning, Smythe got a page from one of the emergency nurses about the stick patient, who had not actually left the hospital.

"When you wrote on the order sheet to send that girl home last night, the nurses weren't too happy, so they kept her in the department. She's stayed overnight. Dr. Goldberg reassessed her this morning, and he thinks she has peritonitis."

Smythe sheepishly went back to the emergency department, thankful that the nurses had disregarded his orders. When he arrived, the woman looked too ill to be the self-conscious twenty-four-year-old Smythe had talked into a quick peek in the rectum. Her pulse rate was 120 and her temperature was 39 degrees Celsius; clearly she was in trouble. Smythe put a hand on her abdomen and her muscles tensed involuntarily. Her abdomen was tender all over and there were no bowel sounds.

"You need an operation. Clearly, the stick penetrated further than we thought, and something is going on inside."

Unlike her reluctance to have a sigmoidoscopy fourteen hours previously, she was glad to have an operation offered now. "Go ahead. Whatever it takes."

Smythe lined up surgery and anxiously awaited the findings. If she ended up with a colostomy bag, he'd feel awful. But to everyone's surprise, the stick had penetrated and advanced parallel to the rectum, skewering three loops of the small bowel in the pelvis. The result had been slow leakage of small bowel contents over the twenty hours following the injury; the bowel and other organs were marinating in a couple of litres of greenish intestinal contents. The associated inflammatory response was enough to make her sick and give her the symptoms of peritonitis. There was no sign of the stick—it had been pulled out intact with no clue that it had done so much damage. The abdomen was thoroughly washed out, the small bowel repaired with sutures, and the young woman on her way home a week later.

It wasn't the first time a nurse had saved him, and he was sure it wasn't going to be the last. He learned from this case that small bowel injuries didn't declare themselves immediately. It took time for the damaging effects of small bowel fluid to become apparent. He wished he'd had ready access to a CAT scanner that day. If a CAT scan had identified abnormally located fluid when Smythe first examined her, she might have had her surgery the previous evening.

Now, fifteen years later, Smythe knew the CAT scanner was a good thing. But as Gerri Kennedy and her delayed operation for appendicitis had shown him, a CAT scan did not always add a lot of benefit. There had to be a balance and some intelligence when using technology.

Chapter 8 ~ The Right Call

Amanda looked out the window, sipping her morning coffee. She'd just dropped the girls off at school. Jim was long gone, having left for work at 6:00 a.m. Amanda enjoyed mornings when there was time to relax while she planned what she'd accomplish for the day. She had a lot on her plate.

Over the past year, Amanda had worked to raise awareness of palliative care. As President of the Lakefield Hospice Society, planning and fundraising to build a hospice within two years occupied much of her time. Having seen an uncle with cancer suffer needlessly in hospital because he was too sick for end-of-life care at home, Amanda spearheaded the project. The community was very receptive, with money pouring in to finance the venture.

When Jim had been playing tennis last summer, he'd met a young man who said, "Oh, you're the husband of that lady who is building the hospice!" When Jim told this story to Amanda, she was filled with pride. For once, the tables were turned. Although she was pleased by Jim's position in the medical community, she grew weary of constantly being referred to as "Dr. Smythe's wife."

Between her children and her parents, Amanda stayed busy with family responsibilities. Ever since her father had come home with five prescriptions about whose use he proclaimed he "had no idea", Amanda insisted on attending medical appointments with him and her mother. At least Jim was fairly low maintenance these days, but there were times when even he required significant attention.

Two years ago, he'd inadvertently cut a patient's common bile duct while taking out her gallbladder. He'd stewed for months afterwards. She tried to convince Jim he didn't need to fret excessively over his surgical complications. She figured if Jim cut a common bile duct, any surgeon could have; Jim had done more laparoscopic cholecystectomies than any surgeon in Lakefield, and until then, he'd not had a common bile duct injury. *His tendency to agonize about problems after surgery is probably why Jim is Jim*, she thought. Amanda could think of other surgeons who probably should worry a little more about complications.

The only surgeon who came close to Jim's ability was Dylan Ross. Dylan was slick, no doubt about it, but unlike Jim, he was also full of himself. His blue eyes and curly brown hair might be enough to make him the nurses' favourite, but Amanda knew he didn't have Jim's surgical experience.

As the latest surgeon to join the Lakefield surgical group, Dylan had replaced a retiring surgeon and in the process raised the general surgery division's profile considerably. Ten years younger than Smythe, he had good hands and equally adept surgical judgment. The problem, as far as Amanda was concerned, was that he knew he was good. And his arrogant flashiness was off-putting: Dylan always seemed to have a new car and a girlfriend to match. Jim was willing to overlook some of Dylan's social indiscretions because he was such a good surgeon. Amanda recognized that regardless of the younger man's irritating qualities, if Jim ever required help above what Jared could provide in the operating room, or if he needed a solid second opinion on a difficult case, Dylan Ross was the one to ask. It wasn't that the other four general surgeons weren't capable, but Dylan was the only one whose level of competence measured up to Jim's high expectations—standards that he applied most rigorously to himself.

It didn't help that Jim's one and only common duct injury had occurred in December—not his favourite time of year. Jim's father had died suddenly of a heart attack in December many years ago. Although he hardly spoke of it, Amanda knew it must bother him; he was on edge every December. As she poured another cup of coffee, she hoped Jim didn't carry his father's bad genes. Jim had assured her that his father had been overweight and a "type A personality"—stressed out all the time. Jim, on the other hand, was physically fit and he loved the pressure of his job; good stress, he called it. At least Jim had finally gone to Barry Sanderson to get that check-up.

Jim took care of himself, unlike some of her old boyfriends. They all seemed like such losers when she thought of them now, but at the time, they were simply good guys who needed help. Jim attributed Amanda's need to help others to her nursing training. But she knew it was more than that. Even as a girl, she had rescued stray animals in her neighbourhood.

Finally, her parents had set limits on the number and species of animals she could take in. So she began volunteering at the SPCA instead. In high school, she had toyed with the idea of applying to veterinary medicine, but settled on nursing for its wider range of opportunities.

Amanda finished her cup of coffee in time to head to her Hospice Society meeting.

* * *

"Good morning, Jim." An older doctor smiled as he approached the front desk. Smythe looked up from writing on a chart.

"Good morning, Ted," Smythe replied. *At least he remembered my name this time*, Smythe thought. *I guess Barry can't be far away.* Sure enough, Barry Sanderson trundled around the corner and nodded to the nurse in charge. Both bald, father and son seemed ageless. Barry was about fifty. He had a slight build and a high-pitched voice, similar to his father.

"Good morning, Jim," Barry said, glancing at the chart his father was clutching.

Ted had been a family doctor in Lakefield for forty-five years and continued to work in a limited capacity, despite being seventy-two. Ted's memory wasn't so good anymore, so at some urging from Barry, Ted had finally reduced his office practice to part-time last spring. Convincing him to retire was not so easy. Ted Sanderson continued to be listed as the MRP (most responsible physician) when any of his patients were admitted to hospital, as long as they did not require care from a specialist.

Last spring, one of his patients—a forty-two-year-old construction worker—had been admitted with severe facial pain from trigeminal neuralgia, an inflammation of one of the cranial nerves. When Ted ordered soap suds enemas three times daily, most of the staff would have questioned it—except that a student nurse carried out the order, which was only cancelled when the patient refused the third enema.

A thirty-two-year-old woman admitted with gastroenteritis had had slightly low serum potassium on her third day in hospital, due to her diarrhea. When Ted Sanderson ordered twenty milliequivalents of potassium chloride to be injected intravenously over one minute, the order was fortunately caught by a pharmacist and cancelled immediately. Given over one minute, the dose would have been fatal: potassium chloride was the injection of choice for state-sponsored executions, as it caused cardiac arrest when administered quickly.

The issue of Ted Sanderson's competency had been discussed

informally at times, but Ted was adamant about continuing to work. Rick Abbott was looking for a concrete reason to remove his hospital privileges. A medical diagnosis of dementia would help, but a psychiatrist hadn't formally assessed Ted's cognitive abilities yet. Most people viewed the enema order as innocuous, and Ted defended the potassium chloride order as a minor error, claiming he had meant one hour, not one minute. Besides, the hospital had checks and balances in place to deal with such errors.

Three physicians older than Ted worked at the hospital. They were all bright, and the eighty-one-year-old was top-notch. So, it was tricky for Abbott to hone in on Ted without some decent, objective information. Age alone could not be cited in mandating retirement.

While Abbott was ready to pounce at the next possible opportunity to force an assessment on Ted, Barry Sanderson had agreed to keep a close eye on his father. Whenever Ted was in the hospital, Barry was not far behind, quietly checking each of his father's orders. It was all very informal, but it provided nurses with the reassurance that they would not be the subjects of a scandal due to Ted's misguided orders.

Barry Sanderson was such an agreeable type to help his father in this way. Smythe had chosen to see Barry for his check-up several weeks ago because of Barry's easy-going personality. He had visited Barry a couple of times at his office since then and was pleased with their rapport.

* * *

"What's the purpose of the gallbladder?" Smythe smiled at Jared as they prepared to make the umbilical incision.

"It stores and concentrates bile. It's like a side-storage container off the common bile duct, releasing bile into the small intestine after a fatty meal."

Smythe made a one-centimetre cut into the skin above the man's umbilicus, preparing to insert the laparoscope. "Tell me about bile, Jared—what is it, and why do some people form stones?"

"Bile is made in the liver to digest fats. It's released from the liver and travels through the bile duct into the small intestine, although it's stored and concentrated halfway along in the gallbladder. It's made up of bile salts, cholesterol and phospholipids—when the proportion varies, bile becomes lithogenic and is more likely to form stones."

"What else contributes to stones?" Smythe inserted the camera through the umbilical port as the abdomen continued to insufflate with carbon dioxide. On the two TV screens, they viewed duplicate images of the anatomy of the upper abdomen, brightly lit and magnified.

"Stasis. When bile doesn't move, it's likely to form stones. That's why stones usually form in the gallbladder, not the bile duct. After the gallbladder is removed, bile trickles steadily from the liver to the small intestine without being stored along the way. People seem to be fine, with normal digestion."

"Who gets gallstones?"

"More often women, especially with pregnancy, older people and those with a family history."

"What about lithotripsy? Why not blast them with ultrasound?" Smythe asked.

"Lithotripsy is great for kidney stones, but gallstone fragments getting stuck on the way out can be a bit of a disaster."

"Why does the gallbladder need to come out? Why don't we just take out the stones?"

"New stones would form."

"Excellent, Jared."

The patient, Mr. Obutu, was a sixty-year-old man who'd had upper abdominal pain and vomiting for three days. The ultrasound didn't show gallstones, although Smythe was fairly sure it had to be the gallbladder. Either the ultrasound missed a small stone blocking the outlet of the gallbladder, or he had the much rarer "acalculous cholecystitis", inflammation of the gallbladder without stones. The CAT scan showed some "stranding", indicating inflammation in the right upper quadrant, but imaging did not confirm a diagnosis. Normally, a HIDA scan would be arranged to see if the gallbladder filled with bile. After intravenous injection of a radioactive isotope, lack of filling of the gallbladder would confirm cholecystitis and the need for surgery. Operating without a HIDA scan in the presence of other non-diagnostic tests could be considered reckless. However, there happened to be an isotope shortage at the time, and a HIDA scan would not be available until next week, leaving Smythe to make the decision based on clinical judgment.

"Does this hurt?" Smythe had asked, pressing into Mr. Obutu's right upper quadrant.

Mr. Obutu winced. "A bit."

"Take a deep breath in," Smythe said, pushing under the patient's ribcage.

"Ow!" Mr. Obutu shrieked.

"Despite the tests being inconclusive, I think it's your gallbladder. We should take it out," Smythe said.

"Whatever you say, doc. Just fix the pain."

In the operating room, Smythe and Jared used three instruments and a camera through four tiny incisions on Mr. Obutu's abdominal wall to expose the gallbladder, which was mostly tucked beneath the undersurface of the liver. Dense inflammatory adhesions to the anterior abdominal wall also hid it. Smythe peeled the structures apart, exposing the top of the gallbladder. Wisps of white material indicating infection covered it. The gallbladder itself had patches of grey and black; a healthy gallbladder should be pale green.

"Well, you called this one right, Jim," Jared stated.

"Yup. Gangrene of the gallbladder—don't see inflammation advance like that very often," Smythe replied proudly.

Removing Mr. Obutu's gallbladder would not be easy. Smythe proceeded to dissect it away while Jared held the camera and retracted it upward, exposing the lower end. Smythe moved on to the attachments at the bottom of the gallbladder, preparing to separate it off the undersurface of the liver.

"What's the most important complication to avoid when removing a gallbladder, Jared?"

"Common bile duct injury."

"Exactly." He remembered his only common bile duct injury. It had caught him totally off guard; he was doing what he'd thought was an easy cholecystectomy. But the lower end of the gallbladder was more inflamed than he'd realized, distorting the anatomy. By the time he'd cut what he thought was the cystic duct—the small duct joining the gallbladder to the side of the common bile duct—it was too late. Bile trickled from the vicinity of the liver. He called his surgical colleague, Dylan Ross, to come in from home to help out. They converted to the big, old-fashioned incision, confirmed the complication, and sent the patient to the university for a definitive repair. Smythe had felt awful.

When laparoscopic cholecystectomies were introduced in the early nineties, common bile duct injuries increased, some occurring at the hands of repeat offenders who hadn't learned the technique adequately. Smythe hated the possibility of being lumped in with that group—even if this had been his first one in over 1000 cases.

The problem with the innovation of laparoscopic surgery was the speed with which the change occurred. In 1988, most surgeons hadn't even heard of laparoscopic cholecystectomy, but within four years, the open technique had been abandoned except in the most difficult circumstances. Patients and surgeons shunned the few cautious doctors who recommended a randomized trial comparing open versus laparoscopic cholecystectomy. Patients said, "Why have it out the old way when it can be done with the laser?" The fact that lasers had nothing to do with laparoscopic gallbladder surgery was disregarded: everyone wanted the new high-tech method and surgeons were excited to be part of the change.

Smythe remained silent as he worked on the most treacherous part of the operation. Beads of sweat formed just below his surgical cap. As he elevated the lower end of Mr. Obutu's gallbladder away from the expected location of the common bile duct, Smythe's mood lightened. "When I get to this stage, I can relax. It's all downhill from here. And yes, I did make the right call on this one."

* * *

Mr. Obutu's case wasn't the first time Smythe made the right call without full diagnostics, and it wouldn't be the last. Earlier in the year, Jason Malcov had asked Smythe to see a seven-year-old boy with vomiting and abdominal pain. "I just want you to put a hand on his belly. His tummy is soft, but he is in a lot of pain. I think he's got gastroenteritis, so I'll probably refer him to pediatrics if you think he's not surgical."

Kyle was gaunt, and he grimaced while lying on the emergency room stretcher. Smythe took a history from his parents and found no recent medical problems. Kyle had had surgery as an infant to correct a problem with his urinary system that caused frequent infections. Doctors had also told his parents that Kyle had a congenital heart valve problem that might require surgery someday.

Now, at ten o'clock at night, Kyle had been vomiting several times each hour since supper. At home, his pain had come in waves, but it had been constant and severe over the last hour. Smythe pressed on the boy's soft, distended abdomen. He seemed to be in pain whether Smythe was pushing there or not.

Smythe went to review the X-rays with Malcov looking over his shoulder. "There's not much to see here, but he does have some dilated small bowel," Smythe pointed out. "I think with all his distension, we're just not seeing much bowel on the X-rays because it's all fluid-filled."

"What do you think, Jim?" Malcov asked.

"I'm worried about him. He's in a lot of pain. He's not passing any flatus. You did know he's not passing gas, didn't you?"

Malcov's face flushed. "Well—"

"Jason, you've got to ask these questions," Smythe interrupted.

"Sorry."

"Don't say sorry. Just get it right next time."

"Do you think we should scan him?" Malcov asked.

"I think this fellow needs an operation," Smythe replied.

Malcov's eyes widened. "Really? But his white blood cell count is normal. And his belly is soft. What about a scan first? There's not much to lose, is there?"

Smythe wasn't sure which infuriated him more: Malcov's lack of appreciation for how sick this boy could be, or the disrespect he was showing in questioning Smythe's opinion.

"His pain is out of proportion to the physical findings in the setting of a bowel obstruction. I think he's got a lot to lose if we don't operate soon. If the blood supply to his intestine is in trouble, then we could be looking at infarcted intestine in a couple of hours. We're operating."

Forty minutes later, as they draped Kyle's abdomen in the operating room, Jared asked Smythe, "What do you think we'll find here, Jim?"

"I'm not sure, but I'll sleep better tonight knowing we've had a look. Kyle's previous surgery raises the possibility of a bowel obstruction from adhesions. The fact that he had some problems soon after birth also makes me wonder about a congenital problem causing a bowel obstruction. We have to look, whether we find anything or not."

Smythe started by making a six-inch vertical incision, taking care to curve around Kyle's umbilicus midway. The abdomen was quite distended, but there was virtually no fat. Smythe took great care in penetrating the final layer to avoid inadvertently cutting into Kyle's intestine. A gush of blood-tinged fluid emanated from the small opening. Smythe quickly inserted his finger, lifting the abdominal wall while he deepened the entire incision through all the layers. With more fluid, the small intestine began to bulge out through the opening. The small bowel was greyish purple and swollen.

"Wow!" Jared said incredulously.

"You're not kidding," Smythe replied. "His entire small bowel is in trouble." He inserted his right hand, feeling for any firm areas that could be points of fixation around which Kyle's bowel was twisting. Without a word, Smythe lengthened the incision in both directions and then placed both hands in Kyle's abdomen. He then proceeded to turn the small intestine 360 degrees in a counter-clockwise direction. "Let's cover this with some warm, moist towels and see if it pinks up," Smythe said to the scrub nurse.

Before they could get the bowel covered, Jared exclaimed, "Jim, the bowel looks better! It's starting to get pink!"

"That's a relief." Smythe took a deep breath. "You know what this kid has, Jared?"

"No, what?"

"He's got a malrotation of his gut. Ever since birth, his intestine has been abnormally positioned. In utero, it failed to do the usual 270-degree rotation and fixation. As a result, the small intestine has been floating on a narrow pedicle ever since. I'm surprised this didn't happen sooner."

"What do we do now?" Jared asked.

"Now that the bowel is untwisted, we have to reduce the chance of recurrence. I think it's the Ladd's procedure. We try to broaden out the mesentery, so it's less likely to twist. I need a little help with this. I'm going to scrub out for a few minutes."

Smythe went to the lounge and pulled a large surgical textbook off the shelf. Yes, it was the Ladd's procedure. He'd only seen one before, while he was a resident. After perusing the textbook, he phoned the pediatric surgeon on call at the university to go over the procedure. They agreed that it was better if Smythe could do it, rather than sending Kyle up for a second operation. Smythe scrubbed back in.

For the next twenty minutes, Smythe carefully divided Ladd's bands between the duodenum and the right colon, thus broadening the pedicle from which the bowel derived its blood supply. It would now be less likely to twist in the future. He also took out Kyle's appendix, which was now situated on the left side and would result in some diagnostic difficulties if Kyle ever got appendicitis in the future.

Smythe felt satisfied as he began to suture Kyle's abdominal incision. "That was close, Jared. Another hour and his bowel might have been infarcted. We'd have had to take out his entire small bowel, and he'd've been dependent on intravenous nutrition for life."

"You made the right call here, Jim."

"Yes, Jared. I think you're right."

* * *

Slogging through his office consultations Tuesday afternoon, Smythe could finally see the light at the end of the tunnel. Moira had booked far too many patients that afternoon. He'd have to talk to her about that.

With only six patients left, he introduced himself to Mrs. Smithers, a sixty-four-year-old woman who had been referred for assessment of hemorrhoids. They chatted briefly, and Smythe determined she would need a colonoscopy at the hospital to exclude pathology higher up, but he'd like to see what the hemorrhoids looked like today since she'd passed a small amount of blood with her morning bowel movement. He asked her to take off her clothing from the waist down and to cover with a sheet. He'd be back in a couple of minutes to examine her.

Smythe walked down the hall to the washroom, thinking about the office renovations that had given him more space than he needed. He couldn't wait to get his small gym up and running. Locking the washroom door, he relieved himself—he'd been an hour behind all day and hadn't emptied his bladder for several hours. He washed his hands hurriedly as he remembered Mrs. Smithers lying half-naked on the examining table.

As he grasped the door handle, it rotated, but the door wouldn't open. He was locked in. He remembered that the door had been removed for a few days during renovations; clearly, it hadn't been reinstalled properly.

He banged on the door five times in quick succession. No response. He then reached for his cell phone before realizing he'd put it in his desk charger only thirty minutes ago. Smythe thought of Mrs. Smithers and her hemorrhoids awaiting his inspection. "Moira! MOIRA!"

He couldn't believe what was happening. *No one could hear him!* A lot of good the extra space in his office did him now, putting additional distance between the bathroom and main reception area. Then he remembered how the privacy officer had advised him to pipe music into the waiting room, discouraging people from hearing confidential information. *Great, my patients' privacy is protected while their surgeon dies of starvation locked in the washroom!*

After about ten minutes of yelling and banging, Smythe heard some rapid footsteps coming towards him down the hall. "Jim?" Moira asked. "Are you in there?"

"Of course I'm in here! Where do you think I've been for the last ten minutes?"

"You'd better come out. Mrs. Smithers is waiting."

"I can't get out. Tell Mrs. Smithers I got called to the hospital." He could hear Moira trying the door handle.

"I can't," Moira replied. "She came out to the waiting room wrapped in a sheet, asking if you'd forgotten about her. Then she said she thought she heard you yelling."

"Get me out of here, and I'll see her in a couple of minutes." Smythe thought this would be funny if it had happened to *anyone* but him.

"You don't have to yell, Jim. I can hear you just fine. I'll be back in a few minutes."

Smythe scanned the washroom for something—anything—to help him escape. He thought of MacGyver and what *he* would do in one of his heroic TV moments. After another exasperating five minutes, Smythe heard more footsteps approaching.

Moira said, "I've called Dr. Abbott. He's coming over from emerg. He'll be here right away."

"Abbott? What does Rick know about breaking into washrooms?"

"He was all I could think of, Jim," Moira responded, her voice quivering.

Within a few more minutes, Smythe could hear Rick and Moira talking outside the door. The next time Moira spoke to him, she sounded more confident: "Don't worry, Jim, Mrs. Smithers said she'll show you her hemorrhoids tomorrow. I've rebooked your remaining patients, and we'll have you out of here in no time."

Rick added, "I've got something that'll get you out, Jim. I'm sliding it under the door!"

Smythe looked at the small crack between the floor and the bottom of the door, where the pointed end of a miniature Phillips screwdriver emerged.

"Oh great, Rick. Just what I need if I want to adjust a pair of glasses! What the hell am I going to do with that?"

Abbott responded, "It's stuck. If I can just break the handle off, you can use the stem."

"Never mind," Smythe exclaimed, eyeing a thin metal light-switch cover sitting on the floor in the far corner. He ran over and grabbed it, then wedged it into a small gap in the door hinge and banged upward with the base of his hand. At first, there was no effect, but eventually the hinge bolt shifted slightly. Buoyed by his success, he continued to hammer until his hand hurt. Within a minute, the hinge bolt popped out, landing on the floor. He repeated the maneuver with the upper hinge, and suddenly the door fell off its hinges into the washroom. He was free!

* * *

The next morning at the hospital, Smythe entered the empty doctors' lounge anticipating a relaxing cup of coffee before the workload began to heat up. As he sat down, he noticed a hand-written sign on the washroom door. It read: "Reminder—Bring cell phone to prevent entrapment." Smythe chuckled, then recognized the sign was in Sandi Tremaine's handwriting. He hadn't realized she had the sense of humour to write a sign like that. *Well, good for her*. He left the sign untouched.

Smythe sat down beside Jared, who had just seated himself and was thumbing through the morning newspaper.

"Hey, Jim, did you see this? They just published a report that you're seven times more likely to get an infection in some hospitals in the province than in others! But the government won't release the names of the hospitals studied."

"Oh, another one of those reports," Smythe replied casually.

"The government won't release the hospital names," Jared repeated emphatically. "Sounds a little shameful to me."

"Good for the government."

"What d'ya mean?"

"You've got to be careful how you interpret statistics like those. Who collected the data and why? If different people gather each hospital's data, it can dangerous to make comparisons."

"I suppose—"

"The last time this happened was fifteen years ago down east, about complications from gallbladder surgery."

"I never heard about that."

"Of course you didn't," Smythe explained. "You were probably in grade school at the time. Someone pulled stats on common bile duct injuries. The results were truly troubling if you believed them. D'you want to know how they screwed up back then, Jared?"

"How?"

"Hospitals get paid by the complexity of the cases they handle. Some hospitals encouraged their coders to be much more liberal than others in order to secure as much funding as possible. When they assigned diagnostic codes to a patient's hospital stay, some hospitals were very aggressive, calling just about any minor problem occurring after gallbladder surgery a common bile duct injury."

"Doesn't sound right to me," Jared commented.

Rick Abbott entered the lounge and sat down, listening intently as Smythe continued. "Some eager reporter pulled the stats and naturally was horrified at the discrepancies between hospitals. But the problem was it didn't pass the sniff test. The article implied that common duct injuries were happening on a regular basis at most hospitals. It just reeked of bad data."

"Are you going on about bile ducts again, Jim?" Abbott asked. "That was years—"

"Even when the media was corrected," Smythe continued, "the story kept re-circulating in different newspapers and on the television. Some surgeons successfully sued and a year later, a tiny retraction was printed. As a result of the original article, hundreds of patients were scared and inconvenienced unnecessarily. Many of them delayed or cancelled their surgery—all because of the bile duct newspaper story, all based on bad data."

Abbott was now staring intently at Smythe, squinting.

"What?" Smythe asked.

"I'm just waiting to see whether you're slamming just the media. Or are you going to take a run at health administration as well today?"

"Very funny, Rick. The thing is, this type of fiasco rears its head every ten years, and the people who propagate it are too young to remember the last time it happened."

"I agree that the bile duct article was based on erroneous data," Abbott said. "But there *was* a problem with bile duct injuries early on. *We* need to provide the real numbers to reassure the public that they're safe, and to identify problems when they come up. If the medical profession is silent on these issues, someone is going to go digging and take the numbers out of context. That's when it spells trouble."

"Thanks for your input, Rick, but I was talking to Jared about this recent report on infection rates in hospitals." He turned to Jared. "Good for the government for not releasing the hospital names this time around. They're not concealing any horrifying treatment of our citizens; they just recognize that it's more complex than some people would like us to think."

Jared rubbed his chin. "I never thought of it that way."

"Of course you didn't, Jared. *And you're a doctor.* And if you didn't, what do you think the rest of the population thinks about it? They don't know. So, when you read an article like this one today, just take it with a very big grain of salt."

"But we've still got to question how we're doing, Jim. We've got to review our own results," Abbott added.

"Of course. But the conclusions are uncertain when you have hundreds of people collecting statistics at different hospitals, often at different times and *with different motivations*. That's just common sense." Smythe gulped his remaining coffee, stood up and bolted out the door.

Chapter 9 ~ Everything I Touch

Shirley Carver pushed her tray away from her after a leisurely lunch. She sat opposite Angela Beaumont, a much younger nurse who had been in the operating room for the past year. Shirley had worked in the hospital for twenty-one years, the past sixteen of them in the operating room. She preferred the late lunch. If she timed it correctly, slipping away five minutes early and returning five minutes late, the lunch could be extended to forty minutes. In addition, the cafeteria was not busy at this hour, allowing more relaxation time before going back to work. And by the time she finished lunch, there was not much left to the workday—just one final push before going home.

As far as nurses went, Shirley Carver was one of the best. She'd put in her time in the emergency department and intensive care early in her nursing career, so she was certainly comfortable attending to sick people.

Angela had been spending a busy day in Smythe's operating room while Shirley had been in orthopedic surgery. Angela was twenty-three years old and unmarried, taking an interest in the single doctors in the hospital, especially in the operating room. Shirley tucked a strand of grey hair under her O.R. cap as Angela inquired about Jim Smythe.

Ever since she had scrubbed on the Rory Harbin case, she was enamoured with Smythe. Over a matter of minutes, Angela had witnessed a frenetic bloodbath turn into an incredible save, all because of Dr. Smythe's quick actions.

"Why does he work so hard?" Angela inquired.

"It's always been that way for Dr. Smythe."

"He can't need the money. He must be loaded!"

"Of course he doesn't need the money. Dr. Smythe doesn't need to work at all. He's *never* needed to work."

"You're kidding!" Angela looked incredulously at Shirley.

"Dr. Smythe's father dropped dead of a heart attack when Smythe was thirteen years old."

"So?"

"His dad had a chain of successful restaurants. When he died, the company was sold and he left his son ten million dollars."

"Wow!"

"And you probably haven't seen Dr. Smythe waste ten million dollars, have you? He's generally pretty tight with his money. I suppose that's why some rich people stay rich."

"So why does he work?"

Shirley paused. "He loves life as a surgeon—the challenges and successes. And I think he's afraid of dropping dead like his father. The only way to take his mind off it is to work all the time. He's trying to pack as much excitement into his life before age fifty as he can. Dr. Smythe is now in his mid-forties. I think that's about the age that his father keeled over."

"I can think of better ways to get excitement than from working all the time."

"You have to understand, Angela, Jim Smythe's work is a bit different from ours. He calls the shots, and he works as much or as little as he wants. For the most part, he's not watching the clock when he's at work. Make no mistake, I don't dislike my job and I'm very proud of what I do, but for me, *it's a job*. For Dr. Smythe, *it's a way of life*."

"It just seems strange, to have all that money and still work all the time."

"Dr. Smythe is not typical. He's more like a surgeon back in the days when I was a student. The younger ones don't make it their lives nowadays. But for whatever reasons, Jim Smythe has chosen to do it the old-fashioned way."

"I suppose if I needed an operation, I'd want him to do it."

"I'm with you there." Shirley paused. "What's he up to today?"

"When I was leaving for lunch, he was about to reverse a colostomy." Angela looked at her watch. "Speaking of that, I should probably get back up to help him. I'm supposed to relieve Liz at 2:30." Angela picked up her tray and headed for the operating room while Shirley took a few more minutes to relax.

*   *   *

The day of Cecil McNaughton's colostomy reversal had finally arrived. His bladder problem had been completely cured by his previous surgery. For this operation, he was placed with his legs in stirrups in case Smythe wanted to pass a circular stapler up through his rectum to join the bowel. Developed in the seventies, staplers had revolutionized the way bowel surgery was done. In good hands, a sutured join was as safe an anastomosis as any. However, staplers were quicker and sometimes invaluable in difficult situations, such as a join low down in the pelvis—too low to hand-suture.

Smythe made the abdominal incision by removing Cecil McNaughton's old lower midline scar and then simply dividing deeper layers until reaching the peritoneal cavity. He entered the abdomen through a few adhesions—small bowel adherent to other loops of small bowel—that had to be separated. Once all that was sorted out, he made a circular incision on the skin in the left lower quadrant around the colostomy. The bowel was dropped back into the abdomen while they searched for the lower end. When they found the distal segment, it was simply a matter of joining up the two ends of bowel.

"Well, Jared, should we suture this or staple it?"

"It's up to you, boss. What do you think?"

"To tell you the truth, I think it will be difficult to get a stapler all the way up through his rectum as high as we need to join the bowel. My vote would be to hand-sew this one."

It took about fifteen minutes to suture the two ends together. The stitching looked perfect. There was no tension between the two ends of joined bowel, nor was there bleeding. *A great operation*, thought Smythe.

After closing the abdomen, they were finished for the day in the operating room.

Later on, Smythe visited Cecil in his room to tell him that the operation had gone well. Again, Cecil hardly looked like he'd had surgery. He was sitting up.

"I have no pain. This is great!"

"I want you to move, Cecil. If it means taking painkillers to keep moving, then take them."

"When can I eat?"

"Not so fast. I'll let you know. It'll be a few days."

As with the previous operation, Cecil had been bridged with heparin injections for five days before surgery. He was then off all blood thinners after the operation until it was safe to restart heparin injections. Smythe visited him daily. Since things had gone well, Cecil restarted heparin injections forty-eight hours after surgery. On Thursday, Smythe succumbed to Cecil's daily requests to eat and allowed him to start with clear liquids.

On Friday, Cecil was pale and he wore a pained expression. He complained of nausea and a bloated feeling in his abdomen. Smythe decided to order blood tests. To his surprise, Cecil's hemoglobin had dropped from 135 before surgery to 85 on Friday.

"You must have had some bleeding."

"How do you know that?"

"Your hemoglobin has dropped. I think we need to stop the blood thinners."

Smythe decided to get a CAT scan that day to confirm his suspicions. The scan showed fluid around the anastomosis, where the bowel had been reattached. There was no air in the fluid collection, which meant there probably wasn't an infection, an abscess or a leak. Cecil's bowel upstream from the join was rather dilated. This was probably a result of the hematoma or collection of blood preventing forward flow through the anastomosis.

By Sunday, Cecil still had not passed any gas out the rectum. Smythe was beginning to get worried. When he saw Cecil Sunday morning, he looked at the wound. A gush of pink fluid spurted between the surgical staples on the skin. Such a gush could signal an impending wound dehiscence. If the deeper layers came apart, sometimes the entire wound could open up.

"Keep the staples in and put on an abdominal binder," Smythe instructed the nurse.

He stopped at his office on the way home to do paperwork, not in the mood just yet for being cheerful with his family. He had over a hundred messages on his computer to review, and although it wasn't all that appealing, at least he didn't have to pretend to his computer that he was having a good time. At four o'clock, his cell phone rang. He found it amongst the clutter on his desk.

"Where are you?" Amanda didn't sound pleased.

Smythe closed his eyes, leaned back in his chair and tilted his head towards the ceiling. "At the office. Trying to get caught up on—"

"You do remember Sara's school band party? It starts at four and you're not home."

"Of course I remember. I was just on my way out the door. I just lost track of time. I'll meet you at the school in five minutes." Smythe was shutting down his computer as he spoke.

"It's in the gymnasium. There'll be lots of food. I'm bringing broccoli salad."

"Great. I can't wait to try it."

At the school, Smythe walked into the gymnasium, where about forty parents were gathered around the food table and thirty children played at the far end. He recognized only about half of the parents, a fact that made him feel slightly uncomfortable. Amanda was setting up her salad on the long table spanning the width of the basketball court at the north end, while other parents unveiled their culinary creations.

Smythe caught Amanda's attention when she finished. "I'm sorry, I've just got a tough case going on—a post-op that's not doing well."

Amanda looked up sympathetically. "I figured something like that was going on. Try to enjoy this just for a while, and you'll feel better. I made the salad just the way you like it—lots of bacon in it."

"Thanks, sunshine."

When the food was ready and after the children had loaded up their plates, Smythe piled up a variety of salads and hot foods—some of them unidentifiable—until his plate was full. He hadn't realized how hungry he was. Standing beside Amanda, chatting with other parents, Smythe was able to forget for a while about Cecil McNaughton and his rocky post-operative course.

On the way home, Smythe stopped in at the hospital to see Cecil while Amanda drove Sara, picking up Emily, who had been at a friend's place for the afternoon. Smythe found Cecil no better or worse. It was calming to see that nothing bad had occurred in his absence.

Still, Smythe was not entirely surprised to get a phone call from the surgical unit shortly before midnight. Cecil's wound had burst open, and a student nurse was holding a sterile towel over two and a half feet of small intestine protruding through the wound.

Shit, thought Smythe. It was almost midnight and Cecil had to go back to the operating room. Mrs. McNaughton was not pleased when Smythe phoned her with the news, but she did end the conversation by saying, "I trust you, Jim."

During the operation, Smythe repaired Cecil's abdominal wall after pushing the intestine back where it belonged. There were no obvious signs of infection in the abdomen, but Smythe was worried. He was also becoming weary of Cecil and all his problems. He had spent half the weekend at work, despite the fact that this was supposed to be a weekend off.

On his way home, Smythe felt a burning in his chest. He glanced at the digital clock on the dashboard of his Lexus SUV: 1:32 a.m. As he pulled the vehicle off to the side of the road, he retrieved a bottle of Maalox from the glove compartment and took a gulp, then closed his eyes and waited. If the pain wasn't gone in five minutes—by 1:37—he'd turn around and go back to the emergency department to finally get this checked out. Either that or he'd put himself on a regular acid reducer to avoid these bouts of heartburn.

During the five minutes, he contemplated the idea of going to the emergency department with chest pain. The first thing they'd do was tell him he was confined there for at least twelve hours until his initial cardiac work-up was completed. Then they'd stick an intravenous line in his arm and get him to chew down some aspirin tablets before they had any answers to the tests. After a series of three blood tests and three electrocardiograms, they might let him out, if all was well. By this time, it would be 2:00 in the afternoon, and his whole day of surgery would be shot. He'd have to sign Cecil over to one of his colleagues, which would be fine if there were no new problems, but he had to stay on top of this and didn't care to involve anyone else at this stage. Not to mention that he'd have to find a way to reschedule his other operations, and when would he do that? He opened his eyes, started up the car and pulled away from the curb, heading for home.

It was 1:36 a.m. The pain was better—nearly gone. He kept driving, purposely not looking at the clock. When he pulled into his driveway, it was 1:40 a.m. and the pain had all but vanished. No need for an emergency visit, not tonight, anyway. *Shit*, he thought. *What next?*

Despite only four hours of sleep, Smythe climbed out of bed at 6:00 in the morning, getting ready for another Monday in the operating room. His joints ached. Trying not to disturb Amanda, he slipped into the en suite bathroom and turned on the walk-in shower. He stepped under the steady stream of hot water and initially it felt good, soothing his sore knees and shoulders.

As he massaged his scalp with shampoo lather, he started to feel warmth that was no longer placating his aches and pains; instead, it tormented him from within. He imagined beads of sweat forming on his body. As he turned down the water temperature, he noticed that he was salivating excessively, to the point that he had to spit towards the drain. A sudden wave of nausea accompanied discomfort in his upper abdomen. Reflexively, he held his mouth closed, which only worsened his situation as his gastric contents were then forced up his esophagus. With his lips firmly held together, the vomitus followed the path of least resistance, out his nostrils until finally his mouth opened, allowing the bulk of his stomach contents to spew onto the shower floor. Despite the burning in his throat and nose, he felt much better. After washing all he could down the drain, Smythe turned off the shower and cleaned up the residual bits of broccoli and other food with some toilet paper and flushed them down the toilet.

As he towelled himself down, Smythe thought about the possibilities. It was unlikely he had a bowel obstruction or early appendicitis because he didn't have much abdominal pain. It had to be the food from the potluck. *One crappy hour at the school, and now this*, he thought. He quietly dressed himself, noting that Amanda remained sleeping and would know nothing of the vomiting episode. He slipped a few Gravol and Tylenol tablets into his shirt pocket. He felt better, but just in case, drove to work and left his bike at home. He had to get through his day of surgery. He was convinced it wouldn't be easy to substitute another doctor for him, especially at the last minute. All of the other surgeons were booked, and he was not going to cancel his surgery day unless he absolutely had to.

His first operation was a laparoscopic cholecystectomy on a forty-nine-year-old woman. In the preoperative holding area, Smythe reviewed Mrs. Wozniak's history and asked her if she had any questions about the imminent surgery. She sat up in the stretcher, looking directly at Smythe.

"Did you get a good sleep last night?" There was a gleam in her eyes.

"Never better!" Smythe responded with quickness that could only come with many years of practice.

Towards the end of Mrs. Wozniak's gallbladder surgery, Smythe began to feel unwell again. He excused himself just in time to let Jared close all of the incisions, including the deep fascial incision at the belly button, normally one that Smythe closed himself. Smythe dashed into the washroom next to the operating theatre. *Thank goodness I'm alone*, he thought, vomiting into the toilet.

By midday, Smythe was actually feeling a bit better, having managed to sneak some Gravol and Tylenol in between cases, washing them down with a sports drink from one of the vending machines. Just as the third operation was finishing before noon, scrub nurse Shirley Carver asked, "Are you feeling okay, Dr. Smythe?"

"I feel great," he retorted.

"Because if you wanted to reschedule—"

"Reschedule nothing!" He fixed his gaze on Shirley. "Yes, I felt a little under the weather earlier. And yes, I feel better now, so don't you *or anyone* suggest that I rearrange my day. *I'm the one* who decides when I'm well enough or not well enough to work." He paused, then added,

"But thank you for your concern."

The operating room staff was silent for the rest of the day, apart from the obligatory communication required to make each operation successful.

Despite Smythe's illness, the day of surgery actually went well. He continued to keep himself hydrated and took pills to control his symptoms. Feeling better, he went up to the ward, only to find that Cecil had spiked a fever of 39 degrees Celsius late Monday afternoon. He had also been off his blood thinners since Saturday, and the risk of a stroke was always in the back of Smythe's mind.

As Cecil McNaughton's condition worsened, Jim was getting more vexed with Mrs. McNaughton. Every day, it seemed she had a question for him.

"Can we feed him, Jim?"

"What about an MRI, Jim?"

"Jim, why are we feeding him?"

Every time she asked a question, it increased his self-doubt. He knew how to handle complicated patients who were having trouble after surgery. Why couldn't she just leave him alone and let him do his job? As she wore him down, he began doing his ward rounds earlier in the morning and later at night in order to avoid her. It was bad enough having to go in to see Cecil, each day in worse shape than the day before. Cecil's steady decline irked Smythe—all this trouble after surgery for a benign condition! He could handle it if someone developed life-threatening complications after a cancer operation, but all this was after an operation purely done for patient preference, not out of necessity. *Why the hell did he want his colostomy reversed?* wondered Smythe. *And why the hell did I agree to do it?*

One evening, Mrs. McNaughton caught Smythe in the hallway. It was long past visiting hours, but the sicker the relative, the more likely the nurses were to turn a blind eye to family members staying late. It was 11:30 p.m., and Smythe was making a quick stop into Cecil McNaughton's room before going home.

"Is he going to be okay, Jim?"

"I think so, Mrs. McNaughton. But anything can happen. He's had so many things go wrong. We just have to support him and hope no new bad surprises pop up."

"What's the worst thing that can happen?"

"I'd rather think positively at this stage. Look, I was thinking, we could get another opinion, either from one of the surgeons here, or from the university."

"No, I trust you, Jim. I know you're doing the best you can."

Then why don't you lay off? he thought. "Well, it's always an option," he said out loud.

When Cecil's fever spiked again the following day, Smythe arranged another CAT scan. This time, the scan showed air bubbles in the abdomen around the anastomosis. There was free fluid throughout the abdomen and the bowel wall looked thickened. It confirmed Smythe's worst fears.

That night, Smythe and Jared took Cecil back to the operating room to open him up. His abdomen was full of putrid fluid and fecal material. It took an hour just to get down to where Smythe had previously reattached the bowel. Despite its perfect appearance at the end of surgery ten days ago, there was now a one-centimetre hole where the anastomosis had disrupted.

There was no choice but to bring out another colostomy. After cleaning up the infection and doing the colostomy, they closed Cecil's abdominal wall for the third time. By now, the swelling in the abdomen was so substantial that closing the wound was difficult. Smythe knew there was no way Cecil could come off the breathing machine that night, so he was wheeled off to the intensive care unit with an endotracheal tube in his airway for mechanical ventilation. This would likely continue for several days until Cecil's infection cleared with broad-spectrum antibiotics. He would remain heavily sedated while on the breathing machine. Cecil also remained off blood thinners.

The next morning, after hardly sleeping, Smythe went to the intensive care unit. By the expression on the nurse's face, Smythe knew something was wrong. She explained that Cecil's cardiac enzymes and electrocardiogram had changed for the worse since the most recent surgery. It appeared that Cecil had sustained a massive heart attack, and would definitely have to be on the breathing machine for several days. But because of the heart attack, Cecil was put back on the blood thinners through heparin injections.

*　*　*

Later that day, just as Mrs. McNaughton thought nothing else could go wrong, she got another phone call from the ICU physician.

"Mrs. McNaughton, this is Dr. Downey. Your husband appears to have had a gastrointestinal bleed."

"Yes?"

"He's passing a lot of blood out his colostomy. We've stopped the blood thinners, but he's still bleeding. Do you want us to transfuse him?"

"Of course I do! Why are you asking me that?"

"Mrs. McNaughton, I think you'd better come in."

When she arrived, Dr. Downey explained that things were not good. Despite stopping blood thinners and transfusing three units of blood, they had not stopped the bleeding. It was probably an ulcer, which under normal circumstances would stop on its own or with medication. But now they would have to do a gastroscopy to find the ulcer and possibly clip or burn the bleeding vessel. Dr. Downey said he would call Dr. Smythe to have him come in to do the procedure.

"No, not Smythe," Mrs. McNaughton said with conviction. "Is there anyone else who can do it?"

"Yes, I could call the gastroenterologist on call."

"Then do it."

After the bleeding had been stopped by clipping a single vessel during gastroscopy, Dr. Downey sat beside Mrs. McNaughton in the ICU family lounge.

"We need to talk about care level, Mrs. McNaughton."

"What for? What do you mean?" she said, dabbing her eyes with a handkerchief.

"Every time we fix one thing, something else goes wrong. He's been bleeding. His lungs are dependent on the ventilator. The abdominal infection is not completely controlled. If one more thing goes wrong—say, for example, if his kidneys fail—"

"What are you saying? That my husband is some kind of farm animal who you can just leave to die, or better yet, shoot to put out of his misery?"

"I'm not saying that, Mrs.—"

"Then what are you saying?"

"There may come a point when we can't help him any further. We need to discuss that in case it happens—before it happens."

With two of the four McNaughton daughters present, Mrs. McNaughton agreed that certain heroic measures would not be in the care plan, should Cecil take a turn for the worse. It was not an easy decision; however, it was clear that several of his organs were failing. It was one step forward followed by two back.

That night, with his wife by his side, Cecil McNaughton had a cardiac arrest. As they had discussed, there was not much that could be done, and so nothing was done, apart from keeping him comfortable. It was only a matter of minutes before Cecil's electrical cardiac activity stopped completely. With tubes coming out of every possible opening, Cecil McNaughton was now dead in the intensive care unit, awaiting a review by the coroner. No autopsy was performed. The coroner was satisfied that the course of events was explicable solely on the basis of the medical record. No additional information was required.

* * *

Smythe got the phone call at 2:36 in the morning. Cecil McNaughton was dead. He offered to come, but the nurse informed him it wasn't necessary; Dr. Downey was currently talking with the family. Smythe lay awake until 5:45, when he drifted off into a restless sleep. Fifteen minutes later, his alarm awakened him to face the workday. *One less sick patient to look in on*, he thought. He felt depressed, but he knew the only way to carry on was to keep working. As long as he could do surgery, Smythe knew he'd be fine.

But the next few days were tough. Hearing people talk, reading the obituary in the newspaper and catching a brief spot on the local television news about Cecil McNaughton was all Smythe could take. Just as the depressing talk of Cecil was starting to fade, his funeral was announced throughout the community.

Smythe didn't know whether it was proper etiquette to attend McNaughton's funeral. He eventually concluded that he could not stay away, but ensured that he slipped in the back a few minutes late. As he listened to the service, he watched the four adult McNaughton girls up at the front with their own children. They leaned on each other for support, while occasionally letting out wails of despair.

Smythe's mind wandered. If he hadn't started heparin so soon after the colostomy reversal surgery, Cecil wouldn't have bled. If he hadn't bled, then no hematoma. Without a hematoma around the anastomosis, he wouldn't have been partially blocked and become distended. No distension—no wound dehiscence—no evisceration—no re-operation. The stress of all that probably caused the bowel to leak, which resulted in peritonitis. He wouldn't have had the heart attack if he hadn't leaked. And the bleeding ulcer was just icing on the cake. Smythe felt a lump in his throat that wouldn't go away. When he was certain no one was looking, he slid a small bottle of Maalox out of his suit pocket and took a swallow.

As the service concluded and family members made their way out, Mrs. McNaughton's eyes locked on Smythe's. Without saying a word, her eyes spoke directly to him: "YOU—KILLED—HIM."

And for a benign condition, to boot, thought Smythe as his eyes welled up.

After the funeral, Smythe headed over to the office. He would have cancelled the entire afternoon, except that it would have involved moving several patients, and there was nowhere else to put them with only a month left until Christmas break. At least he was appropriately dressed for the office in a dark suit, white shirt and tie.

He arrived a few minutes late, and the waiting room was half-full already. He never could figure out why patients would show up half an hour early for an appointment when Smythe was often half an hour behind. Sometimes he wondered if it was a deliberate plan to blame him for their one-hour wait before seeing him.

The first two consultations were routine with nothing unusual or interesting. His next patient was a familiar face. Smythe had fixed this man's hernia eighteen months ago; unfortunately, the hernia had recurred.

"I remember you telling me it could come back. I just didn't think it would come back so soon." The man was clearly somewhat annoyed but didn't want to show it, as he probably knew that a prompt repair of his hernia recurrence was dependent on Smythe's availability and willingness to get him in for more surgery.

A couple of quick follow-up patients were jammed in between new consultations. Smythe didn't like seeing follow-ups in the office because occasionally there were wound issues that he was better equipped to see at the hospital. One woman came in with redness around her abdominal incision. When Smythe examined her and gently pulled on the wound, it burst open due to foul-smelling pus under pressure. Mostly draining, but partially spraying, the putrid fluid ultimately hit Smythe's white shirt. The stench in the office was none too pleasant, and of course, this was a challenge that he and Moira would rather be reserved for the hospital.

A few consultations later, Smythe saw yet another person with a wound infection. This time, he managed not to open it up in the office but made arrangements to meet the patient at the end of the day in the emergency department, where he would likely need to do a similar procedure, this time clothed in fresh surgical greens in case it was as messy as the last one.

As Smythe walked over from his office to the hospital, having finished an hour late at six o'clock, he reflected on the afternoon. The funeral had been a downer, but the office wasn't any better: a total of four complications from his surgery in one abbreviated afternoon. As he dodged the busy traffic, he said aloud, *"It seems everything I touch turns to shit these days."*

Chapter 10 ~ Two Sides

The next day, Smythe was recovering from the funk induced by the McNaughton case. If he immersed himself in his work, the satisfaction of great cases could go a long way to improve his mood. The more available he was for his referring physicians and patients, the more likely he'd be doing stimulating work and feeling better about himself. It wasn't always so great for his family life, but he couldn't ignore the threat of depression from the McNaughton catastrophe.

The day had gone well. Smythe had spent half of it seeing new consultations in the office, followed by an afternoon in endoscopy, scoping stomachs and colons. He'd found a colon cancer that would require surgery and had also identified a big duodenal ulcer that would likely heal with medication.

His phone rang. "Smythe here."

"Dr. Smythe, this is Tina, from Dr. Abbott's office."

Smythe didn't want to speak to the Chief of Medical Staff so soon after his bad outcome with Mr. McNaughton. He took a deep breath. "Yes?"

"Dr. Abbott was wondering if he could meet briefly with you. Are you free this afternoon?"

What now? "Sure. What time?"

"He's here now doing paperwork, so any time in the next hour would be fine."

"I'll be there in about twenty minutes." Smythe had a bad feeling about this. To be called down to Rick's office without a stated reason felt a bit like being called to the principal's office. It was not likely going to be a chat about the weather.

Within half an hour, Tina ushered Smythe into Dr. Abbott's office, where she seated him in the only chair facing the large desk. "Dr. Abbott just stepped out for a few minutes. He won't be long."

Smythe looked at the walls, which were covered with certificates and diplomas. About half were related to Abbott's medicine practice. The others reflected the administrative side of his work. Completion of "Physician Manager Course, Level 3" and "Medical Administration 2" were a couple of prominently displayed achievements. *He sure has turned to the dark side*, mused Smythe. On Abbott's cluttered desk was a cut-out magazine article entitled "Handling the Disruptive Physician".

Abbott strode into the office at that point and promptly sat down behind his desk. "Sorry I'm late, Jim."

"No problem," Smythe fibbed.

Abbott paused while he rubbed his eyes. When he'd adjusted his glasses back into place, he leaned forward and looked directly at Smythe. "There have been a couple of complaints about your behaviour in the operating room recently."

"My behav—Oh, is it about last week when I yelled because they weren't giving me the equipment I wanted?"

"That was one episode."

"That wasn't my fault."

"Not according to the nurse in charge that day," Abbott countered.

"When I have a patient asleep on the table, the nurses have to get me what I need right away. There's no question."

"I agree. But yelling at a junior nurse and making her cry is not a solution."

"C'mon. I can't be responsible for every tear that falls in the operating room just because someone is a bit oversensitive."

"This isn't 1985 anymore, Jim. What may have been acceptable for one of your teachers doesn't fly nowadays. There's a lot going on about disruptive physicians and how to deal with th—"

"Are you saying I'm disruptive?"

"You were perceived that way. The mere perception of a disruptive physician is a problem."

"You're kidding!" Smythe snorted.

"No, I'm not. In a hearing, if a doc says he was behaving appropriately but one nurse and a witness say otherwise, it could be troub—"

"What do you mean by a hearing? Are you threatening me?"

"Of course not," Abbott reassured. "I'm calling you in now to help prevent problems. If the perception continues, it could be difficult for you."

"Seriously?"

"Yes, seriously. This is all fairly recent, Jim. Have you been under any extra strain lately? These are the first couple of episodes I've heard about in a long time."

"I've had a bad case or two," Smythe admitted. "So what about the second complaint—you said there were two."

"The second was very similar. One of the junior nurses in the operating room claimed you made her feel stupid. She said you asked for some warm saline to irrigate a wound. When she set aside some water and asked another nurse to go run for some saline, you upset her by the way you told her water was good enough, and why the hell didn't she know that water was fine, even though you asked for saline."

"Oh, c'mon!"

"After the case, she ran into the nurses' lounge and burst into tears. She was sent home for the rest of the day."

"It's not my fault if she's fragile. I simply looked at her to indicate I expected a little more from a nurse working in *my* operating room. So she went bawling to the head nurse. It's not my problem."

"You know, Jim, it never ceases to amaze me how two individuals or two groups of people can be present at the same event and the end result is two completely different versions of the same experience. It's like football. Or a hockey game. Fans view the same play and have completely different interpretations of exactly what happened. It's the referee's job to sort out what actually occurred or what's fair. And in this case, I'm the referee—only I wasn't there. I have to sort it out after the fact."

"In this case, there *are* two versions—there's my reality, and then there's hers—the wrong one."

"No, the versions are merely perceptions of one occurrence. The two perceptions can be completely different, yet neither contradicts the facts. They simply describe the same incident from opposing angles."

"It was no big deal."

"You know, if you're stressed, there are progr—"

"I'm okay. It's not my fault. I'll be fine. And I'll be more careful."

"That's all I can ask for. Thanks for stopping by, Jim."

Smythe bolted out the door, somewhat shaken. Surgery was his life. He couldn't let some kind of administrative barrier prevent him from doing what he was meant to do. Taking a deep breath, he walked across the street to his office to finish paperwork before the end of the day.

* * *

There it was, finally! Hazel Kowalchuk's chart sat on Smythe's desk. He now had what he needed to respond to the Medical Licensing Authority about the complaint. Smythe took one look in the file and it all came back to him. He could write a detailed response to the Authority; he didn't even need the file anymore, except to confirm the dates.

Gelatin bezoar—those two words brought everything about Hazel Kowalchuk flooding back. Hazel had been fifty-five at the time. Smythe was dragged out of bed at 2:00 a.m. to see someone who was in septic shock, possibly from perforation somewhere in her abdomen. Her infection was so advanced that her blood pressure was hardly measurable. They weren't even sure Smythe could make it in time to do anything for her, but would he mind coming in? When Smythe arrived, Hazel lay looking moribund. If they didn't act soon, she'd be dead. Smythe told the emergency doctor to go ahead and intubate her; if they wanted him to do something, Hazel would have to be alive for him to do it.

He reviewed her information. Hazel had no immediate family nearby, just a landlord who had become suspicious when she hadn't been seen out of her apartment for several days. At the urging of a relative over the phone, and after a number of efforts to contact Hazel, the landlord let himself into her dwelling at nine o'clock in the evening. The place was a mess, with dirty dishes and unwashed laundry strewn everywhere. Half-eaten tins of dried luncheon meat littered the counter, and cigarette butts were all over the place. Hazel was unconscious on the living room rug, half-dressed in an old tracksuit. On the table were several empty bags of gummy bears. Three more empty bags lay on the floor by her head, while her right hand cradled a nearly empty fourth one. Each bag was 500 grams—a little over a pound. If Hazel had eaten four bags of these gelatin critters at one time, she'd have close to two kilograms of them sitting in her stomach.

Afterward, Smythe speculated about what had happened. She must have formed a massive gelatin bezoar in her stomach. A bezoar was basically a clump of matter in the gastrointestinal tract. A phyto bezoar consisted of a massive clump of undigested vegetable material, while a tricho bezoar was related to clumps of hair—a big hairball. Surgeons didn't often encounter bezoars anymore, so when a bezoar did require an operation, it was usually a beauty. Perhaps better management of patients at risk—chronically institutionalized individuals—was the reason for reduced incidence. Bezoars could be silent, but when they caused complications requiring surgery, it was usually because of obstruction.

Smythe had never heard about gelatin bezoars—he wasn't sure if they'd ever been described. With a gelatin bezoar, the fluids in the gastrointestinal tract combined with the substance, causing colossal swelling of the material after it had been consumed. In this sense, Hazel's situation may not have been a bezoar by the classic definition, as it may have been acute rather than chronic, and its presence may have been multiplied exponentially by swelling after she'd eaten the candies. Regardless, combining two kilograms of gummy bears with liquid was a recipe for disaster.

When Smythe examined her, she clearly had signs of peritonitis despite being comatose. Her plain X-rays showed large amounts of free air in the abdomen, signifying a perforation of something, somewhere. There was no need for a CAT scan—the diagnosis of "perforated viscus" had been made. Her white blood cell count was severely elevated and toxic cells were identified, signifying advanced systemic infection. Under Smythe's direction, she was resuscitated with large amounts of intravenous fluids and drugs to support her blood pressure. Then she was given powerful antibiotics and taken to the operating room. Surgery was arranged under a two-doctor consent, as Hazel was in no position to agree to anything.

At 3:45 a.m., Smythe opened her up and found, as expected, a perforation with extensive contamination of her abdominal cavity. The perforation was in the anterior wall of her stomach—a linear rent five inches long, three-quarters the length of her stomach. Gelatinous material ballooned the stomach, exuded through the opening and filled her entire abdominal cavity. Her insides resembled a rare malignant condition called "pseudomyxoma peritoneii", a situation in which cancerous, gelatinous tumours deposit throughout the abdominal cavity. Hazel Kowalchuk's deposits were in all the colours of the rainbow and shaped like swollen bears, dogs and cats, allowing Smythe to discern that she did not have pseudomyxoma. He could tell it was not a recent perforation because it had to have taken days for the body to create the stench and accompanying pus. How long she had actually been lying on the floor was a matter of inference, but it was likely at least a day or more.

Through remarkable feats of critical care medicine, Hazel Kowalchuk was saved that night, not without the help of Smythe's valiant efforts to clean out the gummy bear and water concoction. He also did a partial gastrectomy, removing unhealthy stomach edges, before reconstituting her gastric anatomy. Hazel made what Smythe judged to be a full recovery, but unfortunately, she did not agree.

In her statement to the Medical Licensing Authority, she alleged her weight loss since the event was due to Smythe's careless surgery. He failed to diagnose her condition fully ahead of time, and his work had resulted in long-term, troublesome symptoms. Hazel now had early satiety and was unable to eat as much in one sitting. She also had intermittent bloating and diarrhea.

Smythe leaned back in his chair and contemplated his response to the Medical Licensing Authority. He was confident he could provide sufficient information for them to assess the situation objectively and be convinced of the truth: Hazel Kowalchuk was a nut-bar. It wasn't her fault and he didn't blame her. *There are two sides to every story*, Smythe thought. In this case, though, he was on the right side. Even if it took him all night, he was going to get that letter done and in the mail to the Licensing Authority. That would take care of one problem. Then, he just had to get Abbott off his back.

* * *

Angela Beaumont and Shirley Carver sat down for coffee in a far corner of the cafeteria. Their meetings were becoming regular events. Shirley had told Angela that chatting with a young, enthusiastic nurse helped take her mind off her divorce. "I heard that Dr. Smythe will be operating on the mayor's daughter soon," Angela said, her voice concerned.

"We're not really supposed to discuss these issues, but in a word—yes," Shirley replied.

"But she's so young to have breast cancer."

"If you think thirty is young now, Angela, just wait until ten years from now. Then, you'll start to think forty is young."

"It's all relative, I guess." She paused. "I've kind of wondered . . ."

"What?"

"Why does it always seem to be Dr. Smythe who operates on the important people?"

"When you've been here as long as Dr. Smythe has, and you do as good a job as he does, word gets around. I would go to him in a heartbeat."

"But he must be difficult to get in to see. I mean, the wait to get into his office must be fairly long."

"If you're somebody in this town, and you have a problem that needs surgery, you find a way to get in to see Jim Smythe. If you *know* someone, a few words will do wonders to get an urgent appointment."

"What do you mean?"

"If you know you need to see a surgeon, and it is a real surgical problem, Jim Smythe will see you. You just have to talk to the right people. I think he views himself as the surgeon for the rich and famous."

"That's not fair," Angela interjected.

"But actually, he'll see anyone at any time. It just so happens that those who are important seem to find a way into his operating room."

"I heard that Dr. Kravchenko's son didn't get in to see him."

"That was different. Dr. Kravchenko's son got appendicitis when Dr. Smythe was on vacation. As it turns out, no other surgeon here was good enough, according to Dr. Kravchenko's wife, so they all drove down the road ninety minutes to have his appendix taken out at the University Hospital, the mecca of academia and surgical excellence." Shirley rolled her eyes. "It took hours to get him into the O.R., and by the time Clarke Kravchenko had his appendix taken out, it was ruptured. Plus, it was probably just a first-year resident who did the surgery. And poor Clarke, he's such a nice boy. It's a damn good thing everything turned out fine in the end."

"I hope the mayor's daughter is okay."

"So do I, Angela."

*   *   *

Jim Smythe got a call to see T.J. Singh, a doctor who had been admitted as a patient to the medical ward. *I'm not even on call*, Smythe thought. *Why do I have to see him?* And then he remembered how long he'd known T.J., and that his practice unfortunately had been shut down for the last six weeks because of illness. T.J., a thirty-seven-year-old family physician, had trained in India but had been practicing in Canada for the last twelve years. He had been admitted to the University Hospital for a month and then convalescing at home for a couple of weeks, but just as the word on the street circulated that he'd be back to work soon, he was admitted to the medical ward in Lakefield with no clear diagnosis other than "malaise". They were still waiting for his medical records to come from the University Hospital. Smythe couldn't comprehend why it took a week to have medical information sent when it would take literally nanoseconds for the electrons to get here—something to do with bureaucracy or consent issues. Smythe received all this information over the phone from the unit secretary. In a nutshell, he had no idea why he was being asked to see Dr. Singh, but what the hell; of course he'd see T.J. at the end of the workday.

It was 8:00 p.m. when Smythe finished up his clinic and hospital work, having phoned home to let Amanda know he'd be late for supper again. He climbed the stairs two at a time to reach the medical unit on the fourth floor.

In the hope that he might find something on the medical chart first, Smythe went to the nursing station to check T.J. Singh's file. The unit secretary had been correct: there really was no background information, just some lab test results, a hand-written history by the admitting physician and a note on the order sheet: "Consult Dr. Smythe re: central line for nutritional support."

The documented medical history simply stated, "Admitted with malaise. Was in the University Hospital for a month. Getting better, but started feeling unwell again." *That's helpful*, Smythe thought sarcastically.

He walked down the corridor to find T.J. in a semi-private room. His roommate was either out for a walk, or had recently been discharged, as the bed was still dishevelled but there was no sign of an occupant. Smythe's eyes shifted over to the thin figure in the B bed. That couldn't be T.J. But it was. He must have lost fifty pounds. Trying not to let his surprise show, Smythe reached out to shake hands.

"T.J., it's good to see you. What's up?"

"Oh, hi, Jim." T.J.'s sunken cheeks were more obvious when he spoke.

"You're in the hospital again. You not feeling so hot?"

"No, Jim, I just can't seem to snap out of this." His voice was hoarse, his breathing laboured. "First it was pneumonia, and then they were thinking chronic fatigue syndrome. I was vomiting over the last few days, so I went to emergency, and here I am." T.J.'s eyes were vacant.

"They say you need a central line for nutritional support. Are you okay if I put one in tonight?"

"Sure, go ahead."

"Listen, T.J., there's not much information on your chart. They're still trying to get some records from the university, but those haven't arrived yet. Can you tell me anything about your illness—what tests you had done, what they're thinking is going on?"

"No, not really. They did a whole bunch of tests."

"Have they tried a feeding tube? If you need nutritional support, that's a lot better than intravenous feeding, you know." Smythe really didn't want to micromanage T.J.'s care, but he did want to know if inserting a central line was reasonable. If it was, he'd insert it and let the attending physician take care of the ongoing management of T.J.'s nutrition and illness.

"No, I wouldn't let them. What's the point of ramming a tube down my nose to feed me when I'm vomiting? It won't work."

Smythe looked at the clock. Eight-thirty in the evening. Amanda wasn't going to be too pleased. He wasn't even on call—he should be home. But there was no better time to do it the following day. And heck, for a medical colleague, he could stay late. T.J. would do the same if their roles were reversed. A central line would only take about half an hour, including set-up and clean-up time, if all went well. The intravenous just under the collarbone was like the first step of a pacemaker. He walked quickly to the nursing station, grabbed some equipment, found a nurse to assist, and started at 8:40.

With T.J. lying flat on the bed, his right chest and shoulder were cleansed with iodine solution. Sterile drapes were applied, creating a window through which Smythe would work on the right upper chest. He didn't need to make a significant incision for this, as he would have done for a pacemaker. Xylocaine was injected to freeze the area. At the last possible moment, Smythe instructed the nurse to put T.J. in the Trendelenberg position, with the head of the bed tipped down. Smythe's desire to distend T.J.'s veins and avoid an air embolism outweighed the memory of Harley's death-by-Trendelenberg experience. The nurse pushed the button on the side of the hospital bed, and the electric motor whirred as T.J.'s body tilted down. The veins on his emaciated neck became prominent. On the first stab, Smythe's syringe located the subclavian vein behind the collarbone. After drawing back dark venous blood, he disconnected the syringe, leaving the large needle protruding from T.J.'s thorax. Smythe passed the wire through the needle without resistance. After removing the needle and passing a dilator, he advanced the catheter over the wire. Without the need for an introducer sheath, as in the case of a pacemaker lead insertion, the chance of air embolus was small. However, Smythe took great satisfaction in seeing prompt back-flow of blood through the catheter. The nurse was visibly unimpressed by the amount of blood that was trickling out of the catheter, making a mess on T.J.'s bedding. But Smythe didn't care, as his mind briefly flashed back to Mr. Bellini. If blood was coming out, air wasn't going in.

They were done shortly after nine o'clock and Smythe went out to the nursing station to review T.J.'s chart. As he rescanned the lab tests, a warm rush of nausea overcame him. T.J.'s INR—the international normalized ratio, a measure of blood clotting ability—was abnormal at 2.7. T.J. wasn't on blood thinners, so what was going on? Why was his blood so thin? If Smythe had taken note of that result earlier, he wouldn't have inserted a central line. He'd have to follow T.J. closely for bleeding complications. He had just assumed that T.J., being another physician, would volunteer such relevant information about his health. Smythe would have to be more careful next time.

Smythe checked on T.J., wished him a comfortable evening and went home to see Amanda and the girls.

The next day, he went up to see T.J. at 7:30 a.m. He assumed someone would have notified him if there had been a problem with bleeding overnight. T.J. looked no worse than he had the night before, but he sure did look chronically ill. Smythe also thought his eyes seemed a little yellow.

While passing the nursing station, Smythe called out to no one in particular, "Have Dr. Singh's records from the University Hospital arrived yet?"

No answer.

He turned to the unit secretary, who was seated at the front desk. "Well, have they?"

She looked up at him and said, "I'll check into it this morning, Dr. Smythe. We'll let you know when they arrive."

"Well, thank you." His words were drawn out and loud enough for anyone on the nursing unit to hear, if they happened to be interested.

Two days later, the phone call came: T.J.'s records had finally found their way to the unit. Too much to send by fax or any other electronic means was the excuse, so paper copies had eventually been sent from the university by courier. Smythe arrived on the unit to find that T.J. had been moved to a private room. His file was three inches thick but it didn't take Smythe long to figure out what was going on, despite the voluminous package of records. By the look of things, T.J. also must have known *exactly* what was wrong with him.

T.J. Singh had been admitted to the University Hospital for liver failure. He had hepatitis B; the source was unknown. He also had cirrhosis of the liver, likely secondary to the hepatitis virus. His condition had stabilized, but he was considered to be advanced enough that no specific treatment would be offered. Care was meant to be "supportive". T.J. had been assessed for a liver transplant, but his blood tests suggested he had not cleared the hepatitis virus and that his bodily fluids were highly infectious. They would thus be infectious to a new liver, or to anyone who came in contact with his bodily fluids. *You bastard!* thought Smythe. *You let me put in a central line, knowing you are on the edge of advanced liver failure and are infectious with the hep B virus! If I had stuck myself with a needle contaminated with your blood, I could be looking at a similar fate to yours. Because you were too cagey to tell me what was going on, I put myself at risk for no good reason.*

Smythe went down to T.J. Singh's room to give him a piece of his mind. Upon opening the door, he observed two nurses positioning T.J.'s head up on a pillow. T.J. was clearly in worse shape than he had been two days previously. His eyes were now sunken and unmistakably yellow, his facial expression was utterly blank and he wasn't responding to verbal stimuli. T.J.'s blood was so toxic with built-up chemicals as a result of liver failure that he was becoming encephalopathic; higher brain function could no longer exist in the milieu resulting from his liver failure.

A quick perusal of this morning's blood test results confirmed Smythe's fears. Bilirubin was high and serum proteins were low. INR was now off the map. The liver had been unable to synthesize clotting factors. T.J. was a mess. T.J. was going to die.

That afternoon, Smythe stormed into Rick Abbott's administrative office; Wednesday was Rick's half-day, which he devoted to administrative duties. He found Rick sitting behind his desk, fiddling with a paper clip and a large stack of paper.

Smythe was livid. "What the hell's going on here with T.J., Rick?"

Abbott looked up from his desk and gestured for Smythe to sit down. "What do you mean, Jim?"

"You know T.J. Singh was admitted to hospital here?"

"Someone mentioned he was here, yes."

"Do you know he's got hepatitis B and that it's terminal?"

Abbott glanced down at his desk, then at the ceiling. "I'd heard something about it."

"Why didn't you tell me?"

"You didn't ask. Why should—"

"Because I just put a central line in him earlier this week, that's why!"

"What's your point, Jim?" Abbott appeared to be trying to hide his irritation.

"Rick, I put a central line in T.J., putting myself at risk of contracting the virus. It seems everyone but me knew he had hepatitis B and was infectious. But it wasn't on the chart. So I was at risk."

"You didn't poke yourself with a needle, did you, Jim?"

"No, but I *could* have."

"So what's your point?"

"Protection of the patient is always a big deal. Any minor breach that might put the patient at risk is huge. But where does protection of the health care worker come in? Who's looking out for *my* interests and safety?"

"We do have—"

"*No one*, that's who. Nobody told me about T.J.'s hepatitis B because *his* right to confidentiality superseded *my* right to safety. They took so goddamn long to send his records from the U because of his right to confidentiality. If you can't tell, Rick, I'm pissed off. You know, this confidentiality thing has gone way too far these days. Did you hear the latest rule around here?"

"I suppose you're going to tell me."

"Two patients can no longer ride in the same ambulance anymore, *even if it's built for two people*."

"Why's that?"

"Confidentiality, that's why. I thought you'd know. I thought guys like you made these rules, Rick. It doesn't matter if two patients urgently need to be transferred ninety minutes up the road to the University Hospital. It doesn't matter how sick they are, how conscious they are or whether they give consent to ride together. It can't be done. One poor guy has to wait for a second ambulance because it's supposedly unethical for them to ride together and hear about each other's medical problems. Never mind the fact that on daily ward rounds, I go into patients' double rooms, asking about their flatulence and their bowel movements and telling them about their cancers, all in front of their roommates. Or perhaps I shouldn't be telling you that because you'll close all the double rooms in the hospital."

"Are you sure that's not just a rumour? I hadn't—"

"And pathology reports! They're killing me! Did you know it took six weeks for me to realize my patient had cancer because they didn't send me *my* patient's pathology report? So you know why?"

"Are you going to tell me?"

"Because the clerical staff that filled out the form didn't put my first initial on it. The primary copy went to the family doctor—T.J. Singh, as it happens—who was off sick. At the bottom of the report, it said they weren't sending a copy to Dr. Smythe because no one specified which Dr. Smythe it was to go to! I'm the only goddamn Smythe that's worked at this hospital for the last hundred years! Tell me, Rick, if you were a patient, would you want your pathology report to go to five Dr. Smythes in the province and breach your confidentiality, or would you prefer that no Smythes get the report? I'll tell you what, Rick, when I get cancer, you can put it on the front page of the newspaper if the only alternative is nobody getting the report and the treatment being delayed. Where's all the common sense gone?"

Abbott shifted in his chair and quickly interjected, "Look, Jim, many of these privacy issues are growing pains—related to computerization of medical records. They'll be sorted out over the next few years. But let's deal with one problem at a time. Why did you come down here to see me?"

"T.J."

"Okay, did you get stuck with a needle?"

"No."

"Do you want to go through the needle stick protocol anyway—be followed for the next six months to see if you contract hep B?"

"No, thank you."

"I can't change the University Hospital, but would it help if we worked on a policy here?"

"Such as?"

"Perhaps mandatory flagging of a patient's chart if the patient is a risk to health care workers. So hopefully you'd know next time before you put in a central line."

"Yes, that would help." Smythe began to calm down, feeling resigned. There was nothing that could be done for him now. Rick was correct. They could only plan to prevent a similar episode in the future.

As Smythe stood, Abbott asked, "Aren't you presenting grand rounds in early January?"

"Yes." He moved sideways towards the door.

"What's your topic?"

"I haven't decided yet. Or shall we say, I'm not ready to reveal that to the public."

"Well, I'm looking forward to it. I'm sure you'll do a bang-up job, Jim."

Smythe smiled and nodded as he backed out of Abbott's office.

Walking down the hall, he found himself feeling satisfied.

*   *   *

The next day, T.J. was clearly on his way out. His breathing was laboured. His care level had been altered to comfort measures only and he had been moved again, this time to a private room next to the nursing station. *Good thing I inserted that central line*, Smythe thought sardonically. He dropped into T.J.'s room the next two days, despite the fact that the encephalopathic coma prevented any appreciation of Smythe's visits. On the third day, T.J.'s room was empty, apart from the hospital cleaning staff scrubbing every square inch of the floors and walls. At the nursing station, the charge nurse explained that T.J. had peacefully stopped breathing just after four o'clock in the morning.

It was Smythe's second funeral in two weeks, but at least he felt better about attending this one. Even though he was still angry with T.J., he was also bonded to him. They'd been medical colleagues, on staff for a similar length of time. Smythe couldn't recall who had come to Lakefield first; they had probably arrived the same year. T.J. had referred many patients to Smythe, always good referrals—well thought out and supported by good investigations.

The church was packed. Although T.J. had no family locally, he had hundreds of friends and supporters. Smythe was amazed by the number of people who got up and had something funny or nice to say about Dr. Singh.

Smythe speculated about how T.J. had contracted the hepatitis virus. He couldn't believe T.J. had abused intravenous drugs. He could have picked up the virus back in India, but who knows? Perhaps he'd picked it up through a sexual encounter. It didn't matter. T.J. hadn't told him, so Smythe didn't want to know.

Smythe wondered how many people would attend *his* funeral. He questioned whether it would be this many. *Not bad, if you must die at age thirty-seven.*

Chapter 11 ~ Call an Ambulance

The next evening on call, Smythe was operating on Mrs. Poon, a seventy-year-old woman from China. She had resided in Canada with her son and his family for the past fifteen years, but her son reported that she had not learned English to any meaningful extent. With her daughter-in-law and son translating, Mrs. Poon had related the unfortunate history of increasing abdominal cramps over the past few months, accompanied by a twenty-pound weight loss. As she was barely taller than five feet, the drop was significant. Today, she was vomiting material that resembled feces; Mrs. Poon's denial that something was seriously wrong could not continue.

Smythe had told the family before surgery that he had a bad feeling about this case. Although the CAT scan did not demonstrate any definite tumour mass, there was some free fluid, and the possibility of cancer needed to be considered. By this time, her bowel was completely obstructed. Rather than doing more tests, Smythe knew it was time for surgical treatment. Just before Mrs. Poon was wheeled out of the emergency department towards the operating room, her daughter-in-law cautioned Smythe, "If it's cancer, don't tell her."

"Don't tell her?" Smythe replied. He feigned surprise even though he'd received requests like this before.

"No. She couldn't take it. You can't tell her." Mrs. Poon's son nodded in agreement.

We'll see about that, thought Smythe. He'd seen this type of family dynamic before. He couldn't simply lie to Mrs. Poon. After all, she was the patient. Sure, he could delay the bad news or tailor it in a way that he judged appropriate. But he wasn't going to disregard his implicit contract with a patient just because the family members wanted to call the shots.

Unfortunately for Mrs. Poon, Smythe's suspicions were confirmed. Upon opening her abdomen through a long midline incision, he found fluid and multiple small tumour nodules. The cancer had probably originated in one of the ovaries, and then extensively spread throughout her abdominal cavity. She had nodules on all surfaces of the peritoneal cavity, ranging in size from tiny grains of sand to ball bearings. One of the lumps tethered her small intestine so intensely that it was the clear point of blockage: upstream, the small bowel was markedly swollen and dilated, while the bowel below this particular lesion was collapsed and empty. Such a transition point was a sure sign of the site of obstruction. Smythe knew there was nothing he could do to stop the progression of her cancer, but he could deal with her bowel obstruction—at least temporarily. If he could bypass or remove the blockage, she could continue eating for some time. But while some chemotherapy could give Mrs. Poon a chance at a longer life, Smythe wasn't holding out much hope that she'd survive much beyond a year.

Fortunately, he was able to resect the particular segment of small bowel, thus relieving Mrs. Poon's blockage, but he wasn't sure how long it would help.

The next morning, Smythe entered Mrs. Poon's room expecting to find her alone and sedated from the post-operative analgesics. Accompanied by the ward nurse and her clipboard, he was planning a quick visit; with the language barrier on his side, he could defer the discussion about operative findings until she, and perhaps the family, would be more receptive to the news of incurable cancer. But to his surprise, when Smythe walked into her small hospital room, he saw at least ten people. In addition to her son and daughter-in-law, three other adults and several children, from toddlers to teenagers, were present. Without any encouragement from Smythe, the teens promptly escorted the younger children out of the room. Smythe performed his usual ritual of looking at the chart and then checking his patient's abdominal wound by lifting up the bed sheets and peeking under the large abdominal dressing.

"Everything looks fine," he said to Mrs. Poon and her son, who was standing at her bedside. "We found. . ." He paused and surveyed the relatives, whose collective glare was chilling. ". . . a blockage. We removed it. You're better now."

Mrs. Poon winced in pain as she sat up in bed. She stared into Smythe's eyes and asked, "Is it cancer?"

Mrs. Poon's son and daughter-in-law stared at each other, jaws dropping and wide-eyed. Smythe hesitated. The delay was nearly enough to reveal his unequivocal opinion about Mrs. Poon's condition. He said, "Quite possibly. But we won't get a final pathology report for about a week. Then we'll know for certain."

The entire room breathed a sigh of relief. Smythe speculated on the mood of his patient and her family. Mrs. Poon appeared happy that someone was finally being frank with her. The family seemed grateful for the ounce of uncertainty Smythe had injected into the discussion after their mother's unexpectedly bold question. He'd just got himself a one-week reprieve, and could deal with the family and the follow-up discussion later. He might even get through this with minimal headache. The last thing he wanted was to involve the Ethics Committee in Mrs. Poon's case. As far as Smythe was concerned, although family opinions should always be considered, Mrs. Poon was the patient. She was the one he should deal with directly.

One week later, her son and daughter-in-law agreed that Smythe could tell the family matriarch the truth about her health. Not only did Mrs. Poon accept the diagnosis, but she also told her family she'd wanted to know and was glad they weren't trying to hide anything from her.

*   *   *

As Smythe sat down for a cup of coffee in his office, he reflected on some of the issues that had infuriated him lately. Sandi Tremaine had particularly annoyed him earlier this year when she'd extended her tentacles into administrative business. It was common knowledge that Tremaine was like a dog fixated on a bone when she took on a cause. Any opponent need only consider how she'd handled her divorce. A couple of years ago, she had formalized a protocol outlining how surgeons could book emergency surgery. Under the guise of efficiency and fairness, her plan struck Smythe as a means for anesthesiologists to wrestle control of the operating room from the surgeons. The changes resulted in a lot of hard feelings, but eventually there was a system in place that seemed to work. Blind luck, thought Smythe. Surgeons should control surgery, but this concept was being eroded over the years. Now everyone had to have their say in how surgical care was provided—everyone except the surgeons.

As he leaned back in his office chair and placed his feet on the desk, Smythe's mind wandered further into the past.

Soon after he'd arrived in Lakefield, a case illustrated Smythe's disdain for what he called BBS—bureaucratic bullshit. In the 1990s, the ambulance dispatch system had been a bit primitive. The university hadn't yet gotten its act together with air ambulance or critical care services, so the responsibility of sending in an urgent case lay totally with the sending facility. The system in Lakefield was governed by a patchwork of rules, which some people referred to as an algorithm. Exactly which ambulance went and when it was dispatched depended heavily on this bureaucratically created algorithm, a complicated pathway of decisions. Health care experts had constructed it during the calm and unemotional hours of nine to five.

Several years ago on a Friday night, Justin Van Dorp and his friends were having a pool party to celebrate the beginning of summer. They decided to play touch football along the pool deck, and at some point Justin went for a long pass right next to the house. Fun turned to horror in a matter of seconds. Justin didn't realize how close he was to the building when he dove forward to snag the ball, and he slammed into the sliding glass door with his outstretched right arm. Had he not been accelerating at the time, he might have avoided shattering the glass, but it took him completely off guard. His outstretched arm leading the way, he went through the glass door. At least a friend had taken first aid, which was fortunate for Justin. As bright red blood instantly began soaking through Justin's clothing, a classmate tightly wrapped the arm from shoulder to elbow with a couple of towels. The young man was then quickly thrown into the back of another friend's car and driven to the Lakefield Regional Hospital emergency department.

That evening, Jim Smythe was not on call but he happened to be walking through the emergency department when Justin Van Dorp was brought in by his hysterical friends.

Blood could often appear more copious than it actually was. A couple of tablespoons dripped into toilet water from a bleeding hemorrhoid could convince some individuals that they'd be dead from shock within minutes if they didn't get to the nearest emergency department.

But in Justin's case, he probably *would* have been dead if his friends hadn't acted so quickly and responsibly. With his life out of imminent danger, ER staff whisked Justin into Trauma Bay Number One. It was clear to all involved that the prospect of keeping his right arm was in doubt.

Smythe would not normally have been called about such an injury, but he was always excited to get involved in something that included either bleeding or pus. So, when the blood-covered Justin was brought crashing through the emergency department doors, Smythe was only too happy to find out what was going on.

First, Justin's clothing above his waist was cut off with scissors, and the right upper arm was reinforced with more pressure dressing. The emergency physician and Dr. Smythe then tended to Justin together. They felt it was safer to take the dressing off only once, which meant that the two doctors should see the injury at the same time.

Justin's blood pressure was low and his pulse high; he was in the early phase of shock, and the usual trauma protocols were applied, including rapid infusion of intravenous fluids. When both physicians were ready, Dr. Jansen removed the tight dressing from Justin's upper arm.

As a student, Jim had learned that when bleeding was audible, it was *serious*. As they cautiously removed the dressing, Justin's arm sounded like a faucet turned wide open. They really didn't see the area of injury well before they quickly re-wrapped Justin's arm, just as his friends had done minutes earlier. He clearly had a limb-threatening injury, if not a life-threatening one. Not being a vascular surgeon, and recognizing that Justin would likely require surgery to treat damage to vessels and nerves, Smythe recommended that he be sent to the university promptly. He quickly got on the phone, and the vascular surgeon on call at the University Hospital agreed.

One of the senior nurses phoned ambulance dispatch. While this was being done, Justin's arm was tightly reinforced in an additional dressing that would not be removed until the ultimate surgical treatment was ready to commence. His right hand was cool and somewhat bluish, and he had limited movement of his fingers. It didn't take much experience to recognize this was urgent.

Smythe was dumbfounded when the nurse came back into the trauma bay and stated that an ambulance would be on its way at some point, but that no timeline had been provided.

"You mean you don't know when it will be here?"

"I think it has something to do with the fact that he's already in a hospital. Patients in the hospital are a lower priority than those outside, such as someone at an accident scene."

"You've got to be kidding!" Smythe's voice escalated. "You mean to tell me they can't send an ambulance now, but they can't say why not, or when it might be available?"

Smythe knew there were emergencies and *emergencies*. If Aunt Martha at the nursing home was having difficulty with her bowels, she might need to be sent to the emergency department, and if there were no family member available to drive her, an ambulance would be called. Now, here's where Aunt Martha had one over on Justin Van Dorp that night: he was *already in a hospital*, and she was not. He was considered safer and lower-priority than Aunt Martha, according to the algorithm. In this case, they didn't even know an "Aunt Martha" existed. All they knew from the ambulance dispatch was that no ambulance was available. Dispatch met any efforts to request diversion from Aunt Martha to Justin with polite refusal. Smythe got on the phone, since the nurse in charge was getting nowhere.

He started calmly. "We need an ambulance immediately to take Justin Van Dorp to the University Hospital."

"We can't do that now, sir, but we'll send one along as soon as one becomes available."

"I need an ambulance *now*. Get me one."

"As soon as we can, sir."

"I need an ambulance diverted from wherever it is, to come and pick up this kid and transport him. Now!" By now, Smythe was starting to holler.

"We can't divert, sir."

"Why not?"

"Because your patient is already in a hospital. Ambulances out in the field are attending to clients who are not in hospital and therefore are considered higher priority."

"Listen, here. This kid needs a vascular surgeon. There is no vascular surgeon at this hospital. So, he is effectively *not in a hospital with necessary resources*. Send me an ambulance now!"

"I can't do that, sir."

"Let me talk to your supervisor!"

"I can leave a message, and he can get back to you Monday morning, sir."

"That's not soon enough. What is your name?"

Silence.

"What is your name?" Smythe repeated at a volume that could probably be heard by five ambulances in the surrounding area.

Silence.

Smythe continued, "If I don't have an ambulance here in five minutes, I'm going to take this kid, throw him in the back of my car, drive him half a block and dump him in the street. Then, I'll call you and you'll have to send an ambulance because he won't be in a hospital!" Smythe was now shaking. He slammed down the phone.

Within three minutes, an ambulance pulled up to the emergency entrance. Fifteen minutes later, Justin was on his way, with lights and sirens, heading for the university.

Smythe never did hear whether or not Justin and his arm made a full recovery.

*　　*　　*

At 8:30 on a mid-December Saturday morning, the sun was still not completely up. Amanda sat in her bright green tracksuit opposite Jim at the breakfast table, reading the paper and finishing a cup of coffee before going for a run; her usual route would take her about forty minutes, slightly longer today with the blanket of fresh snow.

Jim looked up from his newspaper and said matter-of-factly, "I don't think I can go skiing between Christmas and New Year's this year."

"You what?"

"I don't think I can go skiing."

"Why not?"

"Dylan Ross was supposed to work then, but his girlfriend ended up booking a trip. He wondered if I could cover his call and pick up some of his operating time."

"You knew we were planning on taking the girls skiing!"

"But Dylan—"

"But Dylan, nothing! Tell Dylan to sort it out with his girlfriend."

They'd had these discussions before, but Jim realized he was walking a fine line this time. Shortly after they were married, he'd explained to Amanda that in some circumstances, work would come before family. She had accepted the fact that if a patient were dying at hospital, some of Jim's family obligations would simply have to wait. Jim recognized this wasn't quite the same—but he'd already told Dylan he'd cover for him. "You know how I find this time of year difficult. I must work. We can go somewhere warm—in February," he said meekly.

Amanda bit her lip, got up from the table and walked to the front door. "You know, sometimes you can be such a bastard, Jim."

"First week of February—somewhere warm—go ahead and book it." The back door slammed shut before he could add anything.

Amanda didn't return home for two hours.

*　　*　　*

Smythe was filling out paperwork to book a boy for an appendectomy when he noticed Jen Boyer hovering in front of him. He realized she wasn't wearing her usual smile. He briefly glanced down at his papers to finish writing the necessary admission orders. With an obvious gesture of satisfaction, he slammed his pen onto the page, signifying that he was done, then looked up at Jen.

"Hey, sunshine. What's up? Why the long face?"

Jen suddenly turned beet red. She briefly looked away, obviously flustered. Turning back, she took a deep breath and asked, "Can I talk to you for a minute?"

"Sure. What's going on?"

"It's my mother. I think she's sick. Can you help?"

"Absolutely!"

"She's been having abdominal pains. I think she's lost a bit of weight. She's tired all the time and I think she needs to see a doctor. Her family doctor was Dr. Singh, so I'm not sure it's best to go through the process of getting a new doctor right now."

"I can see her in my office at the end of the day, if that suits her."

"Yes, thank you so much! What time?"

"I'm supposed to be done at 4:30, but I'm usually late. Can she come over a little before 5:00?"

"For sure."

At 5:30, Smythe stood up as Elizabeth Boyer was shown into his office. He could see why Jen was so attractive. At fifty-two, Elizabeth Boyer was also a pleasure to Smythe's eyes. Unlike Jen's, her hair was quite short, and any grey she may have had was covered. She had no glasses on, and wore bright red lipstick as well as a moderate amount of makeup around her eyes. It was hard to assess her body type because she was wearing a heavy sweater.

As he shook her hand, he said, "It's nice to meet you. Jen's a terrific nurse. I'm sure you're very proud of her."

"Thank you. I am. And thank you so much for seeing me, especially on short notice."

"No problem."

"I'm not as worried about me as Jen seems to be, but I have been having some abdominal pains these last few months. Nothing I can put my finger on. It's just not right."

After Smythe took a full history, inquiring about dietary factors that might incite her pain, along with the other usual questions, he concluded that Elizabeth Boyer was likely not suffering from anything too serious. He took her into the adjoining room and did a limited physical exam, which did not turn up anything unusual.

Back in the consulting office, he looked up from his notes and reassured her. "I don't think there's anything seriously wrong, but I do think that we should probably do some tests. It's unlikely we can get much done before Christmas, but I might be able to arrange for some endoscopy between Christmas and New Year's. If you're available, that is."

"Oh, yes, I can be available."

"I'm also going to put a request in for a CAT scan of the abdomen. Again, I'm not suspecting anything all that serious, but in order to be certain of that, we need to check into a few things."

"Such as?"

"Well, the first thing we need to be sure about is that you don't have a tumour. I don't think it's likely, but we need to address that. A colonoscopy and a gastroscopy would be important. We would also be able to check for other problems, such as diverticulosis, polyps, ulcers and celiac disease. The CAT scan likely won't get done until early or mid-January."

"Thank you." She smiled broadly, her eyes beaming. "I appreciate it so much. I know that Jen's mind will be put at ease now that we're looking into this."

After Mrs. Boyer left, Smythe proceeded to tell his secretary to arrange the appropriate investigations. As he was leaving, he called over his shoulder, "Also, can you order that rowing machine for me, Moira?"

"Where from, Jim?"

He was running out the office door in the direction of the hospital. "Hell, I can't remember. Just go online and look up rowing machines and Vermont. Order it today. And get them to ship it priority. I don't care how much it costs. Just get it here ASAP."

* * *

Putting down the newspaper on the kitchen table, Amanda Smythe picked up the telephone to call her best friend, Linda. The line was busy. Amanda sighed heavily, ready to unload her latest frustrations on any ears that would listen. Before she pressed the numbers into the phone again, she thought back to the early days of their marriage, when Jim was a chief resident and Emily was only a few months old. Jim had not taken for granted the way Amanda had coped with a new baby. Yes, he was busy, but Jim was a good husband in those days. He made sure Amanda was looked after and that she *felt* appreciated. The early days of the marriage had been tough, but Amanda knew what she was getting into. She had been an O.R. nurse, so she was accustomed to the fact that life for a surgery resident—or for a surgeon—would not be easy. She knew it would involve long hours, and that sacrifices would be necessary along the way. She also knew money would not be a problem.

In his final year as a chief resident, they rented a small apartment across the road from the University Hospital. Although Jim could have bought the nicest house in the area and paid cash for it, he preferred that they do things "normally". He didn't want his co-workers or staff surgeons thinking he "had it made", so he kept his financial affairs to himself, and Amanda was content to do the same.

One particular story stood out in Amanda's mind. She'd heard Jim tell it so many times, it was as if Amanda had witnessed the entire event.

One night, Jim had received an urgent call from the hospital at about eleven-thirty. "Dr. Smythe, we have a gunshot wound to the chest coming in by ambulance. ETA is four minutes." Jim's heart fluttered at the thought, and he quickly jumped out of bed. He wasn't sure he could make it there in less than four minutes. He hadn't quite been asleep because they had both been getting Emily settled a few minutes previously. But even if he had been, he would have awakened instantly for such a call. A gunshot wound to the chest—penetrating chest trauma—was one of the few reasons to do an emergency room thoracotomy. Opening the chest cavity of an arresting patient without anesthetic in the emergency department was a life-saving maneuver that most residents got to do perhaps once or twice in their five years of residency—if they were lucky. At least, this was the case in Jim's part of the country where penetrating trauma wasn't very common. Years later, Jim would lament the fact that no one considered this fact when planning surgical training. If a resident were available a full three quarters of the time during the five years, then he or she would be three times more likely to encounter such a rare but important case during training, compared to someone who was available a quarter of the time. How the new generation of surgeons would acquire the necessary experience garnered by surgeons of Jim's era was a bit of a mystery to him. On this occasion, nonetheless, Jim was very excited by the call: a gunshot wound to the chest, arriving in ER in four minutes.

Jim threw on his clothes, kissed Amanda and explained why as he ran out the door in less than a minute. He darted across the empty winter street, which was slick with snow and ice. Arriving on the hospital grounds, he could see the emergency department entrance not far away. As Jim ran out of the parking lot at full speed, he jumped over a snow bank about two feet high. Like a hurdler on the final sprint, his legs were outstretched, one forward and one back to avoid the bank. Out of nowhere, a tree branch caught the side of his face, sending a cold, searing crack through his forehead and left cheek. Good thing he hadn't put in his contacts! His glasses protected his eyes, the loss of which could be rather career-limiting for a surgeon.

His objective in mind—a gunshot wound to the chest—was only minutes, if not seconds, away. He blasted through the emergency department entrance to find a bunch of staff who stopped and stared at him, so he looked behind him to see if they were gazing at anyone else. On his chin, Jim felt a big drop of sweat which, when he wiped it, turned out to be blood. In fact, the entire left side of his face was covered with fresh blood from his encounter with the tree branch. Since no one volunteered the information, he asked, "Okay, where's the gunshot wound to the chest?"

"It's over there, Dr. Smythe. In the minor injury area. The call was a little mixed up. Sorry about that. It was actually a gunshot wound to the *chin*, not the *chest*. And it just grazed the chin." The nurse pointed over to the minor injury area, where an older gentleman was sitting up in a chair as another nurse applied Steri-Strips to his chin. "He was cleaning his gun," she added.

By the time Jim had his own face cleaned and stitched, the man was long gone. Jim walked home, disappointed.

When he entered their dark bedroom, Amanda commented, "That was quick for a gunshot wound to the chest. I guess he didn't make it."

As he turned on the light, Jim replied, "I would have been quicker, but I had to get a tetanus shot."

With one look at Jim's face, Amanda burst out laughing. Jim reciprocated, fully appreciative of the hilarity of the situation.

Amanda reluctantly let go of her daydream. Sitting at the kitchen table, she took another sip from her coffee cup, picked up the phone and called Linda again. This time the line was free.

"Linda, it's me."

"You sound depressed."

"I *am* a bit depressed." Amanda sighed despondently. "Jim is working so hard these days. I'm worried about him. He has no time to spend with us. I know this is a tough time of year for him, but he can't indulge himself completely. . ."

"You don't think he's having an affair, do you?"

"No, he wouldn't do that—I don't think. It's work. He's there all the time. He leaves the house in greens and he comes home in greens. I had to ask him to at least put on a fresh pair once every twenty-four hours."

"Wow. Amanda, you've got to talk to him—"

"And I think he's exercising. It's great he wants to be in shape, but at our expense? He's just not around that much."

"Don't take this the wrong way, Amanda, but sometimes I wonder why you even stick around. Jim seems so self-centred. Why do you put up with it?"

After an awkward moment, she replied emphatically, "Because he needs me." Amanda wiped her eyes and blew her nose into a Kleenex. "And I love him. And the children."

"What do *you* need?"

Amanda paused, leaning back in her chair. "*I need to support my husband.* Even though it's hard at times. It's what I have to do. Besides, I think it'll blow over. After Christmas. It's always a rough time of year for him. It's not like it's the first time he's been this way. It just seems a little more extreme, that's all."

After another twenty minutes of conversation, Amanda said, "Thanks for listening, Linda."

Chapter 12 ~ Chantal

At the scrub sink, Smythe and Jared Chong were diligently washing up before Chantal Wharton's mastectomy. The thirty-year-old mayor's daughter and mother of two had received the bad news early enough in December that her breast cancer surgery could be completed in time for her to be home for Christmas.

"So, Jared, have you got your application ready for surgical residency?"

Jared stared ahead intently as he scrubbed his hands; his eyes looked tired. "I missed the deadline for July but I'm hoping for the next—"

"You what? How could you let that one slip past you?" Smythe's voice was a mixture of incredulity and dismay.

"I know, Jim. I'm sorry. It's chaotic at home. Our little girl is up every night, and Hilary needs my help. I promise, next time around."

"It's not me you have to make promises to. You're the one that has to live with your decisions—or lack of them."

"I *do* want to go into surgery. It's just that I watch you—how hard you work and the pressure you're under—and I'm not always so sure. But I'm thinking long and hard, so if it does happen, I'll be going for it one hundred percent."

"You've got to *make* it happen, don't *let* it happen, Jared. Listen to me: the last thing in life you want to live with is regret. At my age, it's nearly impossible to go back for more training. Don't put yourself in the position of saying 'what if?' twenty years from now. And besides, I'll write a great reference letter for you—just let me know when, and it's done."

"I appreciate that, Jim, I really do."

Silence fell between them as they continued to scrub, and Smythe's mind wandered to his training days as a fourth-year resident.

Dr. Calvin was one mentor who remained indelibly etched in Smythe's psyche. Calvin was slim and of medium height, with grey hair that was thick and a bit dishevelled since he always wore it slightly long. Most of the time, he was mild-mannered and polite—a true gentleman. However, in the operating room, nurses and residents feared him. Calvin always had a fourth-year resident, a rotation that was anxiously anticipated by all trainees from the first day of their residencies. Probably all surgical training programs had, in one form or another, a Dr. Calvin—a typical old-fashioned surgeon whose dedication and experience fortunately benefited patients and residents alike. Smythe recalled more than once when his mentor had held back tears at the scrub sink, preparing for a tough operation on a young patient with cancer.

It was common knowledge that Calvin's residents found working with him to be the toughest rotation; over the years, at least two residents had been off sick with a bleeding ulcer before the end of it. Thirteen of fourteen mornings for three months—he took every other Sunday off—the resident had to meet Calvin on the surgical unit at 6:00 a.m. to start ward rounds. For any resident who wanted to do well, this meant showing up at 5:15 to go through all his patients' charts before Calvin arrived. The alarm clock was therefore set for 4:30 a.m. Residents had many coping strategies to get through these three months. One of the most basic measures for male residents was to shave in the evening before bed at 9:00 p.m. Why waste any time in the morning when valuable sleep was at stake?

Dr. Calvin used to scream at his resident in the operating room louder than any staff surgeon in the city. If a resident ever complained to the program director, the whining didn't go far; how could any surgeon in the city have an ounce of sympathy for a new trainee when they all owed a huge debt of gratitude to Calvin for his dedicated teaching? *Suck it up, boy, we've all been through it. You'll be better for the experience with Dr. Calvin.*

Dr. Calvin became somewhat competitive with one particular resident, Dr. Kuong. Calvin began arriving an additional fifteen minutes earlier each day, catching Kuong unfinished in his preparations as he wrote daily orders on each patient chart. When Calvin showed up smiling at the hospital at 5:00 a.m., Kuong was flustered; he hadn't completed his orders on all of Calvin's patients' medical records, despite having arrived at 4:15. Not to be outdone, Kuong returned to the hospital in the early hours of the next day, at about 12:15 a.m., wrote and dated orders on all of Calvin's patients and went home to catch a few hours of sleep.

To Calvin's surprise, orders over the next few days were all completed before his arrival, no matter how early he showed up. This went on for several days, with Calvin coming in earlier each morning, trying to catch Kuong before the daily orders had been written. Finally, a nurse spilled the beans to Calvin, who couldn't help but be impressed by Kuong's ingenuity. They ended up calling a truce, with the regular 6:00 a.m. meeting time restored.

Like all the residents who'd gone before him, Smythe was deeply affected by Calvin's teaching. If a case was depressing, Dr. Calvin yelled even louder. One day at the scrub sink, Calvin shared his teaching philosophy with Smythe: "You've got to have a thick skin to work with me, son. But if I'm yelling at you, it's because I care. The time you have to start worrying, Jim, is when there's complete silence. If I'm not hollering at you in the O.R., you're probably in big trouble."

Smythe remembered one case when a young man was diagnosed in the operating room with pancreatic cancer. Calvin was quiet until it came time to close the abdomen. Every stitch Smythe placed seemed to be wrong. The screaming didn't let up for the twenty minutes it took Smythe to reapproximate the wound edges, layer by layer. Smythe wondered if all of this had been the surgeon's emotional reaction to a young patient with a bad disease. As an independent surgeon himself now, Smythe felt the same emotional attachment to his patients. Although Calvin had passed away five years ago, Smythe could still hear his voice during critical points of most operations.

When Smythe was tying a delicate stitch, Calvin's voice boomed: "Don't break it! If you break that stitch, son, you're in deep trouble!" Over-sewing a bleeding vessel, Smythe could still hear Calvin shrieking, "That one had better not keep bleeding. Do it right for once in your goddamn life!"

Although no one enjoyed them at the time, Calvin's antics had lasting beneficial effects on surgeons who were now scattered across the country. Smythe wondered how surgeons could be so well trained nowadays, with political correctness preventing teachers like Calvin from emerging. But there wasn't a former resident or patient around who would say anything bad about Calvin. Despite all the yelling, his patient care had been superb and his work ethic exemplary.

Sandi Tremaine's voice interrupted Smythe's reverie as she popped her head between the operating room doors to find him still scrubbing his hands.

"If you scrub any longer, your hands are going to fall off. The patient's asleep. Can we get started?"

"Of course," Smythe responded, making his way into the room.

Jared followed behind, adhering to the age-old unwritten rule that dictated students scrub for fifteen seconds longer than the staff surgeon. No matter how long the scrub, when students demonstrated the indiscretion of entering the room before the surgeon, somebody—anybody—later quietly explained the ritual to ensure that such recklessness was not repeated. Jared was smart enough that no one had ever had to spell out the implicit protocol to him.

Chantal Wharton had found a lump in her left breast in late November. Her initial reaction was to assume it was nothing, since she did not have a family history of breast cancer. Chantal's memory of statistics class was a little fuzzy; otherwise, she would have known that although a positive family history increases one's chance of having breast cancer, the majority of those with the diagnosis actually don't have a close family member with the disease. Women were repeatedly falsely reassured that if they didn't have a relative with breast cancer, they were safe—when in reality, no one was safe.

Chantal happened to mention the lump while the family was having Sunday evening supper. Chantal's husband, Dave, wasn't all that worried about it, and their two children were too young to know what was going on. But Denise Wharton—Chantal's mother and the mayor—was on the phone to Jim Smythe within five minutes.

"Jim, it's Denise. Sorry to interrupt your Sunday evening."

"What can I do for you?"

"Chantal found a breast lump a few weeks ago. She's done nothing about it and we need to get this sorted out before Christmas. Can you help?"

"Of course. Most breast lumps in thirty-year-olds aren't serious, but I'd be happy to check it out. If she can come to my office at 4:30 tomorrow afternoon, I'll see her when I'm finished with surgery."

Smythe would have responded the same way to any acquaintance who called his home with that type of problem, whether it was the mayor or not. Smythe had met the Wharton family years ago, soon after moving into town, and his in-laws had known Denise since she was a young child, long before political aspirations guided her to City Hall.

"Who was that?" Amanda asked as Jim made his way back to the supper table.

"Just someone with a breast lump I'm going to see tomorrow."

Amanda would know there was no point inquiring further. If Jim didn't tell her when she asked the first time, he wasn't going to break under more formal cross-examination.

Smythe saw Chantal the next day. He was somewhat concerned about the texture of the two-centimetre lump in the upper outer quadrant of her left breast. It was a little harder than he would have expected in a benign lump such as a cyst or a fibroadenoma. He also wondered if he felt a node or two under her arm. Chantal had put on some weight after her second pregnancy a couple of years ago, so it was a bit difficult to tell.

A week later, Smythe sat with Chantal in his office to discuss the results of her mammogram and needle biopsy. Her two children were running around his desk playing tag. Rather than face each other across the large desk, Smythe and Chantal both sat in chairs side by side. No adult family members were present. Smythe wondered if he should have warned the family that it wasn't going to be good news. But how could you do that without outright telling them over the phone?

"There's reason to be optimistic," he said, "with newer treatments available."

"Like what? You don't mean chemotherapy, do you?"

"It's possible," he lied. He knew full well chemotherapy wasn't just possible; it was a certainty in her future. "Possible" was a word to let it sink in gradually.

"Take them both off," she said, gesturing to her breasts.

"We can talk about all the options. There's no need to rush," Smythe reassured her.

"No, I've thought about it. If it ever came to this, I want both breasts removed."

"First of all, it doesn't spread from one breast to the oth—"

"I want them both off," she interrupted.

"We need to talk about the options from start to finish. No decisions need to be made today."

They discussed the implications of her diagnosis and its treatment for another twenty minutes. Not surprisingly to Smythe, however, Chantal was back in the office two days later with her husband and parents to go over it again; she'd really retained nothing the day the bad news was initially communicated.

"Would a total mastectomy help me avoid chemotherapy?" she asked for the third time.

"No," Smythe replied. "Chemotherapy is for systemic treatment—to treat disease or prevent it from showing up elsewhere in the body. Radiation can usually be avoided if you have a mastectomy because it is for local treatment—to prevent the disease from recurring locally in the breast or chest wall. But I think either surgical option would be reasonable." Living in a city without radiation available and facing the possibility of further surgery if local control was not achieved with a partial mastectomy, Chantal opted for a total mastectomy. She complied with Smythe's suggestion to deal with the right breast down the road, if that was what she wanted. The last thing she'd need would be a surgical complication on the "good side", which could delay needed chemotherapy.

She decided on a total mastectomy in part to avoid radiation, but also due to the size of the lump compared to the size of her breast. Smythe found more of his patients preferred a wide lumpectomy or partial mastectomy, but some patients, like Chantal, were determined to have the breast removed. Smythe would also check lymph nodes under the arm. If she wanted reconstruction of the breast, then that would wait until later. Chantal didn't want to deal with reconstructive surgery yet, preferring to focus on her two small children and Christmas.

Now in surgery, Chantal was asleep with her left arm extended at ninety degrees and her left breast and underarm prepped with iodine solution. In the X-ray department four hours previously, her breast had been injected behind the nipple with radioactive material. With her now asleep, Smythe performed a similar injection with blue dye. The first place cancer in the breast usually spread to was the lymph nodes under the arm on the same side as the cancer. By identifying the earliest nodes in the lymphatic drainage, or sentinel nodes, Smythe might be able to avoid the extensive surgery traditionally required to clear numerous nodes from under the arm, if Chantal's sentinel nodes were free of cancer.

"So, Jared, what happens if we clearly identify two sentinel nodes under the arm, and one looks like it might have cancer in it?" Smythe made two curved incisions across the breast, each joining on either side of the nipple-areola complex.

"We get them tested on the spot—if there's any cancer in either, we do a formal axillary dissection, trying to clear ten to twenty nodes from below the axillary vein."

"Sounds like a plan," Smythe proclaimed. Cautery was used under the skin above and below the incisions to separate the breast from overlying skin. The breast was then separated off the pectoralis muscle from medial to lateral, until the only remaining attachment was to tissue in the armpit. Smythe then took the radioactive counter and searched the sentinel nodes. The high-pitched squeal of the instrument easily identified three lumps under the arm. They were all "blue and hot".

Smythe's expression behind his surgical mask was visibly one of dismay. "Two of these nodes are enlarged and hard. They don't look good to me." He handed three nodes off to the scrub nurse, who sent them off for immediate analysis in the pathology department. Two of the nodes were identified as cancerous. Smythe proceeded to delicately sweep tissue down from under the axillary vein, high in the armpit, to remove more nodes as planned.

"I'm not happy about several of these either," he said.

When they were finishing up, Smythe asked Jared to close the incision. The tension was getting to Smythe, and he had the incredible urge to scream at Jared, just as Calvin had yelled at him about fifteen years previously under similar circumstances. He resisted the temptation. They placed a couple of drains under the skin flaps across Chantal's flat left chest to drain off excess blood that could accumulate over the next twenty-four hours. Smythe thought of her two children and then of her parents.

In the family room, Smythe spoke to Chantal's husband and parents, with the two youngsters running around.

"I think we got clear around the lump in the breast, but I'm concerned about lymph nodes under the arm. We'll have to wait and see, of course. For now, the task is to get her over the surgery and recovered, in case more treatment is recommended. The pathology report won't be back until after Christmas, so we'll just have to wait for that and focus on recovery."

Chantal's family was silent. They then thanked Smythe and waited for Chantal to be moved from the recovery room to her bed on the ward.

Smythe rode his bike home, despite the smattering of ice and snow on the streets. He couldn't stop thinking of Chantal and her family and her axilla full of suspicious lymph nodes. She'd certainly get chemotherapy. Her hair would fall out. She might even get radiation, due to the advanced spread under her arm. If she didn't get recurrent disease in the first year, they could remove her other breast. She could get the whole thing done with bilateral reconstruction, if she wanted, but not now. Her main priority would have to be to get through this phase of her treatment.

Smythe pulled his bike into the driveway and realized that he couldn't remember one stoplight or any landmark on his way home. He looked at his wristwatch: 6:00 p.m. Not bad. On time for supper for a change.

Entering the front door, he got the usual enthusiastic reception from Sara, followed by the equivocal welcome by Emily. Amanda gave him a big hug.

"Would you like a glass of wine? I just opened some."

"No thanks, honey. Not tonight for me."

"Everything okay?"

"Sure. Everything is fine."

"You sure?"

"Of course I'm sure."

"Jim, you've been working so hard lately. We hardly ever see you." Amanda took a deep breath and added, "You need to make more of an effort for your family."

"No problem. I'll be more available," he lied.

"You don't think there's a problem, do you?" This came out as half question, half statement.

"Of course there's not a problem. And besides, I'm up most mornings before 6:00. I'll make you and the girls pancakes any day at 6:00. It's not my fault you sleep in until 7:00. It just so happens that by that time, with nothing to do around here, I might as well be at work."

"You've got to be kidding! You really don't see a problem."

"Like I said, Amanda, there's no problem. I will be as attentive as you'll let me."

Amanda escaped to the kitchen without saying a word, then finished preparing supper and placed it on the dining room table.

Over supper, she asked, "Did you operate on Chantal Wharton yet?"

"How'd you know? Was her mother speaking to you?"

"Yes. She called me the day you gave them the diagnosis."

"I operated on her today."

"And?"

"I said, I operated on her today. It's done."

Amanda bit her lip and looked down at her plate.

As Jim took his first bite of blueberry crumble and ice cream, the telephone rang. Sara jumped up and looked at the call display. "It's the hospital, Daddy."

"I'll take it in the kitchen." Jim moved to the next room and picked up the phone.

"Dr. Smythe, I know you're not on call tonight, but I'm a bit concerned about Chantal Wharton." It was Rosalyn, an experienced surgical nurse. If she was worried, that was enough to get Smythe's attention. "There's a fair amount of blood coming from her drains—about 200 cc's over the last two hours. She's looking a bit pale."

"How are her vitals?"

"They're all okay—BP 125 over 90. Pulse is 86 per minute."

"Can you get her hemoglobin checked, get a type and screen, just in case—I'd rather not transfuse her if we don't have to."

"No problem."

"And Rosalyn, can you take down her dressing and look at the wound for signs of bleeding? If there's a hematoma there, I'd like to know so we can take her back to the O.R. sooner rather than later."

"I'll call you again when the blood test result is back, or sooner if I have concerns about the wound."

"Thanks, Rosalyn. Talk to you later." Jim hung up the phone. *There's a good nurse*, he thought. She'd call him with all the information later, rather than calling every fifteen minutes. Also, he knew he could trust her judgment about the wound.

Jim returned to the supper table.

"Everything okay?" Amanda asked.

"Yup, everything's fine." He proceeded to gobble up his blueberry crumble and ice cream, including a second helping.

Emily and Sara escaped from the table without clearing dishes, an intermittent lapse that occasionally required Jim to reorient the girls with reality. Unfortunately, the pendulum had been swinging in the wrong direction the past few weeks. *So close to Christmas, you'd think they'd smarten up*, Jim thought.

"Get back here!" he bellowed. "Can't you two ever learn? I thought we'd been through this a time or two before. Haven't we?"

"Jim, it's okay. I'll clean up. Leave the girls alone, will you? It seems you're always giving them a rough time when you're home."

"I expect a bare minimum from my children, and they aren't making the grade at the moment, Amanda." He yelled again: "Get back here immediately and clear the table!"

"Jim, your mind is obviously at the hospital right now anyway. Why don't you unite your body with your brain? Go back there and take care of whatever it is you're stewing about."

"Fine. I'll be back later. I'm not sure when." Jim stormed out the door and drove to the hospital.

When he arrived on Unit 23, Chantal looked a bit pale, but she was cheerful. Smythe avoided the topic of her bad axilla and the local spread of her cancer. Rosalyn was attending to her, checking her blood pressure.

"Couldn't stay away, could you? I thought you'd be dropping by for a visit." Rosalyn had known Smythe for ten years, and sometimes he thought she knew him better than Amanda did. Rosalyn was about ten years older than Smythe, with a round figure and short grey hair.

Smythe took down Chantal's dressing, peering at the left side of her chest, trying not to let Chantal get a view. It was bad enough for her to see her breast missing for the first time; but if there were 500 cc's of blood collected under the incision, he didn't want her to see that until he'd decided what to do about it. To his surprise, it actually looked all right. There was a fair amount of bruising and perhaps a small amount of blood trapped under the incision, but nothing the body wouldn't take care of itself, as long as the amount didn't increase.

Rosalyn had stepped out of the room and come back in. "Her hemoglobin is 95, Dr. Smythe."

"Fine, Rosalyn. Thank you." He turned to Chantal. "Things look all right here. I don't think we'll need to do anything further this evening. Have a good night, Chantal. I'll see you in the morning."

"Thanks, Dr. Smythe. You have a good evening, too."

"I will," he lied.

At the nursing station, Rosalyn asked, "Dr. Smythe, when would you transfuse her? At what hemoglobin would you want to give blood?"

"Blood transfusions increase the risk of recurrent cancer by suppressing the immune system. So I would take her back to the operating room to stop bleeding long before I'd transfuse her. But her bleeding appears to have stopped. So no surgery or transfusion tonight, unless things change."

Smythe left the surgical unit at 8:30 p.m. but didn't feel like going home, so he walked across the street to his office to do paperwork.

Only a few days until Christmas. Then the girls would be off on their ski holiday, with Smythe left in town. He could get some real work done then. Hopefully, some good cases would come in. Smythe could hardly wait. Five days on call out of eight would keep him busy. As he checked the final outstanding lab report on his computer, he looked at the clock in the bottom right corner of the screen. It was 11:00 p.m. Perhaps he should work on his presentation for grand rounds in January; it would be here before he knew it. He opened his desk drawer, pulled out the material he had so far and set to work. *Just like a meal, good presentations take time*, he mused.

He envisaged his upcoming grand rounds; he was going to nail it this time. Then he started picturing the medical awards dinner in late January.

A great presentation at rounds wouldn't clinch the Lifetime Achievement Award, but it couldn't hurt. If the award came his way, who knew what other opportunities might result? Smythe dreamed of possibilities for the next twenty minutes.

Still not in the mood to go home, Smythe started to surf the Internet. In a short time he found himself on an athletic wear site he'd never seen before. Within a few minutes he had a bright orange ski suit picked out in his size. He entered his credit card information, not really certain that he was going to follow through on the purchase. He opened up the enlarged photo of the outfit one more time. What the heck. So what if he wasn't going skiing right after Christmas? It wasn't like he'd given up the sport for good. He clicked his mouse and to his satisfaction, his computer confirmed that his online transaction had succeeded. He left his office at 1:30 a.m.

As he climbed into bed, he kissed Amanda and hoped she wouldn't be angry with him for too long.

The following day, Smythe left his bike in the garage so he could drive to a few stores on the way home from work. He left most of the Christmas shopping up to Amanda, but he did need to make a few purchases. After work, he bought some very expensive jewellery. He then decided to pick up a couple of lattes. Amanda always appreciated such an indulgence, and at 4:00 in the afternoon, it was early enough for him to bring home a treat before supper.

The cashier was a tall, skinny, pimply-faced boy. Smythe had to repeat the order twice. *How could he have difficulty with that one? A no-fat and a regular latte—nothing too complicated there*, Smythe thought. He moved down to the end of the counter, where his order was prepared without delay. When he took one sip from his drink, he knew instantly it was wrong.

Smythe pushed his way back to the front of the line. There was no point in talking to the barista—Smythe was sure the daydreaming kid who'd taken his order had messed up.

"Excuse me, there's some kind of sugar or syrup in this latte." Smythe's words were forceful and loud enough to capture the attention of the five people in the line-up he'd circumvented, in addition to the four workers behind the counter.

"What did you order, sir?"

"You didn't remember the first time I told you. Why should I tell you now?"

The cashier was obviously puzzled by Smythe's response. "If you want us to get it right for you, sir, I'll need to know what you ordered."

“Fine. A no-fat latte, and a regular latte. Mine has some sugar or something in it.”

“Which one is yours, sir?”

“The regular latte, of course!”

“One regular latte coming up, sir! Nothing added this time. Sorry about that, sir.”

Several customers behind Smythe were shifting on their feet and huffing when Smythe added to their anxiety by belting out, “Wait! If you messed up on one, it could have been a double header! Let me check my wife’s latte before I lose my place in line.”

“It wasn’t actually your place in line; you kind of forced your way back in,” an attractive blond woman interjected.

Smythe leaned toward her and growled, “I don’t think so.” He gave her a prolonged cold stare.

She added fearfully, “Go ahead, get it right while you’re here.”

Smythe took a sip from Amanda’s cup and replaced the plastic lid. No sugar. It was only his latte that was wrong. With the mistake corrected, he was on his way.

Smythe was fuming all the way home. What right did some spotty-faced kid have to work there if he wasn’t going to do a proper job? Smythe thought of Dr. Calvin, and how *he* would have torn a strip off that kid if he’d been a surgical resident. His anger gradually transformed to excitement as he thought about writing a long letter of complaint to the manager.

Smythe had felt a dichotomy of desires that day. On the one hand, he wanted to rip into that kid like Calvin had torn into him on a bad day back in surgical residency. Yet, earlier at work, Smythe had felt so good that he had fantasized about seducing a couple of nurses. He knew he wasn’t his usual self, yet he felt fine. Work was going well. Home life was okay. He just had to get through Christmas with the in-laws, and he’d have a busy week at work when his girls were off skiing.

He pulled the car into the driveway, determined not to mention the interaction with spotty-face to Amanda. He didn’t want to get into a long discussion with her about the declining work ethic of teenagers these days.

At the front door, Jim fumbled with his keys as he balanced the two lattes in the crook of his left arm. He was beginning to notice how cold his hands were when Amanda opened the front door. When she saw the lattes, her eyes brightened and she reached out to help him.

“Oh, thank you, sweetie, that’s so kind of you!”

"It's a pleasure, sunshine. I'd like to find the time to do it more often."

They made their way into the front hallway and Jim took off his winter boots. Amanda led Jim by the hand into the kitchen, where they sat down to drink their lattes.

"Hungry?" Amanda slid a plateful of home-baked oatmeal cookies to Jim.

"Thanks." He swiftly scooped up a cookie and before taking a bite, blurted, "You know, Abbott can be such a prick these d—"

"Jim!"

"What?"

"You've never talked about Rick like that before."

"Well, he's changing these days, and I don't like it one bit!"

"You've always liked him. What were the words you've used? Fair. Measured. Rational."

"Well, not anymore. He's spiteful. He's getting on my case for being firm with the nurses in the O.R. Simply for my high standards, he's beginning to crap on me."

"You're always good to the nurses, honey."

"I know, but tell Rick that. I seriously think he's trying to reprimand me for something. I don't know why. I wonder if he's just jealous."

"Jealous? Rick?"

"Think about it. He's a part-time administrator, part-time ER doc. I suspect he feels undervalued. Face it, he doesn't get the recognition that surgeons get."

"I'd be careful about what you say about him if I were you—"

"What, you too? Are you on his side?"

"Of course not!"

"You're not rolling your eyes at me, are you?"

"Sweetie!" Amanda's lower lip started to stiffen.

"I'm sorry, sunshine. I'm just a bit stressed these days, and it's important I know you're behind me."

"Of course I am! You and the girls are the most important people in my life!" Amanda slid her chair next to Jim's and hugged him around his neck as tears silently trickled down both her cheeks.

Chapter 13 ~ Rear Admiral

Smythe survived Christmas with the in-laws. It was a typical holiday with lots of food and drink and plenty of visiting. He was off Christmas Day, and with only two patients in the hospital, he'd leave ward rounds up to the guy on call. Besides, he needed to rest up for his busy stretch between Christmas and New Year's.

Amanda had at least partially forgiven him for his long hours at work and for backing out of the ski holiday. She had reassured him that she was aware it was a tough time of year for him. She'd also taken his advice and booked a warm family vacation for February.

Returning to work after Christmas, Smythe opened the locker room door and nearly bashed straight into Dylan Ross, who was exiting hurriedly.

"Sorry, Jim. I was just going to call you."

"What's up?"

"I'm leaving you an appendix, if that's okay with you. Thanks very much for taking call for me. I owe you one."

"No problem. What's with the appendix?" Smythe leaned against the wall, eager to hear the details.

"It's a thirty-nine-year-old man with appendicitis. A classic case. Tender, elevated white count. I saw him at 6:30 this morning and booked him. Would you mind doing his surgery?" Dylan stared down the corridor, fastening the snaps on his ski jacket, gloves tucked under his right arm.

"No problem. I'll take care of it." What could be better than a case of appendicitis handed to him on a silver platter, with no need for a diagnostic work-up?

"Thanks, Jim. They thought they could get him in about a quarter to nine. If you hurry, you can find him in emergency. Otherwise, he'll be in the O.R. soon."

"It's my pleasure. Say, Dylan, can I ask you a favour?"

"Of course."

"Would you consider writing a letter of reference for me?"

"For *you*? Sure. What for?"

"I'm just looking at options—checking out some opportunities," Smythe said, his eyes shifting restlessly.

"You're not thinking of leaving us, are you Jim?"

"I'd rather you keep it quiet right now, if you don't mind. I'm just in the exploration phase at the moment."

"What does Amanda think of all this?"

"We haven't discussed it yet. I'm trying to sort through a few details before bringing it up. I think I'll wait until January—if in fact anything happens at all. But for now, just keep it to yourself."

"Consider it a safe secret. And hey, you know I'd write you a great reference letter, even though we'd all be sad to see you go."

"Thanks, Dylan." Smythe paused and then added, "Have a great vacation."

Slipping on his gloves and already partway down the hallway, Dylan spoke over his shoulder, "I will, Jim. And thanks again for taking my call."

"You bet!" Smythe hurried into the locker room, looking forward to starting the day with an appendectomy.

He was scheduled to start a list of endoscopies at nine o'clock. If he started the appendix before nine, he wouldn't be all that late with his day. Quickly changing into greens, he went over to the emergency department to see his man with appendicitis. He preferred to assess these hand-over cases as early as possible, just in case of the remote possibility that he would modify the plan. Ross was a very competent surgeon, and this was a straightforward case, so Smythe didn't expect any changes.

It took Smythe only five minutes to assess Mr. Nichols. Leaving the patient's cubicle, he pulled the curtain closed behind him and spotted a familiar face across the emergency department. He'd seen her many times over the last year, a teenage girl dressed in a volunteer uniform. Her eyes locked on his for just a few seconds, long enough to be followed by her smile. Her green eyes reminded him of Amanda's, and he guessed she might be a couple of years older than Emily.

"Hey." Smythe beckoned the volunteer with a tilt of his head.

"Me?" She tentatively approached with a surprised look, her smile undiminished.

"Yes, you. Do you want to see some surgery?"

"Me? Here?"

"Yes, you. But no, in the operating room." Smythe loved to showcase his abilities and he knew the girl couldn't refuse.

"I'd love to!"

"What's your name?" Smythe asked.

"Patty."

"Well, Patty, I've seen you around here quite a bit over the last year. It's time you got a reward for your hard work. I'm taking out an appendix shortly, and you'd be welcome to come and watch."

"Thank you! I'd love to watch!"

Forty minutes later, Smythe and Jared were outside the operating room scrubbing as Mr. Nichols was being put to sleep. Patty, now in surgical greens, paced excitedly behind the two at the scrub sink. Smythe paused for a minute and walked over to the operating room door. Not wanting to contaminate his hands mid-scrub, he kicked the door and peered through the glass window into the operating room, trying to get the circulating nurse's attention. Shirley Carver came through the swinging doors a few seconds later as Smythe moved sideways back to the scrub sink, next to Jared.

"Yes?" she inquired.

"Patty is going to watch our appendectomy. I think she should scrub."

"Scrub?"

"You betcha. She'll get a better appreciation for what we're doing if she's right in there."

"You mean you want her to assist you and Jared? *I don't think so.*" Shirley's eyes scolded Smythe from behind her surgical mask.

"No, she'll just observe. But this way, she'll see much better. If it were laparoscopic, she could see it all on the screen, but this is open, and she won't see nearly as much unless she's actually scrubbed and right up close. If I had known you were going to be so obstructive, I would have booked it laparoscopic so Patty could see it better. But it's too late to change the set-up now. So get her scrubbed."

"But—"

"No buts, Shirley. This young girl might turn out to be a top surgeon, a nurse or who knows what else? Even if she becomes an investment banker, as a result of this experience today, she'll be better informed about her career choice."

"But, Dr. Smythe—"

"As a volunteer here, she's registered with the hospital. It's not like I just pulled her off the street. She's given her time to patients over the last year. It's the least we can do for her. The patient gave me permission for an observer. Get her scrubbed." Smythe finished rinsing his hands and darted through the swinging doors with Jared on his tail before Shirley had a chance to reply.

Just as Smythe and Jared were finished draping the patient, Shirley led Patty into the room. After timidly putting on a surgical gown and gloves, Patty tucked in beside Smythe, who was standing on the patient's right side.

"Remember, if you feel unwell, say something to let us know and take a step back. It's nothing to be ashamed of," Shirley instructed Patty, just in case of a common problem with neophytes in the operating room: fainting.

Smythe recalled High School Careers Day a few months ago. Six students had been ushered into the endoscopy suite to watch Smythe do a gastroscopy. By the time he'd finished the procedure and the room lights were turned back on, only two pupils remained. The other four were out in the hallway, sitting on the floor sipping juice, recovering from their near-fainting spells.

"She'll be fine. Patty's worked in the ER many times." Smythe hoped his reassurances would prove true as he pressed the scalpel blade to Mr. Nichol's skin, cutting into his right lower quadrant.

Patty not only survived—she was entranced by the appendectomy. Smythe had her hold a retractor as they were closing after the appendix had been removed.

When the patient was settled into the recovery room, Smythe dismissed Patty, having answered all the usual questions that she was too shy to ask about appendectomies. The young volunteer bounced down the hallway to the emergency department as Smythe headed in the opposite direction to endoscopy. Just before she turned the corner, he glanced over his shoulder, observing Patty leap and perform a triumphant punch into the air. *She's a keeper*, he thought.

Smythe glanced at the clock on the wall. He was half an hour late to start his endoscopy list—not bad, considering he'd already got an appendix under his belt that day. He hurried over to the endoscopy suite to find Elizabeth Boyer waiting calmly on a stretcher.

When he had seen her in the office, she was fully dressed and it was late, so he had only done a cursory abdominal exam. With her sweater pulled up, he'd just made sure she didn't have any big masses in her abdomen. Now, in her blue hospital gown and without the bulky sweater, he had the opportunity to appreciate her physique. She had a beautiful body. There was hardly an ounce of fat on her, but her trim frame appeared healthy; it was not the kind of thinness he normally associated with serious illness.

He observed her abdominal musculature tense as she sat up from the examining table. His mind then wandered back to his three girls, and he scolded himself for looking at Elizabeth Boyer in such a manner. He knew he was safe, however. Surgical training was great at refining the "poker face". If a surgeon could withhold a look that might suggest "cancer" or "serious complication", surely he could disguise his fantasies about an attractive patient.

Smythe proceeded to examine Elizabeth's gastrointestinal tract from top to bottom. Lying on her left side, she closed her eyes only a minute after receiving the intravenous sedation. The assisting nurse placed a bite-block between Elizabeth's lips and teeth as Smythe lifted the gastroscope. He then advanced the flexible black fibre-optic tube down her throat as he and the nurse scrutinized the live colour image on the high-definition video screen behind Elizabeth's head. As they observed the transit down her esophagus and into her stomach, Smythe asked for biopsy forceps to take some routine tissue samples. Passing a long wire with pinchers on the end through the biopsy channel, under direct vision, he sampled her stomach and duodenum for subtle abnormalities. There certainly wasn't anything obviously wrong.

Having completed the gastroscopy in only a few minutes, he changed his equipment. With Elizabeth still half-asleep, Smythe inserted the colonoscope into her rectum. The trip from her rectum to the top end of her colon where it joined the small intestine was long and tortuous, taking about ten minutes. To Smythe's relief, he found nothing serious there either. He slowly withdrew the colonoscope, carefully watching on the way out to make sure he hadn't missed anything. Although finding something like a colon cancer always provided Smythe with a sense that he could help, he did not want to identify cancer in Elizabeth Boyer.

At the bedside in the wake-up room, he talked to Elizabeth and her daughter, Jen. "Everything looks fine. The only part we didn't fully examine was the small bowel, but the chance of finding anything bad there is very small."

"Well, that's a relief," Jen sighed.

"If we need to, we can arrange some more sophisticated tests for the small bowel, but the CAT scan is usually helpful, so we'll wait and see."

"The CAT scan is booked for January 17," said Jen.

"Great. Why don't you come and see me in the office a few days after that," said Smythe, hurrying off for his next endoscopy.

Just before he started the next procedure in the endoscopy suite, the wall phone rang. The nurse answered.

"Endoscopy, Martina speaking."

Pause.

"Dr. Smythe is busy at the moment. Can I give him a message?"

Extended silence.

"When?"

Pause.

"How big?"

Silence.

"I think you'd better speak to *him* about that." Martina looked inquisitively at Dr. Smythe. She said, "I think he can come to the phone now." With her hand over the phone's mouthpiece, she whispered to Smythe, "It's emerg. I think they've got some business for us." It wasn't until Smythe took the phone that he realized why Martina was grinning.

Dr. Smythe walked quickly to the emergency department just before noon. Not only was he behind schedule, but he also always felt better if he was in a hurry. That way, he wouldn't need to stop to talk to anybody in the hallway unless it was *his* choice. In addition, he found these cases gratifying, if not downright entertaining.

Smythe was on his way to assess a forty-year-old man who had lost a vibrator in his rectum. Although this object had clearly been inserted deliberately, Smythe marvelled at the number of tales he'd heard over the years about how objects made their ways into the rectums of Lakefield's residents.

"I sat on it by accident."

"My wife wanted me to insert it."

"I was just trying to treat my hemorrhoids."

Smythe was very trusting and assumed that 80 percent of the people were telling the truth some of the time. He even believed the man who'd stated he was walking in his apartment in his bathrobe and sat down accidentally on a pop bottle. The young lady who'd been inserting hemorrhoid cream and ended up perforating her rectosigmoid junction also told a credible story. When one looked at the tube that she'd used, it was certainly sufficiently long to do such damage, if one were reckless enough to insert it that far. The poor girl ended up with a colostomy, but fortunately, it was a temporary one. Smythe found it harder to believe stories told when the foreign body was, for instance, a foot-long carrot, meticulously carved to the recipient's presumed specifications.

At one point, he considered making a collection of the foreign objects he had obtained over the years. That could be problematic, though, as the vegetable material would go bad. He hadn't yet retrieved any animals, but that would also be difficult to maintain in his collection. So, with a touch of regret, Smythe had to be content with his memories and the knowledge that there would always be another interesting case around the corner.

Smythe was amazed by how many people had fallen on a shampoo bottle, only to have it miraculously disappear into their rectums. One day when he'd been waiting for the endoscopy room staff to prepare his patient, Smythe had done some epidemiological back-of-the-envelope calculations about shampoo bottles. He took the cross-sectional area of a typical shampoo bottle and expressed it as a percentage of the area of the typical shower stall. Assuming each person showered once daily, and fell 0.5 percent of the time, it was possible to estimate how many encounters with shampoo bottles would likely occur per 100,000 people. Assuming (conservatively) that each time a person's rectal area made contact with the shampoo bottle, there was a 1 percent chance of it being irretrievably lost in the rectum, Smythe was able to calculate the population required to support the number of episodes he and his colleagues saw. With some simple algebra, he figured out the expected referral population of Lakefield using the following formula:

$$\frac{\pi r^2 \times 0.005 \times I \times 0.01 \times S}{L \times W} = \frac{1}{P}$$

where r = radius of shampoo bottle cap, I = incidence, S = Smythe's constant, L = length of average shower stall, W = width of average shower stall, and P = referral population. He thought of adding some elementary calculus to the equation to tighten it up, but decided the extra mathematical complexity wasn't worth the incremental increase in accuracy.

His assumption, of course, was that of patient truthfulness: that these events were random accidents as reported, not deliberate occurrences. By Smythe's arithmetic, the population of Lakefield and the surrounding area would have to be sixteen billion if all of those people supposedly landing on shampoo bottles were telling the truth. His inescapable verdict was that some people weren't being honest.

This particular patient, Michael, swore he was being completely honest. He told Smythe his girlfriend had inserted her vibrator into his rectum. Unfortunately, when it was half in, the part of the instrument she—or he—held narrowed as it got farther from the anal opening. Much to their surprise—but not to Smythe's—the vibrator was launched like a watermelon seed pinched between a pair of fingers. The sphincter muscle simply propelled it in a retrograde direction until it disappeared in Michael's poor rectum.

He'd pondered fishing it out himself with his finger, but after one or two fruitless efforts, realized that would not work for him. He'd also thought of driving down the highway an hour and a half to get to a hospital where there was less chance someone might recognize him, but it hurt to sit in the car even for a few minutes. This discomfort was compounded by the fact that the object of pleasure was still in the active vibration mode.

Michael couldn't remember what kind of batteries they had purchased, but he hoped they weren't the variety advertised as lasting three times as long as the nearest competitor.

Smythe was very sympathetic, explaining to Michael that it was reasonable to try to retrieve the foreign body in the endoscopy suite. Such a process was not always easy. If the endoscope did not work, they would need to operate. It was possible that the vibrator or Smythe's efforts to remove it could perforate Michael's bowel. The man was not in a position to argue, and simply made it clear he wanted to have this item removed so he could get on with life. He also emphatically told Smythe, "I want it back. It belongs to my girlfriend."

At the end of Smythe's previously scheduled endoscopy list, Michael got his turn. Lying on his left side with his buttocks towards Smythe, Michael announced, "I think the batteries have finally quit! Thank God she bought the cheap ones." As Michael drifted off to sleep under the sedation, he slurred, "By the way, how many of these do you do in a day here?"

Upon introducing the endoscope into Michael's rectum, Smythe noticed that the inside was blood-tinged, probably from traumatic contact between the vibrator and the rectal wall. It didn't take long for him to locate the vibrator; there was really only one direction to look, and the foreign body had not made its way all that far. Grasping and removing it was trickier. The endoscopy room had a variety of equipment for such situations, but the best one was probably a polypectomy snare, in which a wire was inserted through the biopsy channel of the endoscope; inside the rectum, the wire opened up into a lasso. With careful manipulation of the controls, the tip of the endoscope could be curved in two opposing ninety-degree planes. Once the object was properly lined up, it could be snared and, if the grip was sufficient, pulled gently out through the rectum. Hopefully, no damage would occur during removal. But in cases where the foreign body was a broken bottle or had jagged edges, all bets were off.

When the object was smooth, the snare tended to keep slipping off the end. Perseverance was important. Fortunately for Smythe—and even better for Michael—the vibrator was bevelled at one end, which allowed the snare to grip it. As Smythe made his fifth or sixth lassoing attempt, he thought that this would make a good video game, but wasn't convinced parents would approve of *Retrieve the Rectal Foreign Body* for the family gaming machine. He also realized that finding a strategic partner in such a venture was unlikely, so he abandoned that idea.

With the vibrator successfully grabbed, Smythe gently pulled the colonoscope out. To his delight, the vibrator came with it. By this time, Michael was waking up from sedation. In his gloved hands, Smythe held the object up proudly, as one would hold a winning catch at a fishing derby. He then plunked it down on the table beside him, at which time the batteries briefly came back to life. Smythe and an assembly of nurses watched the vibrator give a few dying spasms.

Although Michael seemed to understand that the procedure had been a success, he would need a few more hours in the emergency department to fully recover from sedation before going home.

During the usual congratulations and discussion about the latest in foreign bodies, the nurses mockingly called Smythe the "Rear Admiral". But the job was done, and Michael was wheeled back to the emergency department. Smythe wrote specific orders on the chart that he wanted to speak to Michael prior to discharge.

After completing his afternoon ward rounds, Smythe went to the emergency department to discharge Michael. By now, it was eight o'clock at night. The night shift nurse informed Smythe that the patient had signed himself out thirty minutes earlier, against medical advice. He said he was feeling fine and to pass on his thanks to Dr. Smythe, but he really needed to go. Joanne, who was a seasoned emergency room nurse, advised Michael as he left to "put a string on it next time".

As Smythe was locking up his bike by the hospital the next day, Joanne was on her way home after a twelve-hour night shift. She was beaming, and motioned for Smythe to wait for her as she ran over to him.

"You remember Mr. Vibrator?"

"Yeah, is he okay?"

"Oh, he's fine all right. But as he was going out the door, I told him to tie a string to it next time."

"So?"

"He came back in at three in the morning, and guess what?"

"What?"

"The string broke!"

Smythe tried not to giggle, but it was difficult. Finally, his smirk transformed into thunderous laughter.

* * *

Smythe kept thinking about Dr. Calvin. It seemed the harder Smythe worked, the more excited he became about cases. He knew he was yelling in the operating room more than he should these days. However Calvin wasn't a bad guy to resemble, he thought; he was the best surgeon Smythe had ever met.

One day he'd been working with Calvin to repair an inguinal hernia. In simple terms, a hernia occurred when something moved out of one compartment into another. The vast majority of hernias weren't urgent, but they could occasionally lead to emergency surgery. Men were especially vulnerable to hernias, since they had natural areas of weakness where blood vessels and other structures travelled from inside the abdomen through the inguinal canal to the region of the testicles in the scrotum.

Calvin's older method of hernia repair included emphatically telling the resident to pull the testicle back down into the scrotum when the surgery was complete. "If you forget that one important maneuver, the patient could permanently have a high-riding testicle stuck in his abdominal wall. He won't thank you for that complication. And neither will I."

While the resident closed the incision, Calvin would leave the operating room to get a cup of coffee, secure in the knowledge that the resident *would* pull the testicle down into the scrotum at the end of the operation.

One busy day early in Smythe's rotation with Calvin, they had completed the hernia repair without problems. Smythe and the anesthesiologist wheeled the sleeping patient to the recovery room and deposited him with the supervising nurse. Smythe then went back to the lounge where, as the resident, he would dictate an elaborate description of the operation to be typed and placed on the patient's chart. When he neared the end of the dictation, Smythe realized he hadn't pulled the patient's testicle down into the scrotum. *Shit*, he thought, eyeing Calvin as he enjoyed a cup of coffee with a couple of other surgeons across the lounge. Smythe quickly finished the dictation and hung up the telephone.

Casually crossing the lounge to the exit at the far side, when he was out of direct vision Smythe broke into a full-out sprint towards the recovery room. He ran directly over to stretcher number nine, where he and the anesthesiologist had left the patient five minutes ago. With the patient still half asleep, Smythe could pull the testicle down into the scrotum, and Calvin would be none the wiser. To the recovery room nurse's horror, Smythe yanked the bedding down and grabbed the patient's right testicle. Smythe found the testicle sitting where it should be—in the scrotum. As an extra precautionary measure, Smythe gave the testicle a brisk tug towards the patient's feet to be absolutely certain it wouldn't be drawn back upwards. Just as the patient yelped, Smythe noticed a fresh cast on his left leg—this patient had just had an orthopedic operation. The stovepipe arms covered with tattoos and the patient's burly beard confirmed it was the wrong patient.

"Your fellow is over there, in number eight, Dr. Smythe." The recovery room nurse did not look happy. "We had to move him to accommodate this man."

Smythe had no idea why "this man" had needed to go in number nine, but he wasn't going to inquire further. Trying to appear as calm as possible, Smythe moved over to number eight and pulled down the testicle of his sleepy patient. On his way out, Smythe apologized to the man with the cast, muttering, "Well, the good news is, you *don't* have a right inguinal hernia; would you like me to check the left side?" When the man glared, Smythe dashed, hoping Calvin wouldn't find out about the mistaken identity episode.

Smythe wasn't sure who informed Calvin, but he suspected the recovery room nurse may have told the story first. As the tale propagated, Smythe worried constantly about how his teacher would react. But when Calvin did find out, he simply chuckled and said, "At least they didn't operate on the wrong leg, son. Then he'd really have a right to complain."

* * *

"I thought you said he was tight with his money." Angela beamed straight into Shirley's eyes, as if to challenge her.

"Well, yes. I did say he doesn't throw his money around. I think I said that's why most rich people stay rich."

"You heard about his latest purchase?"

"No, I didn't. Tell me about it."

Angela appeared smug. "Smythe blew twenty thousand bucks on a sound system for the operating room. So he can play his music. I know he likes music in the O.R., but why do you think he's springing for the entire area? It's not like he can listen to five songs at once while doing five operations in five different rooms."

Shirley sipped her coffee pensively. "I honestly believe Dr. Smythe is a generous man, but he may have some other motives."

"Such as?"

"He's taken some heat the last few weeks over loud music during his operations."

"So?"

"Well, what better way to reduce the complaints than to treat everybody with a top-of-the-line system? It's a bit harder to complain about the guy who's just sprung twenty thousand bucks for everyone to enjoy music in the O.R. And on top of that, he calls it a Christmas present. It got him off the hook buying us chocolates."

"Speaking of Christmas," Angela said, "did you see the O.R. caps his wife made for him this year?"

"Aren't they great? So much colour you practically have to wear sunglasses to look at him! All she had to do was buy some outrageous tropical bird pattern fabric and sew a few caps, and now he's a happy guy for another year."

"It's nice to know he's not hard to please."

"Pleased is an understatement! He forgot he had one on and wore it home in the car the other day. He went into the corner store with it on when he was buying milk!"

"*That'd* be a sight!" Angela laughed. She straightened up in her chair. After a pause, she added, "He's giving grand rounds after New Year's, isn't he?"

"Yup. The Friday morning after."

"What's the topic?"

"He won't say. Normally the topic is published by mid-December for January rounds. But Dr. Smythe wants to keep it a surprise."

"Interesting . . . It should be good. I hear he's been working pretty hard preparing. Are you going?"

"Wouldn't miss it."

"Me too." Angela jumped out of her seat and headed back to the operating room as Shirley Carver finished her second cup of coffee.

* * *

After a hectic week at work, Smythe's last day on call was New Year's. The stretch of work had been good for him. Several nights he'd gone sleepless, but the mix of surgical cases had been fantastic. He was looking forward to telling Amanda about the ones she'd find most interesting.

On New Year's, morning call was often quiet, but the night before was packed with interesting events. The general population normally started the first day of January a bit slower than usual, so Smythe's first emergency consultation didn't occur until shortly after noon. That was probably a good thing, as he had been up until three in the morning patching up a young fellow in the operating room. The patient had been minding his own business downtown when a complete stranger stabbed him in the abdomen three times. Smythe always found it fascinating how these patients were always "minding their own business". In contrast, an elderly woman with perforated diverticulitis would often search for some reason, dietary or otherwise, that the surgical emergency was her own fault. In this case, the stabbing didn't result in serious internal injury, and Smythe only had to repair a couple of holes in the bowel. He climbed into bed at four o'clock in the morning, satisfied he'd had another good year of surgical cases, but wondering if next year could be better.

Shortly after noon, Smythe received a call about another foreign body. Unlike objects stuck in the rectum, there was usually little doubt about the mechanism of getting something stuck in the throat. Typically, it was a famished individual's first bite of food ingested without sufficient chewing. This case, however, illustrated a slightly novel means of getting a foreign body caught in the upper esophagus. After the event, Serge Gagnon explained the full details to Smythe, looking him straight in the eye. Serge was a heavy man with an honest face, thought Smythe.

Just before noon, Serge had taken his wife and two small boys to a New Year's Day brunch buffet. When he headed to his table, his plate was a heterogeneous mound of foods ranging from pancakes to salad to lamb stew. He planned to go back for a slice of prime rib after he consumed his first plate. But he carefully avoided seafood, due to a minor allergy.

As the family sat down to eat, Serge made sure his three- and five-year-old boys were settled in before he attacked his own food. Upon his first mouthful, he knew something was horribly wrong. Serge had taken a rather generous forkful of egg noodles, yet when he swallowed, he felt a sharp spasm of pain in his throat. His first thought was not to panic—at least he could breathe. But no matter what he did, there was now a persistent, sharp pain in the middle of his neck. He took his glasses off and wiped his eyes as tears silently streamed down his puffy cheeks. His problems were compounded when he gingerly took a sip of water, which ended up half going into his airway, and half being shot out across the table at his terrified wife.

Serge was unable to speak more than a word at a time, but signalled to his wife that they had to go to the hospital. Later, he said the object had felt like a bone or a shell—not something you'd expect in even the most generous forkful of egg noodles. Serge's wife gathered up their belongings and their two screaming boys. As they headed out the door, she indicated to the restaurant staff that they were going straight to the hospital. Without any warning, the manager appeared out of nowhere and physically blocked the exit, preventing the family from leaving without paying the bill. With his hands evidently covering his own neck, Serge's honest face was incapable of satisfactorily explaining to the manager that this *was* a real emergency. Serge was in no position to point out the logic that four Gagnon plates, all teeming over with uneaten food, probably meant this was real. Serge reluctantly slammed down his credit card as his wife and children retrieved the car.

Serge made it to the hospital emergency department across town in six minutes, where he had to wait fifty minutes before seeing a physician. In the waiting room, his sputtering and gagging were probably the most important factors moving him up the triage scale: the nurses and other patients were all becoming grossed out.

In retrospect, if Serge had had more knowledge and less honesty, he could have achieved much more immediate attention. As a forty-eight-year-old male, a clearly more successful strategy would have been to indicate to the triage nurse he had chest pain. After being whisked past the full waiting room for an urgent cardiac work-up, he could have provided more detail. It would have been easy as an aside to mention to the doctor that he thought the chest pain was from a gigantic bone caught sideways in his upper esophagus.

An emergency physician saw Serge and referred him to Smythe to have the foreign body removed. Through a combination of sputtering, sign language and his wife's interpretive assistance, Serge made it quite clear that he wanted the object back after Smythe retrieved it.

While Gagnon's wife and children went for a quick bite at McDonald's, Smythe took Serge over to the endoscopy suite. It turned out that the lodged object was not a bone, but a four-inch shell fragment—probably a stray from the seafood section.

Afterward, he held up the article to Serge and his family. "It's hard to believe something this jagged and this size could make it as far as it did, but here's the culprit." Smythe demonstrated it like another prize catch.

"My throat still hurts, doc. It's much better, but it hurts." Serge was nearly fully awake, the sedation having almost completely worn off.

"It'll hurt for a couple of days. You should probably stay on fluids during that time. Remember, if you have increasing pain or fever, you need to get right back in here to see me. I don't think your throat was seriously damaged, but don't wait at home if you are getting worse."

"Can I take that shell with me?"

"Sure."

"I'm going straight back to that restaurant. There's no way this shell should have been on my plate. I don't eat seafood. I'm taking this straight to the manager to get my money back."

Smythe wondered if the fifty-buck refund on the family meal was perhaps a little modest. He knew a few lawyers in town who could probably turn that shell into several thousand dollars. But who was Smythe to become involved in the restaurants and legal politics of Lakefield? "Sure, you take it back. Give 'em hell!"

Chapter 14 ~ Sir George

Angela pushed the last bit of cookie into her mouth. Before she finished chewing, she asked, "What's up with Dr. Smythe these days? I heard he yelled at a couple of nurses last week, enough to make them cry and complain to Dr. Abbott—again."

"Too much work over the holidays, I think," Shirley reasoned. "Too much of a good thing can be bad, even for Smythe."

"If he keeps up this pace, he's going to snap."

Shirley stirred her coffee and looked straight into Angela's eyes. "Is he going to snap because he's working too hard, or is he working so hard because he thinks he'll snap otherwise?"

"I dunno." Angela stared blankly across the cafeteria, then gathered up her dishes. "I'll see you at rounds Friday morning? It's Smythe's big talk."

"Absolutely!"

*　　*　　*

Dr. Abbott closed his office door and motioned for the two other physicians to sit down opposite his desk. It was 5:30 on Thursday afternoon and Abbott had called a special meeting of his latest subcommittee.

Sandi Tremaine sat down in the chair closest to the bookshelf. Katrina Jaworsky settled in nearest the door. The younger Jaworsky, who was now leaning back in her chair tracing the eraser end of a pencil around her lips, drew Abbott's gaze.

As Chief of Medical Staff, Abbott chaired the Medical Advisory Committee. This body consisted of twenty physicians who met six times a year to make decisions regarding policy pertaining to medical staff. Most M.A.C. business was mundane, but occasionally controversial topics arose, awakening its members. Tremaine had been on the M.A.C. for three years. She was both seasoned and one of the gutsier members. Jaworsky was the newest. It was unusual to have such a recent addition to the medical staff on the M.A.C., but Jaworsky's psychiatry colleagues were happy to abandon the committee now that she was on staff. When the latest psychiatrist had suddenly resigned from the committee, Abbott appointed Jaworsky to maintain balance. He was delighted with the decision, as she had all the intelligence and common sense her references had indicated before her arrival at the hospital.

The topic of the day was Smythe. For this discussion, Abbott had created the small subcommittee that now sat in his office.

"This is a culmination of a number of complaints. There's no *one* problem that stands out, but Dr. Smythe seems to be popping up on my radar quite frequently lately." Abbott peered over his glasses, first at Tremaine in her operating-room garb, then at Jaworsky, who was dressed in her usual work clothes, as if she had just come from a cocktail party.

"He clearly needs to smarten up," Tremaine declared.

"I have spoken to him once recently," Abbott retorted. "But right now, we have no particularly glaring hospital by-laws violations, and we don't have a single criticism of his patient care, in or out of the operating room."

"He is good, I'll give him that," Tremaine admitted, her stance softening.

"Good, but disruptive," Abbott stated. "What do you think, Katrina?"

"Being on the psychiatric end of things, I hardly ever cross paths with him. I think I've spoken to him only two or three times since I came here. And there were no problems. Can you give some examples of your concerns?"

Abbott opened a manila folder on his desk and pulled out a page of handwritten notes. He ran his stubby index finger down the left margin, his lips moving as he totalled the complaint categories.

"I have basically four areas of concern here. One: he's made nurses cry six times in the last three months—yelled at them a little too hard in the operating room. Two: three complaints about loud music in the O.R. Three: he bullied a nurse into allowing a volunteer to assist at surgery."

"He *what*?" Tremaine looked incredulous.

"I thought you would've heard about that one. He plucked a thirteen-year-old volunteer out of the emergency department and made Shirley Carver suit her up to assist at an appendectomy."

"You're kidding!"

"He already had Jared Chong assisting, so it wasn't like he was relying on the girl, but he did make her scrub in on the case."

"What'd she think of that?" Tremaine queried.

"She was thrilled, of course. But that's not the point. The patient didn't know it was a thirteen-year-old when he consented to an observer. *And she was scrubbed assisting*. Not exactly forthright of Smythe, even if the kid wasn't doing much. And what if her parents objected afterwards? We don't have a leg to stand on."

"What does Dr. Smythe say about it?" Jaworsky asked.

"He claims he didn't know she was thirteen."

"That's not always the best defense," Tremaine muttered. "What else? What other problem?"

"Let's see, where was I? Oh yes. Four: he pulled some scam in medical records to delay dictating about forty charts a couple of months ago. Of course, he denied it to staff downstairs. I haven't had a chance to discuss it with him yet."

"There doesn't seem to be any one item that's *too* terrible," Jaworsky observed. "Just the sum total that's a bit worrisome."

"The way he treats nurses has obviously deteriorated. He claims they don't get him what he needs, when he needs it." Abbott looked up at both physicians. "Any thoughts?"

"Is there any history of substance abuse? Is he a drinker?" Jaworsky asked.

"Not that we know of. And no other medical issues as far as I've heard. I'm sure you've noticed he lost some weight several weeks back. There was some speculation in the doctors' lounge at that time that he had cancer. But I don't know where it came from and I think it had no basis."

"Any marital issues?" Jaworsky queried. "Sometimes they can contribute to the mix."

"None that I've heard of," Abbott replied. "Although I'm not sure he'd be telling *me*."

"What do *you* think?" Jaworsky locked her eyes with Abbott's.

"I think I need to have a chat with him."

"You need to make it clear to him that it's the *pattern* that's so disturbing. He needs to fix it, or he'll be in trouble." Tremaine paused, then added, "You *can* yank his privileges, can't you, Rick?"

"Yes, but not without good reason. And if he appeals and wins before a committee, then it becomes complicated."

"Well, it's getting to the point that I don't want to give anesthetics for his surgeries anymore. You never know who he's going to piss off next. I've seen him in action. And just because I don't cry like the nurses doesn't mean he hasn't gotten under *my* skin a few too many times. He's the nicest guy when things are going his way, but lately he's been a bastard to more than just the nurses. So if you don't do something, Rick, *I will.*"

"What d'you mean?"

"I've come this close," Tremaine said, gesturing with her thumb and index finger, "to arranging a total boycott of his surgeries by the entire anesthesiology department. If no one from our department will work with him, he's finished."

"That bad?"

"At times, it is. And when there's no getting through to him, something drastic has to be done to make him aware. It doesn't matter how good he is, or how likeable he is most of the time. It's his shitty behaviour that needs to be stopped."

"You should meet with him as soon as possible," Jaworsky stated, making eye contact with Abbott. "He needs to know in no uncertain terms that the pattern must change or you'll make things difficult for him."

"I can probably grab him after grand rounds tomorrow morning. He's presenting. I'll try and catch him for a few minutes at nine. Hopefully, I can talk with him then, as I'm stuck in meetings all day after that." After a pause, he added, "And I *am* serious. If he doesn't cooperate, I'm going to have to take him to the wall on this."

"Good luck." A look of satisfaction permeated Tremaine's expression.

* * *

Dylan Ross cautiously made his way down the steep auditorium steps. It was 7:45 on Friday morning, and the front door down by the podium was still locked. He sat in the second row, tucking his white hospital coat under his seat. He had just put on his crisp surgical greens, grabbed a cup of coffee and was settling in early to get some "paperwork" done on his electronic organizer before rounds at eight o'clock. One Friday a month, the operating room started later so the hospital community could gather for grand rounds. He glanced over his right shoulder towards the empty seats in the auditorium, then looked down at his lap, occupying himself with his handheld device.

Suddenly, a loud clatter sounded from high in the back of the auditorium. When it continued, Dylan turned his head and shoulders towards the back of the room. Dr. Smythe was stumbling down the steep steps, both arms full of paraphernalia for his presentation. He reached the front table and deposited his cargo with a thud, then proceeded to take out his laptop and connect it to the multimedia station. After taking off his soaking wet O.R. cap, he removed his similarly drenched white coat and carefully placed it over a chair in the front row. Smythe's greens were blotched with water, likely from a combination of sweat and melted snow. He was unshaven.

"Are you still riding your bike these days, Jim?" Dylan asked incredulously.

"You betcha," Smythe replied enthusiastically.

"I thought you weren't riding when you were on call—you *do* know you're on call tonight, don't you?"

"Yes, of course."

"You don't look like you got a lot of sleep last night, Jim. Are you going to be okay for call tonight?"

"I got a couple of hours. I had to do the final preparations for this talk."

"A *couple* of hours? *Before* a night on call? Do you want me to cover for you so you can grab some sleep later? You know how busy Friday nights can be. I do owe you one for covering between Christmas and the New Year."

"No, I'll be fine—but thanks, Dylan. Thanks very much."

Rick Abbott walked in the front door of the auditorium and then straight up to Smythe, who was fiddling with his laptop at the podium.

"Jim, can I talk to you for a few minutes after rounds?"

"I'm all yours, Rick. D'ya wanna grab a coffee after?"

"Sounds good. I'll meet you down here and we can go have one in my office."

Smythe looked somewhat surprised, but before he could respond, Abbott was making his way to an open seat a few rows back.

Now, at five minutes to 8:00, the room was starting to fill up. And was it *ever* filling up. Surgeons, anesthesiologists and internists tried to crowd to the front rows. Doctors, nurses and other hospital personnel took any seat they could find. Dylan adjusted himself in his chair as Frieda, the ICU nurse, squeezed into one beside him.

"I'm glad I got a seat so close to the front," she said. "It looks like we'll have a full house today."

"How are you today, Frieda?"

"I'm fine, Dr. Ross. How are you?"

"I'm well."

A loud tapping on the microphone interrupted them.

"Could everyone take their seats, please?" Smythe was no longer in sight. The unfamiliar voice continued. "When everyone is quiet, we will turn off the lights in preparation for the show."

"Show?" whispered Dylan. "I didn't know I was coming to a show!"

The packed room was silent. The lights went off. Suddenly, a familiar sound loudly resonated throughout the auditorium: the opening chord to "A Hard Day's Night" by the Beatles. Instantaneously, the dark room lit up as the title screen flashed up at the front: "Gastroesophageal Reflux Disease (GERD) and the Nissen Fundoplication". From the left side of the podium, Smythe dashed out of nowhere while music continued quietly in the background.

Dylan leaned close to Frieda and quietly commented, "Music, you've got to be kidding!" Then he added, "No wonder he didn't advertise the topic—no one would show up."

Smythe offered a multimedia presentation extraordinaire. Music faded in and out as video clips of laparoscopic surgery played at appropriate times to illustrate Smythe's points. He took the varied audience of 250 from the most basic points to the most complex nuances about his topic. His opening included a history of GERD and the early physicians who had investigated and treated it. Without notes, he continued by explaining that acid reflux could often be managed by simple lifestyle measures such as refraining from lying down after a large meal. Avoiding exacerbating foods was often useful. Occasionally, an antacid such as Maalox would be enough to treat symptoms. More powerful prescription medication was also available. Smythe discussed tests used to rule out cardiac causes of chest pain and more sophisticated investigations to understand the physiology of a particular patient's reflux. Long-term untreated reflux could lead to precancerous changes, or Barrett's esophagus, and ultimately cancer at the gastroesophageal junction, he explained. Smythe then proceeded to discuss the technical aspects of the Nissen fundoplication, the operation to wrap the stomach around the lower esophagus to prevent acid reflux. Colourful diagrams faded as video clips of laparoscopic surgery solidified his description.

For fifty minutes, the entire room was hanging on Smythe's every word.

As he initiated his concluding remarks, a booming voice over the loudspeaker interrupted: "Anesthesia to ER, stat! Dr. Tremaine to ER, stat!" Sandi Tremaine sprang out of her chair, sprinting to the ER.

"Well, that can't be good," Smythe commented with a smile, wrapping up his presentation. "So, in conclusion, the Nissen fundoplication is a very useful operation to treat acid reflux disorders, providing patient selection is carefully done."

Just as his concluding remarks were proudly culminating to a climax, "A Day in the Life" was becoming louder in the background, approaching its pinnacle.

"The last thing you want is to do this operation on a patient who is likely to get complications. The laparoscopic approach has revolutionized many intra-abdominal surgeries, the Nissen being no exception. The Nissen fundoplication!" Jim Smythe savoured the words.

As he stated those final words, the classic piano chord at the end of the song rang out, signifying the end of his presentation. Smythe was now standing on the table at the front of the lecture hall, looking up at the audience members. "Any questions?"

A thunderous applause ensued. Grand rounds hadn't been this entertaining or informative for a long time. Smythe was beaming. He climbed down from the table and raised his right hand to suppress the ongoing clapping. "Any questions?" he repeated.

A doctor from the front row stood up and said, "I enjoyed that very much, Jim. The music and the video clips were great—unconventional but very well put together."

Smythe nodded and smiled.

"My question is how often should a person be screened with gastroscopy if they have Barrett's esophagus?"

"I'm glad you asked that," Smythe replied. He clicked the remote a few times, and six-foot-tall brightly coloured pictograms flashed up on the screen. When he had completed his detailed explanation, Smythe pointed to a dietitian high at the back of the auditorium. "Yes, Trudy?"

Trudy stood up and stated, "I'd never really understood that operation until now—thank you."

"My pleasure."

Trudy continued, "Is a gastroscopy necessary in every person you treat for reflux?"

“The short answer is no. If they are too young to expect cancer, you can probably start medication and see how they respond. But we can’t forget cardiac investigations—individuals with a chance of an underlying heart condition should be tested to ensure nothing is being missed.”

Smythe continued, answering several more questions, and then stated, “We have time for one more.”

Dylan Ross posed the final question. “Jim, that was an excellent presentation. I can’t help but ask, however, why you picked this topic. As you stated early on, the Nissen should be done by only a few surgeons to keep the experience and volume of these procedures sufficient for each surgeon to maintain skills.”

“Yes.”

“But you don’t do the Nissen fundoplication. Why did you pick this surgery as your topic, despite the fact that you don’t do it?”

Smythe paused and looked up at the clock—8:59. “Let’s just say I had a score to settle from my med school days.”

Dylan Ross leaned over to Frieda and whispered, “That makes no sense to me.” And then out loud he replied, “Well, an excellent job nonetheless, Jim. Excellent job.” And, with those final complimentary comments, a second but more abbreviated round of applause was heard as people picked up and went off to start their workdays throughout the hospital.

At that moment, the loudspeaker thundered, “Surgery to ER, stat. Dr. Smythe to ER, stat!”

“Well, that can’t be good,” Smythe announced as he bounded towards the exit.

* * *

Smythe jogged down the corridor, excited that something urgent was waiting for him in the emergency department. He thought about his presentation and how 250 people had sat silently through the entire hour, focused on him. The music and visual effects had been great. Who would’ve thought rounds could be so slick? He felt as if Sir George Martin had personally helped produce the show. Smythe wondered briefly what his life would be like if he’d gone into entertainment instead of surgery. As he rounded the corner into the emergency department, he jolted his mind back to the present task at hand.

Chapter 15 ~ Natalie

Smythe strode into Trauma Bay Number One to find at least twenty-five hospital personnel packed in the room, many of them gathered around an emergency stretcher. In the middle of the stretcher lay seven-year-old Natalie Sinclair, who apart from some gasps for breath was not moving. Dr. Tremaine was at the head of the bed, barking orders. The remains of Natalie's shirt lay underneath her, after scissors had been used to expose her neck and chest. An emergency nurse held blood-soaked gauze firmly over the front of the child's neck, while four other nurses worked on Natalie's arms and legs to get a good intravenous line, the initial one having been lost after only a few minutes. The heart-rate monitor beeped 200 per minute, fast even for a seven-year-old.

"Jim, a Rottweiler mauled her about twenty minutes ago, over on Fortieth Street. There's been a lot of bleeding from her neck, and I'm worried we're going to lose her airway any minute now."

Smythe took everything in. Clearly, the airway was Natalie's most pressing problem. Bleeding could be controlled by pressure, at least for a little while. "Have you tried to intubate her, Sandi?"

"Yes, twice. My first try was my best shot, but I couldn't see enough to get a tube in. We bagged her for a while, then just as I tried again, we lost the IV line. My second look wasn't nearly as good. I think her neck swelling is getting worse. Jim, you've got to help me with this. I think we might need a surgical airway."

A nurse suddenly shouted, "I've got a number 24 IV in the left foot! It seems to be running well."

"Should I try again, or is there something you can do, Jim?" Tremaine pleaded.

Smythe looked over at the oxygen saturation monitor. Barely holding 85 percent, very low for a child receiving oxygen. "Get me a cricothyroidotomy kit—NOW!"

Within about thirty seconds, a nurse was opening the kit while another tied on Smythe's gown from behind and a third fixed his mask.

Smythe then took control, requesting a nurse to apply pressure to the child's neck with a bulky piece of fresh gauze, as far off the midline as possible while still controlling the bleeding. The centre of Natalie's neck was now visible. The bulk of her injuries appeared to be on the left side, as if the dog had picked her up and shaken her like a rag doll, shredding one side but preserving the midline. Thank goodness for that.

As Dr. Tremaine was stabilizing the child's neck, Natalie's respiratory efforts were deteriorating every second. Oxygen saturation dropped below 50 percent, and her heart rate plunged to 45 beats per minute—catastrophic in a child, usually signifying imminent cardiac arrest. Rapidly swiping iodine across her neck, Smythe now passed a needle through it without anesthetic, aiming at forty-five degrees for her trachea. As he sucked back on the syringe, a sudden withdrawal of air signified that his hollow needle was in Natalie's empty trachea. Within seconds, Smythe had passed a wire down then withdrawn the needle. He made a one-centimetre cut on her neck around the wire and then firmly pushed a dilator instrument over top. Natalie's heart rate dropped below 30 and the monitor was no longer picking up oxygen readings. Her lips were blue. People in the room were shouting but Smythe wasn't listening. He quickly removed the dilator, and with the wire still in Natalie's trachea, pushed a small endotracheal tube through the midline of her neck, over the wire and into her airway. After he removed the wire, Tremaine immediately connected oxygen via a ventilating tube and began squeezing puffs of air into Natalie's lungs.

Just as children could decompensate quickly, they could also recover from danger rapidly, and that was exactly what Natalie Sinclair did. Within twenty-five seconds, her dusky blue lips turned pink, her heart rate surged to 150 beats per minute, and her recently limp body began to squirm. Dr. Tremaine ordered sedation through one of the two good IV lines.

While the others in the room breathed a collective sigh of relief, Smythe stared at the blood-soaked gauze still being pressed to the left side of Natalie's neck.

"We've got to get the O.R. ready to fix this little girl's neck," Smythe yelled to no one in particular.

"Jim, you've saved her life once today," said Dr. Tremaine. "Isn't that enough?"

"What do you mean, Sandi?"

"We're just ninety minutes down the road from the university. Don't you think she'd be better off there, in a trauma centre with pediatric and vascular surgery?"

"She's bleeding, Sandi. She needs to go to the operating room. Now. Not in an hour or two. Now!"

"But with pressure on her neck, she'd likely be fine until she reached the University Hospital."

"Likely isn't damn good enough, Sandi. Get the O.R. ready."

"But—"

"But nothing. Listen, Sandi, you look after the airway and I'll look after the bleeding neck," Smythe sneered, his message barely veiled: she *had been* looking after the airway, but if he hadn't stepped up, then Natalie Sinclair would already be dead.

Sandi Tremaine's face was flushed. She steadied herself against the equipment counter and closed her eyes briefly. By now, the participants in Trauma Bay One were dispersed, cleaning up, getting Natalie ready for the O.R. and documenting what had occurred over the past twenty minutes. Dr. Tremaine slipped away to prepare for Natalie's imminent operation.

In the operating room, the nurses were quickly getting Natalie positioned for surgery. They prepared her neck with iodine, while Jared Chong took over maintaining pressure on the left side. The bleeding seemed to be well controlled. Dr. Tremaine stood at Natalie's head while Smythe stood to the left of the child's neck, Jared opposite him. Shirley Carver was right next to Smythe, at the level of Natalie's left elbow. Just as they were about to start surgery, "Stairway to Heaven" started to play over Smythe's new sound system. "A great song!" Smythe exclaimed. "Jared—when was that song released, can you tell me that?"

Smythe's Socratic method of teaching in the operating room didn't usually include music trivia. "I, uh—"

"C'mon! A surgical assistant should know his music! It was 1971. Sally—can you turn that song up a bit for me?" Then to Shirley as he nudged her elbow: "That's not too loud for you, is it Shirley?"

"As long as I can hear you, Dr. Smythe, that's all I care about."

"How about you, Sandi, is that too loud for you?"

"As long as I can hear my monitors, Jim, I'm fine with it."

If anyone was troubled by the song choice, they weren't saying.

"May we start, Sandi?"

"Go ahead, Jim."

"So, Jared, what's our strategy if this is a major vascular injury?"

Without hesitation, Jared responded, "Proximal and distal control."

"Exactly. If you get control of the vessel above and below the injury, it's easy and safe to repair the damage. If you don't have good proximal and distal control, you're done for. Now, let's get a look at where we might need to control."

Jared's right hand was still firmly pressed on the left side of Natalie's neck, and as Smythe rolled the hand further to Natalie's left, a huge gush of dark, venous blood emanated from one of the dog bite holes. He quickly returned Jared's hand to its original spot, minimizing the blood loss.

"How much blood do you think she's lost, Sandi?"

"Difficult to tell, Jim. Her hemoglobin was down below 100. This early in the resuscitation, that could mean substantial blood loss. Her vitals are currently stable, so I think she's well compensated at the moment. But we may need to think of giving her blood if you're going to lose much more."

"We might," said Smythe. He then took his scalpel and made an angled cut from behind Natalie's left ear, down the neck to the midline at the sternal notch, just above the breastbone. When he came to where Jared's right hand was controlling the bleeding, he rolled it away slightly, getting into more brisk bleeding. He then quickly extended the incision the full length of the neck and returned Jared's hand to where it had been. His incision intersected a few of the huge gashes made by the Rottweiler.

"The key to proximal and distal control, Jared, is exposure." He then worked his way through unrecognizable tissue that he told Jared was sternomastoid muscle. "Retract this muscle so I can find the jugular vein up top. By the colour of this blood and the non-pulsatile nature of the bleeding, I think it's unlikely to be an artery. The carotid is probably fine, believe it or not. She's a lucky girl if it is."

Jared's grip on his retractor intensified, exposing the operative field as instructed. As bleeding increased, he shifted pressure from his left hand towards the middle of the neck. At least with Smythe's big incision, they were a little more focused on where the pressure seemed to help. Working well away from this, Smythe gently teased an instrument into the depths and around the jugular vein, high in the neck. Accomplishing this without poking a hole in the vein was paramount; injuring the vein where they were trying to obtain distal control could be disastrous.

Smythe then passed a slippery rubber tube around the vein, which was no thicker than the thinnest of shoelaces. But with this maneuver he achieved distal control. Each step of the way, a small gush of blood came out. The probable sum total was worrisome.

"Jim, I think I should give her a unit of blood now."

"Whatever you say, Sandi."

Smythe achieved proximal control—getting around the jugular low in the neck—with more difficulty and more blood loss. When this part of the vein was secured, Jared could pull his hand off the middle of the neck with no further bleeding. He suctioned the pool of blood from over the top of the jugular vein, exposing a three-centimetre laceration longitudinally—straight down the front of the jugular.

"We've found the injury," Smythe announced loudly enough to overcome the background music.

"That's a relief," said Tremaine. Others nodded.

Smythe didn't share the same sensation of relief because he had *expected* all this to occur. Jared stared at the huge gash in the vein. There was no way she would have made it to the University Hospital without bleeding to death.

"So, what do we do now, Jared?"

"Sew it up."

"Very good. With what?"

"Four-O polypropylene."

"Sounds good to me, Jared. Where do I start?"

Jared indicated the top part of the vein, and Smythe planted his first stitch at the top end of the laceration. As he performed a running stitch from top to bottom, Smythe explained every move to Jared. He reminded him that veins were much more fragile than arteries and more likely to tear. He didn't waste a single move as he placed each stitch perfectly, reapproximating Natalie's jugular vein the way it was supposed to be. Before he finished, Smythe paused and looked Jared directly in the eyes.

"You finish this," he said.

Jared appeared stunned at Smythe's suggestion. With some hesitation, Jared took the needle driver. His hands were shaking.

"Jared, if you have a tremor, you need to know how to cheat. Rest your wrists and the base of each hand on something—anything—and they won't shake."

Jared did as instructed and it worked. He proceeded to place the last four stitches in Natalie's jugular vein. He took longer than Smythe had taken to place fifteen stitches, and Jared's were uneven; one of the gaps looked too large, as if it might allow bleeding. He moved the needle backwards through the vein, when Smythe suddenly yelled, "What the hell are you doing?"

"I want to make it better."

"You try to make it better and you may blow the whole deal, Jared."

"Should I leave it the way it is?"

"You tell me, Jared. If you try to make it better and it ends up worse, I'll kick your ass so hard, you'll feel it 'til Tuesday!"

The music had stopped. In the tension, no one dared restart it. Smythe had ranted in the operating room before, but never like this.

"Leave it. It's fine." Jared didn't sound completely certain.

"Then tie your suture here—*at least six knots* on a running stitch, like this." It seemed like several minutes as Jared laid down the knots squarely, meticulously, his hands shaking. "If you break that stitch—" Smythe hollered as Jared snugged his final knot. Then, more calmly, he added, "Good. Now release proximal and distal control."

Jared took the rubber ties that were securing the vein tight on either end of the repair and began to loosen the top one. As blood welled up around the vein, Jared froze. The bleeding continued. Smythe grabbed the tie from Jared's hand and tightened back on the vein to stop the bleeding.

"What the hell's up with that?" Smythe shrieked.

"I—" Jared was quivering.

"Your stitches weren't so hot, were they?"

"No—sir."

Smythe suctioned away all the blood, then calmly rolled the jugular vein over to expose a one-centimetre laceration on the back wall of the vein. "What the hell are you going to do about this, Jared? Why didn't you check the back wall?"

The dog had bitten right through the jugular vein. Although the major injury was on the front, the back had to be checked. Searching for an injury to the back wall had been drilled into Smythe many times during his training. Jared briefly closed his eyes, only to be startled by more yelling.

"Well, why didn't you check it?" Smythe bellowed.

"But—"

"I'll tell you what, son, I saw the back wall laceration peeking at us when we were repairing the front wall." Smythe looked smug.

There was silence. Then, Jared exclaimed, "But this little girl—"

"What, Jared? What are you saying?" Smythe was now hollering louder than anyone had ever heard him. "Are you accusing me of putting this girl at risk for this little demonstration? *Are you?* Well let me tell you something, Jared. I'm completely in control here. And, let me ask you, will you ever forget this case? Will you EVER forget to check the back wall? EVER again in your life? How many patients might you save in the next thirty years as a result of your experience with this case? Let me tell you, if you save ONE, this learning experience has been worth it, at a cost of four tablespoons of blood to this little girl."

Jared was silent.

Smythe looked around and pointed to the sound system. "What the hell happened to the music? Get me some music!"

They rolled the vein over, and Smythe explained that they wouldn't have closed the back wall through the front anyway. It was best to close the back wall from the outside if you could. That way, all the knots were on the outside of the vein. Smythe quickly repaired the back wall with precision. When they released tension on the ties above and below, the vein distended up quickly with minimal leakage.

Smythe calmed down and carried on teaching. He explained that this small amount of leakage was normal and would be corrected by Natalie's own clotting. He also indicated that it was important not to narrow the vein with the closure. This time it was fine, but they always had the option of harvesting a vein from the leg to create a patch, if narrowing were an issue. They spent the next twenty minutes tidying up jagged edges of muscle and looking here and there for any other hidden injuries.

With Natalie out of danger, the room lightened up considerably. Smythe stopped suddenly and gazed to his left. He focused on Parmita, a petite student nurse.

"Parmita, you've been pushed to the back row this entire case. Do you have any questions?"

"Not at the moment."

"Shirley," Smythe exclaimed. "Trade places with Parmita so she can help us close." Shirley slid sideways, allowing Parmita to tuck in beside Smythe.

"Now Parmita, I need a special retractor to help close the incision. Get me a Henway retractor!"

Parmita looked puzzled. Shirley rolled her eyes.

"Henway!" he repeated.

"What's a Henway?" Parmita asked.

"Oh, about four pounds! Ha!" Smythe's eyes were gleaming. "A hen weighs four pounds!" Parmita giggled.

"Then if you don't have a Henway, get me a Dickfore!" Smythe was beaming.

"*No, don't!*" Shirley said forcefully, looking at Parmita. "*Don't ask!*" Parmita giggled again.

Smythe directed Jared to close the superficial layers of Natalie's neck. Twenty minutes later, she had a sutured gash from her left ear to the top of her breastbone, but she was alive. The tube coming out of her trachea to support her breathing would remain in place until swelling in the neck resolved. With Natalie now stabilized, Smythe phoned the University Hospital to see about transferring her there. Due to her age and need for respiratory support for at least a couple of days, she'd need to be sent to the university's pediatric intensive care unit.

The remainder of the day, the mood was celebratory for Smythe and all those involved. The attending physician from the university phoned Smythe to congratulate him. The University Hospital staff was impressed. No fewer than ten people stopped Jim Smythe in the hallway to congratulate him on a job well done. He was "high-fived" by nurses whose names he didn't know. Later in the day, the local newspaper requested an interview, but Smythe wasn't eager to give it. He wasn't so keen on newspapers since the bile duct article down east, which had left him with a bad taste for media coverage. Also, he didn't have permission from Natalie's parents to talk to the media. Smythe was on call, was the response; no interview would take place right now.

Several patients in the emergency department had to wait hours for Smythe. However, he didn't feel the least bit guilty for keeping people waiting on a day like this one. In his opinion, he was well worth the wait.

He finally finished up at six o'clock in the evening, then headed over to the office to do paperwork and heat up some supper in the microwave before the inevitable Friday evening onslaught of emergency surgical cases.

Chapter 16 ~ Elizabeth

Smythe sat behind his large office desk, wading through reams of insurance forms. He despised this aspect of the job. As he shovelled the last bite of beef stew into his mouth and wiped the excess off his lower lip with a napkin, the phone rang. Call display indicated it was from the emergency department. Friday nights were usually busy, requiring two emergency doctors to be on duty.

"Jim, it's Sheila Abbott." Rick's wife, also an emergency physician, worked occasional shifts in the department.

"What's up, Sheila?"

"This is just a courtesy call. I don't think you need to come and see her now, but Elizabeth Boyer is in the emergency department." Since her gastroscopy and colonoscopy had been normal, Smythe wasn't expecting to hear about Jen Boyer's mum until the middle of January. Sheila Abbott continued, "She's been having more abdominal pain. I ran her through the CAT scanner, and we didn't find a whole lot, but she does have a little bit of free fluid in her belly. I think she might need to see a gynecological oncologist, just in case there's something going on with her ovaries. I sent off a lot of lab work, including tumour markers, but they won't be back until next week."

"I'll come and see her now."

"It's okay, Jim. I can let her go home, but I just wanted you to know that she was here."

"I'm on my way," he said before Sheila had a chance to add anything else.

In less than ten minutes, Smythe was in the emergency department, where he found Elizabeth Boyer in cubicle nine. She was wearing a light blue hospital gown and sitting up on her emergency room stretcher, looking a little haggard. This time she wore rectangular, dark brown framed glasses, similar to Jen's. He also noticed a couple of millimetres of grey at the roots of her chestnut-brown hair. Jen stood by the head of the bed, dressed in a pink tracksuit and looking even cuter in regular clothes than she did in her nursing uniform. Smythe kept those thoughts to himself.

He spent about fifteen minutes examining Elizabeth Boyer after reviewing her file and her CAT scan images. She'd had more abdominal cramping, to the point that Jen convinced her to come in to the emergency department. Although reassured by the negative results of her recent gastroscopy and colonoscopy, she told Smythe the cramps this time were the worst they'd been. "They're worse than my most painful period, not that I remember that too well. Haven't had one of *those* in at least two years."

After completing a careful updated history, Smythe pressed on Elizabeth's muscular abdominal wall. She was tender all over. He stood to the right of the stretcher and looked into her eyes for hints as he probed with his fingers. It was difficult to tell whether her muscles were involuntarily tensing when he palpated her. She winced at times, her eyes watering. After several minutes, he stood up straight and looked at Jen. Elizabeth looked more composed now that no one was pressing on her abdomen.

"I think it might be time for an operation."

Jen's eyes widened. "What for?"

"We haven't found a lot, but clearly something's not right."

"What are you thinking, Dr. Smythe?"

"I'm thinking you have something elusive, Mrs. Boyer. There are a few clues, such as the free fluid. The escalating abdominal pains worry me. It's possible you have a small adhesive band or internal hernia that is causing intermittent obstruction. Sometimes it's better to look and see, rather than wait and see."

"When?" Jen asked.

"Tonight, of course," retorted Smythe.

"That soon?" Elizabeth spoke for the first time in minutes.

"Yes, tonight's the night." He added, "I've never regretted operating early, but I've certainly kicked myself for dithering."

Elizabeth looked at her daughter for reassurance. With an air of complete confidence, Jen said, "If Dr. Smythe thinks you need surgery tonight, then I think you should have surgery tonight."

Smythe excused himself and ducked around a corner to do some paperwork. When he'd completed the necessary admission orders, he sat back and stared across the room, looking through the usual clutter and commotion of a typical Friday night in the emergency department. He heard a baby wailing, monitors beeping and a young man screaming obscenities at a hospital security guard. He wiped tiny droplets of perspiration from his forehead with the cuff of his white lab coat.

"Jim, are you okay?" Jason Malcov sat across the counter, studying Smythe's expression.

"I'm fine," Smythe stated evenly.

"You just look a little stressed, that's all."

"I sometimes get blind-sided by reflux. When it gets bad, I've even thought of seeing one of you guys a time or two."

"Heartburn?" Malcov inquired.

"Occasionally. Usually goes away with Maalox, but not this time, it seems."

"Jim, if you're having heartburn that's really chest pain, it could be serious."

"I know it's nothing—I'm just not sure if I should have it checked sometime. And when it's here, it's never convenient to get tested."

"Maybe that's because you only get it when you're working—and stressed."

"I'm not stressed. It'll settle down soon. If I just wait a little longer."

"That would be your decision," Malcov explained. "If you tell me you've got chest pain, and you want to make it an official assessment, that requires a full work-up. There's no running back and forth to the operating room all evening. If you register here in emerg with chest pain, you're ours for at least twelve hours until serial EKGs and three sets of cardiac markers are completed."

"Hmm," Smythe mused.

"It's your call, Jim. I'm happy to look into it for you if you want. But you've got to play ball with us."

"I'm fine."

"You sure?"

"Ye—" Smythe hesitated. "Yes, I'm fine."

"Okay. But if you change your mind, we're always open."

"Thanks, Jason. I'll keep that in mind."

"No problem. And by the way, great work on that dog-bite kid earlier today. I heard all about it."

Smythe smiled weakly and glanced back at his papers. He closed his eyes for about ten seconds and then bounced out of his chair, around the corner and over to the main patient display, scanning the names on the screen in case he had any more patients to see.

Sheila Abbott came back from a quick supper break and hovered over the unit secretary at the front desk, perusing several charts. She snatched one chart and shot a cold stare at Smythe, who was still standing at the display that listed patients and their cubicle locations.

"What's this all about?" she asked, holding up Elizabeth's chart.

Smythe turned towards Sheila, calmly stating, "I think she needs surgery. I'm going to operate tonight." The two doctors were now facing each other with only a foot of space between them.

"What for?"

"Bowel obstruction," Smythe said assuredly.

"But she's not obstructed on the CAT scan."

"I think she's having intermittent obstructive symptoms, and we're going to fix her."

"But Jim—"

"I've made my decision."

"But Jim, I've ordered other tests. We haven't got her tumour markers back yet. If her CEA or CA 125 is high, that would certainly be helpful to know ahead of time."

"Sheila, I've made my decision. I'm operating tonight."

"But—"

"I said—" He paused, then spoke louder, "*I'm operating tonight.*" Several nurses congregated around the two doctors, perhaps to discourage them from making a scene in front of patients and other staff. Fortunately for Smythe, cubicle nine with Mrs. Boyer was around the corner and likely out of earshot due to the usual excessive background noise.

"But if she has an ovarian cancer, tonight is neither the time nor the place for her to get proper treatment. She might need to be referred to a gynecological surgeon to have further investigations and a full staging laparotomy."

"Sheila, what part of *operating tonight* do you not understand?"

"I'm just thinking of the patient, Jim. More tests—"

"She's *my* patient, Sheila. The only test she's getting tonight is a scalpel scan! I'm asking you to leave her alone. I'm *telling* you to stay out of this."

Sheila Abbott took a deep breath. Before she had a chance to say anything further, Smythe continued, "If Mrs. Boyer gets her bowel strangulated in an internal hernia, she'll end up with six feet of dead gut. Is that what you want, Sheila? Is it? What do you think I'm going to wait for? Do you want me to wait for her bowel to infarct? Do you?"

"But—"

"Sheila, if you interfere and prevent my patient from having the surgery that she needs tonight, I will report you to the Medical Licensing Authority. You know that meddling with my patient could be construed as professional misconduct, don't you? You could have your license taken away for less."

"Are you threatening me, Jim?"

"No. I'm just stating a fact. Elizabeth Boyer is having surgery tonight. Period."

Smythe abruptly turned and walked away, passing at least twelve staff members who had been observing the showdown. They dispersed rapidly. He continued quickly around the corner to cubicle nine without uttering a word.

Smythe pulled the curtain open just enough for him to slip into the cubicle. With a warm smile, he asked Jen, "Where's your mum?"

"You just missed her. She went to the washroom a minute ago." If Jen had heard any of the confrontation between the two physicians, her expression revealed none of it.

"I just wanted to let your mother know she's on the list for emergency surgery tonight. I expect it will happen in the next two or three hours."

"Thank you, Dr. Smythe. I don't know how to thank you enough."

"It's my pleasure. I'm glad to help. Especially for someone like you, Jen." As she blushed and looked up at the ceiling, he glanced at Jen's slender hands. Three rings. Two on the left, one on the right. The absence of a ring on the left ring finger was patently obvious. A sure sign of availability if he'd ever seen one.

As Smythe did more paperwork in preparation for Elizabeth Boyer's surgery, a familiar voice interrupted his thoughts. "Are you okay, Dr. Smythe?"

Sandra, one of the emergency room nurse supervisors, looked at Smythe, who was staring blankly across the room.

"I'm fine. Never better."

"It's just that . . . Dr. Abbott seemed a little upset after talking to you. Is there any way I can help?"

"No, I don't have a problem. I'm not sure what her problem is tonight. But I'm fine. You need to ask Sheila if you want to know what's bugging her. The only thing I have is more patients to see."

Smythe promptly stood up, looking for his next consultation: a man with appendicitis.

Chapter 17 ~ Security

While Smythe was working on the backlog of referrals in the emergency department, three doctors were chatting in the operating room lounge. Sandi Tremaine sat in a large reclining armchair between Jared Chong and Sheila Abbott. Jared sat on a small stool to her left, while Sheila was in the end seat of a three-person couch. Tremaine's seat faced the television, which was usually blaring all day long, whether anyone was watching it or not. She decisively clicked the remote, silencing the TV. "So what's going on?" she asked, looking at Sheila.

"Jim has got this idea that he must operate on Elizabeth Boyer tonight—"

"Jen's mum?"

"Yup—for a bowel obstruction," Sheila continued tentatively. "I don't think she needs surgery tonight, if at all, yet there's no convincing *him* of that."

"Why don't you think she needs surgery?"

"It's supposedly for a bowel obstruction, yet she's been having regular bowel movements, and her CAT scan doesn't show an obstruction. If I had to put my money on anything, I'd say ovarian cancer is up there on the list, in which case she should be seeing gyne-oncology, not Smythe. It certainly doesn't seem like a big emergency to me."

"That's it! I've had it up to here with Smythe." Tremaine gestured with her hand on top of her O.R. cap. She then turned to her left. "What do you think, Jared? Don't you think he's crossed the line this time?"

"Well, he's surprised me before . . ."

"What do you mean?"

"I've seen him make tough decisions under pressure. When you least expect it, Jim's landed on his feet—made the right call. Everyone else would look bad if this patient turns out to have gangrenous bowel tomorrow with no operation tonight. Remember, it's Jim's neck that's on the line—certainly not mine as the assistant."

"I'm not going to let him get away with this just because he yells louder than the rest of us. If he wants to operate tonight on this case, he's gonna have to justify it to me—face-to-face. I don't put anyone to sleep just because some goddamn surgeon tells me to. I have to feel it's reasonable." Tremaine paused, smiling and looking over at Abbott. "Thanks for coming over here to let me know what's going on, Sheila."

Sheila Abbott shrugged awkwardly and stood up.

Jared jumped to his feet. "I'll go talk to him. Perhaps I can find out more detail—or maybe he'll sleep on it, if it's getting late and the patient remains stable." He left the lounge and exited through the main O.R. doors.

* * *

Jared had just missed his mentor over in ER; Smythe had taken a different route, entering the O.R. locker room. When he heard that Smythe had just barrelled out of the department, heading for the operating room to start an appendectomy, Jared did an about-face. He retraced his steps, except this time he went back through the locker room, where he found Smythe standing in the expected aisle, changing into a fresh pair of surgical greens. Smythe pulled off his top, exposing his well-muscled upper body. He then tossed the hospital shirt into a laundry hamper twenty feet away at the end of his row of lockers. He smiled and pumped the air with his fist.

"How's that for a great shot? Didn't know I was a basketball pro in my spare time, did you, Jared?"

"Not exactly . . . What's up with this exploratory laparotomy, Jim?"

"This is going to be another one of our great surprise operations, Jared. I don't know what we'll find, but I know it's going to be good." Smythe was practically vibrating with excitement. He stood opposite Chong, who had just opened his own locker while beginning to change. Smythe was gazing just above Jared's left shoulder as they spoke. Jared turned to look a couple of times in the direction where Smythe was staring, but he seemed to be looking right through Jared's half-open locker.

As he stuffed his shirt into his locker, Jared took a sip of his Diet Coke. “No, seriously, Jim, what’s up with that case? Isn’t that Jen Boyer’s mother you’ve booked?”

As he tied up the drawstring to his fresh greens, Smythe responded, “Jared, my boy, this is a great day!” His blank stare was reciprocated by a nervous laugh from his younger assistant. “Tonight is the night I save Elizabeth Boyer with surgery, and as my reward, I get to have sex with her daughter!”

“Jen? You’ve got to be kidding! Are you fucking crazy? What the hell would she see in you? No offence, Jim, but you’re twice her age!”

“Simple fate,” he yelled. “Save the mother, fuck the daughter! It’s great to be alive, isn’t it, Jared?”

“Does Jen have any say in this?” Jared asked.

“I know she’ll be game, Jared. I just know it!”

Jared Chong scratched the top of his head then combed back his black hair with his hand. They were both fully dressed in their surgical greens. Smythe slammed his locker shut with a loud crash.

“C’mon, Jared, we’ve got an appendix to take out! And then it only gets better!”

“Jim, I have to take a quick dump. You go ahead. I’ll be in the O.R. in a couple of minutes.”

“Dump away, Jared, my boy. I’m sure you’ve got fifteen minutes before this guy with appendicitis is off to sleep. You know how slow things happen at this time of night.” Without saying another word, Smythe disappeared into the operating room hallway, singing no particular tune as he went. He dashed down the hall to room number eight so he could speak to his patient before the man went off to sleep for his appendectomy.

In the room, apart from the beeping monitors, all was silent as Dr. Tremaine prepared to induce the general anesthetic. She quietly motioned to Smythe that it was okay for him to say a few words to his patient before she administered the final medication.

“Everything will be just fine! I’ll let you know what we find in the morning, when you’re wide awake!” Smythe’s booming voice was well beyond what the anesthesiologists preferred for their patients as they were about to go off to sleep. Tremaine swiftly pushed the plunger on the syringe, delivering medication into the IV line. The man lying on the operating table drifted off to sleep, and she inserted the endotracheal tube into his airway without incident. Two nurses commenced the final preparation for surgery, counting instruments while another clipped hair from the man’s abdominal skin.

"Jim, I've been meaning to talk to you about that next case—Boyer, is it?"

"What do you need to know?"

"Why are we doing it, especially at this late hour? It'll be close to midnight before we start."

Smythe gave her a cold stare and said, "Her life is in danger, that's why." He then turned and pushed the swinging doors open, adding, "I just have to run over to the emergency department. I'll be back in *three* minutes!"

Not long after, Smythe and Jared were in the room draping their patient for surgery. This one was a laparoscopic appendectomy. Once the incisions were made and instruments inserted, the abdomen was inflated with carbon dioxide gas to allow working space in the abdominal cavity. As Jared inserted the camera, the overhead lights were turned off, darkening the room significantly. This particular patient was an overweight forty-year-old male whose case of appendicitis had gone misdiagnosed for forty-eight hours. Dr. Malcov had finally referred him to Smythe on the patient's third visit to the emergency department. By this time, the appendix was buried in the right lower quadrant, stuck to everything around it by the body's immune response to the localized infection.

Smythe broke the silence. "You see, Jared, how humbling appendicitis can be at times? Most often it's straightforward. But perhaps because this man is big, his symptoms were not typical, and his appendix is tucked in behind, it was a difficult diagnosis. The day you think you've got appendicitis all figured out should be the day you quit being a surgeon—or any type of doctor, for that matter." The team watched the surgery progress on the screen. Smythe and Jared concentrated as they worked the laparoscopic instruments, Smythe standing to the patient's left side, handling the instruments while watching the monitor positioned beside the patient's right hip. Jared held the camera, exposing the operative field as he stood at Smythe's right side and by the patient's left elbow. The scrub nurse was positioned opposite the two physicians, along the right side of the patient. Despite the technical difficulty of this operation, Smythe was able to carve the appendix out from surrounding tissue with speed and gentleness. Within minutes, the appendix was detached and placed in the retrieval bag.

"I'm impressed, Jim," Jared said evenly. "I thought for sure we'd have to open this guy up."

"Just goes to show the value of a positive attitude," Smythe replied, glancing over pointedly at Tremaine.

After removing the bagged appendix from the umbilical port, Smythe loudly proclaimed, "Time to send for the next patient. Mrs. Boyer, I believe."

"I'm not sure we're quite ready," Tremaine jumped in.

"My case is next, isn't it?" Smythe asked.

"You're next, but I have to run up to obstetrics. You never know how long I'll be up there." Tremaine shrugged.

In the darkened room, Smythe stopped his surgery and gazed towards Tremaine. "We're nearly done. Rather than waste time sending for Mrs. Boyer when we *are* done, perhaps we can send for her now—as we always do."

"This is a bit different, Jim. I don't know how long I'll be tied up on the obstetric unit. I'd rather we not send for her until I know what's going on up there. I can have an obstetric nurse phone down here for me as soon as I know what's happening."

"Sandi—" Smythe began, his voice tight.

"Finish your operation, Jim! The sooner you get done, the quicker we'll get on with the next task at hand." Tremaine's words resonated at a similar volume to Smythe's.

Smythe stared at Tremaine with a look of disbelief. He then turned back to the laparoscopy monitor. "Irrigation, please!" he barked at the scrub nurse.

"As soon as I know what's happening upstairs on O.B., I can let you know if we can send for your patient." Tremaine was firm.

"What do you mean, *if*? You mean *when*, I hope." Smythe finished irrigating where the appendix had been removed. One by one, he removed the laparoscopic instruments.

"Jim, you won the argument about doing the dog bite surgery here, but that doesn't mean you can trample over *everyone* about *every* case. I know your lady's bowel obstruction can wait until tomorrow, and we won't be starting such a case after midnight. Sorry, but that's where I stand on this one."

"Suture!" Smythe bellowed as he prepared to close the incisions.

After a few minutes of silence, Smythe proclaimed, "I have to run over to ER for a few minutes. If you're not willing to send for Mrs. Boyer, then I expect you will discuss that with me, face to face, in front of the patient whose life *you* will be putting at risk."

Tremaine didn't respond.

With the final dressings placed on the patient's abdomen, Smythe tore off his gloves and threw them in the garbage, then whipped off his gown and stuffed it in the laundry hamper and asked, "Is there any Maalox around here? All this shit is giving me chest pain!" Without waiting for an answer, he stormed out of the room, heading for the emergency department.

Jared followed on Smythe's heels and asked, "Jim, can I see you in the locker room for a minute?"

Smythe turned abruptly and glared at his young colleague. "That depends. Are you on *my* side or *their* side?"

"Your side, of course. Actually, we're *all* on your side."

The two stepped into the locker room from the operating room corridor. Without making eye contact, Jared went straight to his locker and turned the dial on his combination lock. The palm of Smythe's hand slammed into Jared's locker, making a crashing noise that would have startled anyone in the vicinity.

"Well? What did you want to talk to me about?"

"Jim, you've got to slow down." Jared pulled down on his combination lock, but it didn't open. He tried the combination again.

"What do you mean slow down? You *are* on their side!"

Jared pulled on the padlock again. "No, seriously. You don't have to work this hard, and you're kind of going overboar—"

"Who are you to tell me I'm going overboard? Slow down? No way! I'm just getting started!"

Jared pulled down on his lock for the third time, finally opening it. He swung the door open, peering into his locker, then pulled out a few items of clothing from the top shelf, revealing a half-finished bottle of Diet Coke. Just as he unscrewed the cap and raised it to his lips for a swig, Dr. Rick Abbott entered the locker room from the main entrance.

As Abbott approached, Smythe stared at him.

"Hey, Ricky my boy, what brings you here on such a fine Friday evening?" Smythe appeared so elated he might not have known he was yelling.

"Jim, I've come to relieve you of your duties, for the time being."

"What the hell do you mean, Ricky-boy?" Jim Smythe was looking right past Abbott as he spoke. By this time, Smythe had stepped up onto a locker room bench, the additional eighteen inches allowing him to tower over Abbott and Chong. Smythe shifted from side to side, as if he were balancing on a ship being tossed in gale force winds.

"Jim, you're not well. Dr. Ross is taking over call for you tonight. You are done for the evening."

"*You* are telling *me* that I'm done? What the hell's that all about, Rick? I'm the surgeon here. I'm the one who decides when I'm able to work. I'm in control! This is about your wife, isn't it, Rick? She put you up to this, didn't she? The bitch is just pissed off because I want to operate on my patient. Well, screw that, Rick. I'm in control here."

"Not tonight, Jim."

Smythe glanced over at Jared. "Oh, it was you! You called him!"

Jared looked at his shoes, then at the ceiling.

"This is my decision." Just as Dr. Abbott calmly spoke those words, two hospital security guards entered the locker room.

"Whoa, what the hell's this all about?" Smythe screamed, prancing from one locker room bench to another.

"Jim, we need to talk, and we need to talk now. You're not well, and we need to address that. I'd like Dr. Jaworsky to have a few words with you."

"Katrina-baby! Bring her on! I'll take Katrina any day!"

"No, Jim, I'm serious. She needs to see you—professionally. She's the psychiatrist on call tonight."

"Well, that's a load of crap if I've ever heard one. Excuse me. I have work to do."

As Smythe pushed his way past Jared and Abbott, the two security guards puffed out their chests and blocked the aisle, preventing Smythe from moving towards the exit.

"Are you going to let me past or—"

"There's no alternative," Abbott calmly interrupted.

Smythe stared incredulously at the Chief of Medical Staff, while Jared silently backed into a corner.

"Oh, yeah, Jared. What do you think about this? Isn't this an outrage?"

Jared was silent.

Smythe suddenly sprinted towards the locker room exit as both security guards tried to grab him. He made it past them both for a moment. But the shorter, stocky one accelerated towards Smythe down the aisle, launching into the air to complete a tackle with Smythe thumping to the floor, face down. Immediately, the second guard grabbed his right arm and pulled it up behind his back, effectively gaining complete control. As Smythe squirmed, he felt his arm nearly snap at the shoulder. Smythe was pinned—defeated.

"What are you going to do, Jim?" challenged Dr. Abbott. "Are you going to run out of here to some other place where you can work without interference? Get real! You're done. Your hospital privileges are suspended. Do the right thing and cooperate."

"But so many patients," Smythe panted, his face pushed into the locker room floor.

Abbott calmly said, "Jim, you *will* be assessed by Dr. Jaworsky tonight. Period. You will be assessed voluntarily or at my direction as a certified patient under the Mental Health Act. The choice is entirely yours. There are always two sides to a story. You'll have your chance to tell your side. Agree to the assessment—or have it imposed upon you. Your choice, Jim. What will it be?"

"Damn, I don't know." Then, to the security guards, "Can you guys ease up, for crying out loud?"

Abbott nodded to the guards, who cautiously loosened their grip without fully releasing it. "I can call Amanda in to be with you, if you'd like."

"No, leave Amanda out of this."

In the end, Smythe agreed to go. In exchange for his cooperation, Abbott allowed Smythe to be assessed in the privacy of Rick Abbott's administrative office rather than go through the usual fracas in the emergency department. Although Smythe thought everyone else "should just chill", he had the sense to know that certification under the Mental Health Act could be a career-limiting move. He therefore agreed to whatever Jaworsky recommended.

After Dr. Jaworsky's preliminary assessment, Jim Smythe was admitted covertly to a private room on Unit 37—the psychiatric ward. He agreed to medication and was heavily sedated; therefore, he did not require physical restraints. Jaworsky diagnosed him as having manic psychosis, secondary to bipolar disorder.

With the help of medication, Smythe slept uninterrupted for eleven hours in his tiny, dark room on the psychiatric unit.

* * *

Early Saturday afternoon, Amanda stomped her boots, shaking off the snow as she entered the main entrance of the hospital. Dr. Jaworsky had called her in the morning about Jim—he was okay. Something about a breakdown. Not to worry, he was safe, she'd said. *Not to worry!* Avoiding the main elevators, she scanned the atrium quickly, making her way to the back corner without encountering any familiar faces along the way. She pulled out her phone and called Unit 37 to have a service elevator sent down to her. As she ascended the empty elevator to the third floor, she could feel a sudden jab in the pit of her stomach. She was breathing rapidly. When the doors opened, a neatly dressed, attractive brunette startled her.

"You must be Amanda," she said with an accent, smiling warmly. She held out her hand and added, "I'm Katrina Jaworsky, one of the psychiatrists."

Amanda shook her hand and responded, "It's nice to meet you, although I wish it had been under different circumstances."

"I understand it's stressful for you. But I want to reassure you, I think Jim will be fine."

"Thank you. And thanks for phoning me this morning. When Jim didn't arrive home last night, I just assumed he was up all night in surgery."

"We would have called last night, but Jim preferred to get some of the initial business done by himself. I'm sure you understand, no?" Jaworsky led Amanda to an interview room at the end of the hall. She knocked lightly on the door, then opened it without waiting for a response, motioning to Amanda to enter the room.

Jim was sitting in one of two chairs opposite the desk. His face was ashen, his eyes blank. He wore blue hospital pajamas and a matching robe. Amanda quickly reached her arms around him without saying a word, then she sat down while continuing to hold his left hand. He turned to her, their eyes converging. "Hi, sunshine. I'm sorry."

"Don't be. I'm here for you."

Jaworsky opened a folder on her desk and, facing the couple, calmly stated, "Jim has been under a fair bit of strain lately. We had a long discussion last night, and it appears that he needs some of our help on the psychiatry unit. Jim has agreed to stay here for a few days with us until he's improved. We gave him a considerable amount of medication to help him sleep and to even out his thoughts, so he may seem a little flat to you, Amanda. But this will normalize over the next few days."

"This is often a tough time of year for him, mostly because of his father's death." Amanda looked at Jim, then at the ceiling. She asked Jaworsky, "What exactly are we dealing with?"

"I'm sorry for not telling you the details over the phone, but I think it's best to share the information with both of you together—that way you'll both be on the same page. Jim has typical features of bipolar disorder. You may have heard of it as manic depression. There are several subtypes, and Jim has been afflicted with the most severe form, as he was becoming delusional of late—"

"Delusional?" Amanda interjected. "Jim?"

"Yes, he's had some thoughts that are out of touch with reality, but the specifics are unimportant right now."

Jim stared into his lap where he was fidgeting with the hospital bracelet on his left wrist, Amanda still tightly holding his left hand.

"I've noticed he's been hyper lately, but I thought that was just Jim. Now that you mention it, the term 'manic' doesn't come as much of a surprise to me. But bipolar? I never thought of it as a diagnosis, just the way he is at times. He's often a lot of fun when he's full of energy."

"Exactly. When people are manic they *are* a lot of fun. But when it becomes extreme, it can be a problem."

"What do you mean?" Amanda asked.

"It's not always just fun. When people are manic, their mood is at an extreme. They can go on spending sprees, become hypersexual, and they can become reckless. Although the person who is at the centre of it all feels great, it can drive family members to distraction."

Amanda gave a subtle nod in Jaworsky's direction.

"Sometimes in a manic phase, a person can harbour grandiose ideas—an unrealistic perception of superiority. Mania is often interspersed with bouts of depression. The condition can go on for many years, only receiving medical attention when there is significant interference with one's life: a marriage, a job, one's financial affairs."

"Well, our marriage is good, isn't it Jim? And money's not a problem."

Jim nodded silently.

"In Jim's case, his work was being affected," Jaworsky explained.

"What happened?" Amanda asked.

"His work performance was being affected," Jaworsky repeated carefully, "but nobody was hurt. It's probably a good thing this finally came to the surface so Jim could get proper treatment. And treatment is often very successful." Turning to Jim, she added, "You're in good company. Famous people like Winston Churchill, Vincent Van Gogh and Virginia Woolf all likely had bipolar disorder. It can often propel people to success—with their abundance of energy. But the extremes need to be smoothed out; that's where medication is important."

"What medication?" Amanda asked.

"Usually lithium, although there are others. We'll talk about them when we know what's best for Jim's situation."

"What next?"

"I think Jim will need to be in hospital for about one to two weeks. And probably off work at least six to eight weeks."

Jim's eyes widened, and he spoke for the first time in minutes: "Six to eight weeks?"

"Yes." Jaworsky replied.

"If that's what it takes," Amanda added.

Dr. Jaworsky continued. "Last evening, we spoke at length about recent events, Jim. We still need to discuss your remote history. Perhaps we can cover that now?"

"Sure."

"Have you had any psychiatric issues before this episode?"

"No," Jim replied tentatively.

"No?"

"Well, there was this one time in pre-med where I got in a little trouble for wandering down the street naked. Except for a flag I—no, we—stole. I was put on medication, but that was primarily to ensure the charges were dropped. I didn't need the meds for very long—I think I only took them for a couple of months, and then I stopped."

"Do you remember the name of the medication?"

"No."

"Anything else—any other episodes?"

"No. Well, yes, actually." He looked sheepishly at Amanda. "I was losing weight, so I went to my family doctor, Dr. Sanderson, about three months ago. He put me on lithium—primarily to gain some weight. I stopped it after a couple of weeks as I didn't need it anymore."

"I see. Did Dr. Sanderson know you stopped it?"

"I don't think so. But I'm not sure. Come to think of it, he probably did mention I had bipolar. But I didn't think so. He wanted to refer me to a psychiatrist, but I declined the offer—I told Barry I'd prefer to keep it between him and me. I went to see him a few times. In the beginning, I agreed to blood tests to monitor me while on lithium. I even renewed my prescription twice—in case he checked with the pharmacist. But the pill bottles just piled up in my office drawer. I couldn't bring myself to take medication. My weight didn't drop any further, and I was feeling so good most of the time."

"Anything else? Any other episodes?"

"No."

"Are you sure?"

"Yes."

"Any mental illness in your family?"

"No." Jim paused, looked at Amanda and took a deep breath in. "Well, yes. My father suffered from severe depression. He committed suicide when I was thirteen. Christmas Day. I tell people it was a heart attack. It's easier that way."

Amanda's jaw dropped open. After ten seconds, she said, "Jim? You never—"

"I know. I'm sorry, sunshine. I hated that I lied to you about my family history. But I despised the stigma attached to suicide even more. I'm sorry."

Epilogue

Monday morning, Rick Abbott ran into Katrina Jaworsky in the hallway. "How's our friend doing?"

They retreated into a small alcove and Katrina leaned up against the wall. "Pretty well, I would say."

"Thanks for spending so much time with him over the weekend. I really appreciate it. You know I feel bad for Jim about this."

"Me too. You know, Rick, it all looks clearer in the rear-view mirror."

"What d'you mean?"

"Well, in the last few months, Jim has been floridly manic, and in retrospect, the clues were all there for us to see. No sleep, lots of energy, fun to be with, pressured speech, bright colours. His delusions of grandeur *were* a bit much."

"Those weren't delusions, were they? He *is* a top-notch surgeon," Abbott replied.

"The ideas he shared with me over the weekend—*they* were delusions. He's *good*, but *not that good*. When he wasn't working, he was dreaming about changing jobs to a top American university: something he neither could do nor would want to do under normal circumstances. Even the twenty-thousand-dollar sound system in the O.R. was something Jim admitted he wouldn't normally purchase on a whim. Choosing his topic for rounds to make up for a mistake as a med student was a little weird. Believing George Martin actually co-produced his rounds was clearly out of touch with reality. But his performance on rounds, and apparently in the operating room, were both fantastic!"

“It’s quite unbelievable.”

“I agree. However, when his sexual fantasies became public and inappropriate, and when his judgment was obviously impaired about Elizabeth Boyer—that’s when he crossed the line.”

“Do you think other patients have been affected? Should we be worried about that?”

“I think it would be reasonable to have someone review Jim’s practice over the last few months, but I doubt you’ll find much. I’m hoping he can be back to functioning safely in six to eight weeks. You’ll need to make sure he stays on his medication, however.”

“I’ll do what I can.”

“His family doctor, Dr. Sanderson, knew about Jim’s trouble a few months ago and put him on lithium. The problem was that Jim didn’t think he needed it. He didn’t bother to tell anyone he was on it—or more importantly, off it. Barry incorrectly assumed that as a physician, Jim would make a good patient. He thought Jim would go for blood tests and take medication as instructed. When Barry finally started getting persistent about asking him to follow up, Jim lied and said he’d changed his mind and would carry on with a psychiatrist—at the university.”

“I still can’t get over how well he has functioned up until Friday—if this was really going on for months.”

“It’s possible he’s been on the edge of mania for years. It’s been the perfect job for him up until now. Being a surgeon has been socially acceptable therapy to him. In a way, he was self-medicating: surgical highs were part of his treatment. His work satisfied his mania, yet he also immersed himself in surgery to rise up from the lows. But it won’t be enough now. He should be on medication long-term—whether he recognizes it or not.”

“When you think about it,” Abbott added, “a touch of mania isn’t a bad quality for most general surgeons. There’s a lot of good in Smythe that other surgeons have in smaller doses. But too much of a good thing was his downfall here.” Abbott paused, then said, “I’m relieved it came to this, in a way.”

“What do you mean?”

“It would have been difficult—if not impossible—to curtail most of his behavioural issues. It was only when he was totally out of line that I could actually do something. Hopefully, it wasn’t too late.”

“It wasn’t,” Jaworsky concluded confidently.

Jim Smythe’s admission to the psychiatric unit lasted only ten days, as he cooperated in taking medication and other therapy, and made excellent progress. His discharge medication included lithium for bipolar disorder and pantoprazole for acid reflux. His cardiac investigations were fine: he had the heart of a twenty-five-year-old.

If it had been anybody else, the rumour mill would have propagated this gossip through every hospital department and back. But Smythe had enough support from his co-workers that people either didn't find out, or chose not to investigate his unplanned eight-week "vacation" during that cold January and February. Smythe's brush with psychiatry remained strictly confidential.

The Medical Licensing Authority dismissed Hazel Kowalchuk's complaint. Her illness and surgery after the gummy bear ingestion was unfortunate, but Dr. Smythe couldn't be held responsible for her troubles. Dr. Smythe's care, according to the Authority's final explanatory letter to Mrs. Kowalchuk, had been exemplary.

The Authority also accepted Rick Abbott's request to have Jim Smythe's mental health observed as a condition of maintaining his medical license. A graded monitoring through the Physician Wellness Program was recommended. Smythe would be under the watchful eye of someone for at least five years, possibly longer.

Abbott enlisted an independent surgeon from the University Hospital to review Smythe's practice. No glaring aberrations were identified. A few select cases were more closely scrutinized, none of which revealed any problem with Smythe's surgical judgment or treatment of his patients. Specifically, Cecil McNaughton's case was reviewed in detail. Although Mr. McNaughton clearly had suffered a string of complications, ultimately resulting in his death, no fault could be found with Smythe's care for his patient. His decisions were described as timely and appropriate. Whether there would have been a more correct time to reintroduce blood thinners after surgery was anybody's guess, and certainly the external reviewer was not in a position to say there had been a more suitable course of action, even with the benefit of hindsight. To Abbott's relief, the external reviewer identified no serious problems in patient care, and none came to light later on.

Elizabeth Boyer had her operation—a proper systematic staging laparotomy by a gynecological oncology surgeon—during daylight hours. Although the diagnosis was ovarian cancer, it was early enough that there was hope with proper treatment—not the outcome Smythe's nighttime surgery would have promised.

Jen never heard a word about Smythe's locker room antics. She simply was told he had changed his mind about her mother's surgery and was now on an extended vacation. Her loyalty to Smythe did not allow her to inquire why; she just accepted the party line that he'd been working too hard and had taken some much-needed time off.

Jared Chong decided against returning to further training in a surgery residency. His wife, daughter and new son were too important to him to embark on the commitment for more training. He continued assisting Smythe in the operating room while also picking up occasional emergency room shifts.

Smythe never gave the interview to the press about Natalie Sinclair. When the family called the hospital to inquire if Smythe could speak to the newspaper reporter, Jim was learning how to relax on a beach in Turks and Caicos. Instead, Sandi Tremaine gave the interview. In addition to praising Smythe's efforts on that Friday in early January, Sandi also answered questions about her recent Clinician of the Year Award.

Smythe didn't win the Lifetime Achievement Award; he never knew whether his nomination had been a baseless rumour, or whether he was voted down to avoid controversy. Awarding this honour to such a young surgeon would have raised some eyebrows, and perhaps out of consideration, his closest colleagues knew that the last thing Smythe needed was controversy. Instead, the award was presented to Ted Sanderson, whose imminent retirement was a relief to the many faithful who had worked with him over the years. If the award encouraged his retirement a day earlier, it was worth it.

* * *

On the morning of his expected discharge from hospital, Jim sat in the small armchair beside the window of his private room, gazing at the cluttered street three floors below. The traffic was heavy for late morning on a Monday. It had stopped snowing a few hours ago, but the road and sidewalks were still covered; it was too cold for the snow to melt, and too soon for the shovels and plows to have done their job. Jim thought about work, and how he'd still be battling the elements daily on his bike if he hadn't had his "episode" ten days ago.

He couldn't remember much about that Friday nearly two weeks ago. His presentation at grand rounds was a blur, but he knew it had been a smashing success; enough people had told him afterwards. His memory of saving Natalie Sinclair from her dog attack was more lucid—another great case to remember with satisfaction. But after Natalie, there wasn't much he could recall about Friday . . . Something about the locker room with Abbott and security. Jim had thought Abbott was being a bastard the last few months, but he realized he couldn't blame him. Rick had been doing his job.

Jim's feelings about his recent diagnosis were mixed. He'd never dreamed he'd have a psychiatric problem, although he'd been aware of it since Barry Sanderson had put him on lithium in the fall. The fact that Barry hadn't realized Jim was off the medication had convinced Jim he really didn't need it. Jim now recognized his logic hadn't been so sound then. But he'd been feeling so good . . . Yet despite Jim's initial revulsion about being treated for a psychiatric illness, he at least felt supported. And it shouldn't have come as a big surprise, given the dark secret of his family history.

The past ten days had been boring, but restful. There had been a small handful of select visitors, who were all very encouraging. Dylan Ross had reassured Jim that his surgical practice would be covered in his absence, and ready for him when he returned. Jim kept mostly to his room and never ventured off the psychiatric unit, not wanting to risk a chance encounter with another hospital worker. With his discharge papers nearly completed, all he had to do was quietly escape down one of the service elevators to have Amanda take him home. Thank goodness for Amanda.

* * *

An hour later, he sat calmly opposite Dr. Jaworsky in the psychiatric interview room.

"You see, Jim, the difference between a psychiatric illness and a personality trait can be subtle. Whether or not one can function at everyday activities is often the deciding factor. Until recently, you were very highly functioning, and I dare say there are many doctors, politicians, lawyers and the like who are probably out there functioning on a knife-edge just like you were. You just have to get back on the other side, which you can do with the help of medication and insight into your mental health. Does that make sense, Jim?"

He didn't give anything away from his expression. "You're comparing me to lawyers and politicians?" was all he could say in response.

"Well, for now, at least we have medication," she replied. "Stay on it, Jim."

* * *

Two hours later, Jim climbed into the passenger seat of the Lexus SUV, happy to be heading home. Pulling away from the curb, both he and Amanda had to adjust their sun visors as the brightness pierced a small gap in the cloudy sky. At a red light, Amanda reached over and took Jim's hand. "You know, at one point I thought you had terminal cancer. Then, I thought you were going to drop dead of a heart attack. And of course, there were moments I imagined you might be having an affair." The light turned green. Amanda returned her hand to the steering wheel as she accelerated the vehicle.

"So, surprise. This is what you got," he replied evenly.

"I don't think I could have handled those possibilities. Jim, I can handle *this*."

"Thanks, sunshine."

"And you know, if you aren't on top of your own health, you can't be good to either your family or your patients. Take care of yourself *first*, and everyone around you will benefit."

"I'll be sure to remember to do that. And if I forget, you remind me."

"I will, Jim. I will."

9781926747637